Antiques
Con

Antiques Con

A Trash 'n' Treasures Mystery

Barbara Allan

KENSINGTON BOOKS
http://www.kensingtonbooks.com

KENSINGTON BOOKS are published by

Kensington Publishing Corp.
119 West 40th Street
New York, NY 10022

All Kensington titles, imprints, and distributed lines are available at special quantity discounts for bulk purchases for sales promotion, premiums, fund-raising, educational, or institutional use. Special book excerpts or customized printings can also be created to fit specific needs. For details, write or phone the office of the Kensington Special Sales Manager: Attn. Special Sales Department, Kensington Publishing Corp., 119 West 40th Street, New York, NY 10018. Phone: 1-800-221-2647.

Kensington and the K logo Reg. U.S. Pat. & TM Off.

Library of Congress Card Catalogue Number: 2013920822

ISBN-13: 978-0-7582-6364-3
ISBN-10: 0-7582-6364-3
First Kensington Hardcover Edition: May 2014

eISBN-13: 978-1-61773-284-3
eISBN-10: 1-61773-284-2
First Kensington Electronic Edition: May 2014

10 9 8 7 6 5 4 3 2 1

Printed in the United States of America

For Kathe

Brandy's quote:
*In human history, the desire for revenge
and the desire for loot
have often been closely associated.*
John McCarthy

Mother's quote:
*By the pricking of my thumb
something wicked this way comes.*
(that Scottish play)

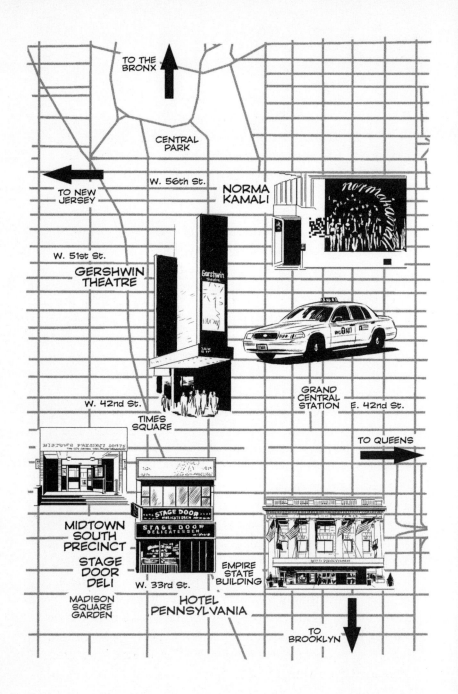

Chapter Two

Con Fusion

No, your eyes are not deceiving you, nor has the publisher made a printing error by beginning this book with chapter two. Rather, chapter one has been omitted, having been deemed by our esteemed editor as inconsequential to the murder mystery about to unfold.

But Mother and I beg to differ!

Mother being Vivian Borne, seventies, bipolar, widowed, Danish stock, local thespian, and amateur sleuth; and me, Brandy Borne, thirty-two, Prozac popping, divorced, and frequent reluctant accomplice in Mother's escapades since coming home to live with her in the small Mississippi River town of Serenity, Iowa, bringing along only a few clothes and my little blind shih tzu, Sushi.

The following is our defense for writing chapter one, however bereft of mystery content it might be.

Several loyal readers have written to inquire as to whether we have as yet found poor Aunt Olive. Olive—actually my great-aunt—wasn't "missing" in the face-on-a-milk-carton manner, since she was, after all, deceased, her ashes encased in a glass paperweight and entrusted to Mother for safekeeping. Unfortunately, during a well-meaning flurry of downsizing our antiques-cluttered home, Olive had gotten herself mixed in with a collection of paperweights and erroneously sold at a garage sale to Fanny Watterson, a third-grade teacher visiting Serenity from Akron, Ohio.

But, as Mother would say, I digress.

Thanks to the prodding of our readers, we—that is, Mother, Sushi, and I—set out by car on an eastern trek to the Buckeye State to retrieve her/it. But, in Akron, we discovered that the third-grade teacher who had purchased Auntie had done so with a paperweight-collecting friend in mind, to whom Olive had been mailed as a birthday present, in Scranton, Pennsylvania. Then, upon our arrival in Scranton, we were told by said friend (a fourth-grade teacher) that she had found the paperweight rather unattractive and possessed of "an odd vibe," so she'd regifted it to a sister (presumably not her favorite one) in Hackensack, New Jersey.

Now, just how Aunt Olive ended up in a torpedo hole of the USS *Ling* at the New Jersey Naval Museum in Hackensack is a fascinating, amusing, and remarkable set of circumstances, but—and here we must reluctantly bow to editorial wisdom—wholly inconsequential to the mystery at hand. (Chapter one *will* be available for your reading pleasure on our website, www.BarbaraAllan.com.)

Just the same, Mother and I would like to point out that if it hadn't been for the quest to recover Aunt Olive, she (Mother) and I would never have considered incorporating into our plans a trip to New York City, where we became innocently involved in yet another murder, giving us material for this, our eighth book.

So forget Akron and Scranton and Hackensack and, for that matter, Aunt Olive (meaning no offense to those cities nor our beloved late relative). Our story proper begins in Manhattan, in late March, where we were on our way to attend a comic book convention, to sell a rare Superman drawing by creators Siegel and Shuster that we had found in a storage locker won in auction last October. (We refer you to *Antiques Disposal*, available from your favorite bookseller.)

Still with us?

Specifically, we were traveling south by car on the Henry Hudson Parkway, having just crossed the George Washington Bridge, when the old burgundy Buick that had done amazingly well for us on our travels thus far began to shudder violently.

Luckily, I was able to ease the car over to an emergency lane before it shuddered its last shudder, dying with a long, mechanical death rattle, punctuated by a final *conk!* and one last steam-heat sigh.

After using my cell to summon help, I was informed by a dispassionate dispatcher (did my lack of a local accent brand me as an outsider?) that our situation was not worthy of a 9-1-1 call in the city, and not to bother her again.

No, Toto (that is, Sushi), we were not in Serenity anymore. Quiet Serenity, where a police car would have been dispatched to assist us toot-sweet. Sweet Serenity, where Mrs. Clyde Martin—monitoring a scanner in her kitchen—would begin preparing an apple pie to present us on our doorstep, in a few hours, as a consolation for our travails.

But no such assistance (and certainly no pie, apple or otherwise) had been dispatched to aid us here on the HHP, where cars cruelly whizzed by two helpless women and a blind dog next to an obviously broken-down car in the late afternoon March wind.

Mother was still quite attractive at her undisclosed age—porcelain complexion, straight nose, wide mouth, large eyes admittedly magnified by her glasses, wavy silver hair pulled loosely back. And I was no slouch—button nose, blue eyes, and shoulder-length blond hair. Plus, Sushi was cute as all heck. Yet our collective predicament failed to soften the hard-hearted New Yorkers, who continued to stir the wind as they passed, ignoring us as if that were a requirement of Big Apple citizenship.

Now might be a good time to mention that Mother was handcuffed. To a black briefcase, that is, which held our valuable Superman drawing. My insistence that the artwork would be safe in a suitcase did nothing to sway her; once Mother got an idea in her head, that was that, even after I pointed out that she would be attracting undue attention to herself (as if that would dissuade Serenity's most notorious diva).

Still, I had smirked. "Why don't you carry a big sign that says, 'Hey world! Here's something so valuable that I'm willing to lose an arm over it'?"

Her frown was almost a scowl. "Dear, I hope you're not going to be a Debbie Downer."

And I had replied, "I hope *you're* not going to be a Nutty Nancy."

Then she said something, to which I responded in kind, none of which can be reported here, if we are ever to have any hope of Walmart stocking our books.

Let's just say it had been a long cross-country trip.

One more thing about the handcuffed briefcase: Mother didn't want to spend the bucks ordering one from her spy catalogue, so she had borrowed a beat-up case from a neighbor, then stole (or as she puts it, "borrowed") cuffs from the police department, where she had recently dropped by ostensibly to give a neighborhood watch report.

Anyway, as soon as we'd crossed the George Washington Bridge, she'd hooked herself up to the briefcase.

And now she and I and the briefcase and our blind dog stood next to our dead car in an emergency lane, where I began to suspect we would spend the rest of our lives.

Mother, pulling her coat collar up around her neck with her spare, uncuffed hand to combat the icy river wind, sighed, "I'm afraid getting someone to stop won't be easy, dear. If you weren't wearing sweatpants, I'd suggest you lift your skirt in time-honored Claudette Colbert fashion."

"What?"

"*It Happened One Night*, dear!"

"You don't want to know what'll happen to us if we are still *here* at night."

Then I had an idea. It could happen.

I positioned Sushi on the car's hood.

"Dance!" I commanded the cute little fur ball.

At first she just looked at me, in the way you're just looking at this page right now.

But then I began singing "Shake Your Booty," and the dear got up on her hind legs and hopped around, wagging her furry ears, flopping her front paws rhythmically, and twitching her doggie booty.

I hadn't gotten to the song's bridge by the time a tan Subaru suddenly veered off the highway, pulling in front of us, then backed up to the Buick.

I gave Mother a self-satisfied smirk. "Who needs Claudette Colbert?"

Grabbing Sushi, I rushed over to the driver's side of the vehicle, just as the woman behind the wheel powered down her window.

"Oh, thank you so much for stopping," I said.

"Car trouble?" the lady asked.

She was middle-aged but nicely preserved, with chin-length honey-blond hair and striking, light brown eyes. She was wearing a red wool coat and black leather gloves. Next to her in the passenger seat was a large gray gym bag.

"Our car *is* the trouble," I said. "I'm afraid we need a junk dealer, not a tow truck."

She gave me a winning smile. "Been there, done that. But with an old Mustang." Then, "Where are you headed?"

"The Hotel Pennsylvania on Seventh Avenue."

She nodded. "Not too far from where I'm going. Hop in."

I thanked our Good Samaritan, then went back to the Buick to collect Mother and our luggage, giving its battered hood a final pat. We'd arrange at the hotel for a proper burial for our old friend.

We filled our savior's trunk with our belongings and settled into the Subaru—Mother in front, gym bag on her lap, the blond Samaritan giving the handcuffed briefcase a curious look; me in back holding Sushi. Then we were once again traveling south on the Hudson Parkway.

Mother introduced herself and me, ending with, "And the little dancing dog that caught your attention is Sushi."

"You should put that mutt on YouTube," the woman said, eyes on the traffic. "But it was your license plate that caught my eye."

Mother's head swivelled toward her. "Oh? Are you another native of the great state of Iowa?"

"Des Moines, originally." She took her right gloved hand off the wheel, thrusting it toward Mother. "I'm sorry, I haven't introduced myself."

She said her first name.

Which prompted Mother to ask, "Do you use a *c* or a *k* in the middle?"

"Two *k*s, actually."

"And end with a *y* or an *i*?"

"An *i*."

I could see our new friend *Vikki*'s face in the visor mirror; she had a sideways smile going, in response to Mother's insistence on detail.

But the woman wouldn't be smiling if she knew Mother's purpose. Before ride's end, she would wheedle from Vikki her last name as well as her address, and the unsuspecting lady Lancelot who'd ridden to our rescue would find herself on Mother's ever-growing Christmas-letter list, receiving—year after year—a long and laborious Yuletide report ("Merry Christmas, my darlings!"), from which the only known escape was death, either the recipient's or Mother's—and Mother felt just fine.

Moved with no forwarding address? No problem. Mother will find you. Returned to sender? Out goes the letter again. Addressee deceased? Next time, it goes to "Family of," so maybe even the Grim Reaper couldn't get you off Mother's Christmas-letter list.

This would very likely be the last time Vikki with two *k*s and an *i* helped anyone ever again on the Henry Hudson Parkway (especially with Iowa license plates).

Mother was asking her, "What's your trade, dear?"

"I work backstage on *Wicked*. I'm a costume dresser."

I interjected, "Oh! That's the show we're hoping to see while we're in town. What theater is it playing in, again?"

Vikki looked at me in the mirror. "The Gershwin on West Fifty-first. That's where I'm going after I drop you off."

With trying-too-hard sincerity, Mother said, "My dear, your job sounds *simply* marvelous." Then, instead of inquiring how long Vikki had been with the play, or how many witches she had seen come and go during its long run, or even if she'd been a dresser on other Broadway shows, Mother shifted the subject to herself.

Just like a wicked witch would.

"Ah, how well I remember waiting for reviews at Sardi's," she expounded.

"Oh?" Vikki replied politely. "You've appeared on Broadway?"

"Oh, my, yes," Mother warbled, as if the woman should have known. "My stage name was my maiden name—Vivian Jensen. But you are so young, and that was so many years ago."

"What were you in?" Vikki asked, interested.

Mother waved a dismissive hand. "I'm sure you've never heard of it, dear. Way before your time."

She had dug herself in a hole.

"Try me," Vikki said.

Confronted with an actual Broadway professional, Mother hesitated, then finally said, "Well, it was just a little production, dear, . . . not so much Broadway as off-Broadway."

"Where off-Broadway?"

"Off-*off* Broadway."

I'd never heard this story before, but my guess? If the play had been any farther off Broadway, it would have been performed in Hoboken.

Mother was saying, "This was in the late sixties, you see, when I was single and had come to Gotham to make my mark."

Maybe in answer to the Bat signal.

"And did you?" I asked, lending her a hand digging that hole. "Make your mark, I mean."

"*I* like to think so," Mother said regally. "As a matter of fact, *I* was the first actress to bare her breasts on a theatrical stage!"

"Oh," Vikki said. "Were you in *Hair*?"

"No, dear, this predated that production by some time."

"Ah. *Old Calcutta*, then?"

"No, this was before *Oh! Calcutta!*, as well. Of course, nowadays I suppose they might call my landmark performance a 'wardrobe malfunction.' You see, the strapless bra I was wearing in a boudoir scene suddenly came unhooked and shot into the audience like a huge rubber band. But this unintentional piece of improvisational business went over so well, the director decided to incorporate it into the production." Mother sighed. "A week later, the police closed us down." Then she added, chipper, "But nothing was held against me!"

Vikki gave me a look of astonished amusement in the rearview mirror, and I smiled back, raising my eyebrows in quick succession. *Welcome to my world.*

Mother was saying, "These days I'm the director of our community theater playhouse . . . along with playing leads."

"She also founded a theater group in our county jail," I offered mischievously.

"That is commendable," Vikki said, seeming impressed. "You go to the jail and hold classes?"

"No, dear," Mother replied. "I was *in* jail—for murder."

The car veered onto the shoulder, then Vikki regained control.

"But the charges were dropped," I said.

The Hudson Parkway had changed to Joe DiMaggio Highway, and then Twelfth Avenue. Soon we were turning onto West Thirty-fourth Street, the crosstown traffic— much to our blond chauffeur's relief, I'm sure—relatively light, and in another few minutes we veered onto Seventh Avenue, where the stately Hotel Pennsylvania loomed on the corner of Thirty-third Street.

Quicker than one can say "Good riddance to bad rubbish," Vikki whipped her car into the hotel's unloading zone and hopped out. Mother and I disembarked, too, to speed things along, and together we got the luggage to the curb.

Holding Sushi tightly, I said to the woman, "Thank you again for helping us."

Mother took her by the hand and said, "My dear, after we take in your show, we would just *love* to visit you backstage."

Vikki smiled nervously and withdrew her hand. "Ah, well, I *am* rather busy back there. Can't promise anything."

I could see the backstage notice board now: *Vivian and Brandy Borne Not Admitted!*

Mother pressed forward, all big eyes and bigger teeth. "Perhaps we could call you and arrange for tickets to be held at the box office. Let me get my cell phone out and add your number. . . ."

But our rescuer was already leaving. "It's been very interesting," she said. "I don't imagine we'll be running into each other again, so I'll just say so long. . . ."

"Don't be so sure," I said with a smile. "It's a *wicked* old world, you know. Always another witch waiting in the wings."

She looked a little startled, then hurried back to her Subaru, relieved to unburden herself of her charges. In another moment, she pulled skillfully out into busy traffic, courtesy of Penn Station and Madison Square Garden across the street.

Pedestrian traffic was no lighter. As we stood beneath the hotel's golden overhang—above which four American flags fluttered between massive Grecian columns—Mother and I made speed bumps in everyone's path.

Sushi gave out a little whimper, bothered by all the big city hubbub, and I held her tighter.

"Welcome to the Hotel Pennsylvania," someone said.

A doorman had materialized, smartly attired in a black uniform with red stripes around his coat cuffs and down his pant legs. Middle-aged, with reddish hair, a ruddy complexion, and friendly smile, he cut an impressive figure.

But the most impressive thing about him? He gave but a brief glance at Mother's handcuffed briefcase, no doubt having seen much stranger things in his line of work.

"Thanks for the welcome," I said.

Mother beamed at him, just a little less crazily than Norman Bates's mama at the end of *Psycho*. "It's a pleasure to be here at . . ." And shaking a forefinger in the air, yowza style, she sang, "*Pennsylvania six five thousand!*"

Then Mother, in response to my horrified expression, waiting a beat for the Andrews Sisters to turn over in their graves, said defensively, "It's a Glenn Miller tune, dear.

Very popular, back in the day. After the hotel's phone number?"

The doorman smiled gamely. "We do get that from time to time. But you're the first one to mention it *today*, ma'am."

"Do I win a prize?" Mother chirped. "A discount coupon perhaps, or a hotel beanie?"

The game smile turned a trifle strained. "I'm afraid not."

Sushi yapped her impatience.

And I yapped mine: "Mother, could we *please* get checked in? Soosh needs to be fed and to get her insulin shot, and I'm hungry, too."

Mother thought about whether to frown or to smile, decided on the latter, and said, "Very well, dear, we could *all* do with some vittles."

If you like, you can just put this book down and wait for the movie: *The Serenity Hillbillies Take Manhattan*.

"Just go on in, ladies," the doorman said. "I'll bring your luggage to the counter."

"Splendid, my good man," Mother said, lapsing into the British accent that was her default setting to impress strangers, and handed him a dollar bill. Apparently she didn't have a quid on her.

I'll give the doorman this much: he didn't flinch. And after Mother turned away, I slipped him a fiver. I mean, five spot.

We made our way into the vast rectangular lobby with its tan-and-gold marbled walls, mirrored columns, and shining floor with a motif of large diamonds and circles.

In case you were wondering why I sauntered into a hotel brazenly brandishing a dog, the Pennsylvania was (and as far as I know still is) pet friendly, playing host every year to the Westminster Kennel Club dog show.

The check-in counter ran the distance of the cavernous room, above which rows of flat-screens projected a variety of cable shows—from business to politics to sports to reality programs. But, despite the possibility of ten check-in stations, only two were open. And to my dismay (and my stomach's), a long line of patrons snaked around, corralled by black nylon ropes, as if they were trying to get tickets to the latest blockbuster flick.

"Well," an unhappy customer said, passing us, having finally checked in, "at least I got to see a complete episode of *Storage Wars*."

"Mother?" I whined. My stomach seconded that question with a growl.

"Courage, dear," she responded. "I just spotted another Good Samaritan." Waving her free hand wildly, she called out, her voice echoing across the lobby, "Oh, *yoo*-woo! Mr. Bufford! It's *Vivian*!"

A heavyset, unmade bed of a man, with a convention bag dangling from a shoulder, gave us a momentarily bewildered look that turned into recognition and a wave back at us before hurrying our way.

Mother whispered, "Mr. Bufford is the convention organizer, dear."

"Yes, I know," I whispered back. She'd had many conversations with him on the phone, and on Skype, arranging for us to come, and I'd spoken to him once or twice myself.

Our host—who I guessed to be about forty—wore wrinkled khaki shorts, a plaid short-sleeved shirt open over the convention's logo t-shirt, and white socks with sandals. His black-rimmed glasses, which rode his night-light bulb of a nose, were adhesive taped at one temple. The combover of his thinning sandy-colored hair seemed to have exploded, and he bore the wild-eyed look of a dude rancher who had just been tossed off a bull.

And the convention didn't even officially start till tomorrow.

Mr. Bufford stuck out a chubby hand to Mother. His smile was as big and sincere as it was yellow. "Vivian, so nice to finally meet you in person!"

Mother had taken the hand. "And you, likewise, young man."

"And this must be Brandy." He had stepped my way. "This is a real thrill. You know, first and foremost, I'm a fan."

"Pleasure is mine, Mr. Bufford, " I replied, my smile straining a little. Frankly, our host could have used a stronger deodorant. But then, after our long day, I probably didn't smell dew-drop fresh myself.

"Please, call me Tommy," he said. "All my friends call me Tommy." He scratched Sushi's head. "Cute dog. Just like in your books!"

Soosh sniffed at him, and (unlike me) seemed to relish his bouquet as she licked his thick hand.

Then his eyes flew to Mother's handcuffed briefcase like magnets seeking metal.

"Is *that* the Superman drawing?" he whispered, eyes wide.

"Yes, indeedy." Mother nodded, patting the case.

"You know, Vivian," Tommy said, an eyebrow arching above a slightly tilted black eyeglass frame, "that might be better kept in the hotel's safe."

"Oh, no," Mother replied, tightening her grip. "This super-duper drawing doesn't leave my sight. It will go to bed with me. It will go to the bathroom with me. Of course, I *will* entrust it to Brandy when I shower, but—"

"Mother," I said, "too much information."

Tommy was looking at me for support, but I shook my head. "I've already tried. She saw a spy movie and got the briefcase idea."

Mother's grin went well with her magnified eyes. "The

character with the briefcase got killed! They had to cut his hand off to get it."

Why Mother found this reassuring is anybody's guess.

"Very well," Tommy sighed. "But it would be a disaster if anything should happen to it—it's the showpiece of the auction, you know."

And the reason we were all-expenses-paid guests.

"Tommy," I asked, "is there any way we can avoid the check-in line?"

"Certainly," he said, grinning big again. "I have all convention guest keycards right here."

From his convention bag, he produced several small hotel folders holding keycards, then, fanning them out like a deck of playing cards, handed one to Mother.

He dug in the bag again. "And here are your badges—which will get you into all the events."

Those, I took.

"I'll get you a schedule later," he said. "You're on a mystery-writing panel Sunday morning."

A striking-looking woman rushed up. She was about my age, tall—at least six feet—curvy but muscular, with raven-black hair worn in a shoulder-length pageboy, à la Bettie Page. Her makeup was heavy—darkened brows, black-rimmed violet eyes—but the pink painted mouth gave her goth look a feminine touch. As did her dress, a fitted black and white polka-dotted number, its low neckline revealing a spray of flowers tattooed across her chest. Red heels with bows on the toes completed her mixed-signals ensemble of hard and soft.

"Sorry to interrupt . . . ," she said, addressing Tommy.

He gestured to us. "Violet, this is Vivian and Brandy Borne. They write the Antiques mysteries." Then he added in a whisper to her, "The Superman drawing," and then to us, "Violet is my assistant."

Which surprised me; I thought her to be a fan or guest professional.

"Hello," the woman replied quickly, with barely a glance our way. Neither Superman nor the Antiques books impressed her much, at least not in the throes of the big job she was caught up in. "Tommy, we've got a problem with the Buff Awards."

"Not *too* serious, I hope," he said, frowning.

"We're missing one."

"Ah . . ." Tommy looked at Mother and me. "Will you excuse me?"

Mother replied, "But of course."

And before I could say, "Nice to meet you both," they were gone.

Mother and I stood for a moment, then I took hold of the brass cart with our luggage, not waiting for a bellhop (I had a limited number of fivers), and pushed it to the elevators, Mother following, holding Sushi in her arms like an unlikely baby.

Our room was on the fourteenth floor, and I had to admit I was surprised by how small it was—my bedroom at home was larger.

"We were promised a suite," I said.

Mother was kicking off her shoes. "Dear, don't be ungrateful. Free is free. Now, where did I put the key to these darn handcuffs?"

"I'm not being ungrateful," I said ungratefully. "But there's only *one* bed."

Which didn't bother Soosh, already snuggled between two plump pillows.

"Yes, that is a problem," Mother admitted. "You *do* snore so. *You* must have the handcuff key."

"*I* snore? You could blow out these windows, on an off night. And I *don't* have the key."

Mother stood with hands on hips and a single eyebrow arched, like Mr. Spock regarding Dr. McCoy. "Dear, I *know* you're tired, but let's not be a Grumpy Gus. If I happen to snore a wee little bit, you can *always* sleep in the tub. We can request extra pillows for that purpose, if need be. You're *sure* you don't have the key?"

"No," I snapped. "Look in your purse."

"Besides," she went on, digging in her bag with her free hand, "this is a *lovely* room—perhaps a trifle cramped, I'll grant you—but this is New York, the City That Never Sleeps. . . ."

"I thought Las Vegas was the city that never sleeps, and with you snoring, I'll be the one that never sleeps."

". . . and simply *no one* comes to the Big Apple to spend much time in a hotel room. Ah, *here's* that naughty key—I had it after all." She unlocked the cuff, which fell to the floor with a thunk, then rubbed her wrist. Her eyes gleamed with possibilities behind the thick lenses. "Do you realize that the Empire State Building *and* Macy's flagship store are a mere block away?"

I had stopped paying attention, having spotted a gift basket of fruit and goodies, compliments of the convention, sitting on a side table.

With my mouth salivating and stomach growling, I moved eagerly toward it.

But Mother blocked my path. "*Oh, no* you don't, missy!" she said. "We're going to send *that* over to the Gershwin Theater to reward that nice woman for picking us up."

Mother made regifting an art.

"Over my dead body," I snarled.

And she grabbed the basket, and I grabbed the basket, and she tugged, and I tugged, and we both tugged, and suddenly the contents were airborne. Then the room was raining fruit and snacks.

A packet of gourmet salmon landed on the pillow next

to Sushi and in a blink of a blind eye she had torn it open with her sharp little teeth.

"*Now* look what you've done," Mother said crossly.

"You did it, not me!"

"You need an attitude adjustment!"

A knock at the door interrupted our squabble.

I let Mother answer it.

"Is everything all right?" Tommy asked, probably having heard bickering through the door.

"Fine, fine," Mother said. Then, "But, Tommy dear, there is a *slight* snafu. . . ."

"Yes, I know," he said, and he looked stricken. "This isn't a suite—my mistake. I know I promised you that, as a perk, for being our honored guests."

"Think nothing of it," Mother said, and I—having joined her—discreetly kicked her in the calf. Not hard. She barely ouched.

"But I *do* have a solution," Tommy said. "You ladies take *my* suite—it's 1537, just up one floor. I haven't moved in yet. Until tonight, it's been easier for me to work out of the convention's office a few blocks from here."

I was feeling a little bad about my behavior, and heard myself saying, "You're sure? Because that would really be wonderful."

"Yes, it would," Mother chimed in. "Not having to share a bed with Brandy is a lifesaver. The girl kicks like a mule."

Maybe so, but not when I'm sleeping. . . .

After exchanging keycards with Tommy, we thanked him again, and he left.

"You forgot to mention I snore," I said.

"Dear, we needn't air *all* our dirty laundry."

"Just mine." I sighed, but my mood was improving. "Help me pick up the fruit."

* * *

Our new digs were a corner suite with two rooms elegantly decorated in gold and blue, the bedroom separate from an outer area that had a fold-out couch, coffee table, desk, and mini-kitchen with sink and small fridge.

While Mother disappeared into the bathroom to wash off the dust from our trip, I put her suitcase on the king-size bed, leaving my things in the outer room by the couch, where I would sleep. Fold-out beds were never wonderful, but compared to sleeping with a world-class snorer, this one would be a magic carpet to slumberland.

After giving Sushi her insulin, followed by a dog biscuit reward for taking the shot, I helped familiarize the blind little darling with the layout of the suite so she could move around and about without bumping into anything.

I also set up a little pee station for her, having brought along a plastic tray with pads designed for emergency situations.

Finally, Sushi and I played the "maid game" I had taught her on other trips (including at those accommodations where dogs were not welcome): I would rap on the door and call, "Housekeeping, housekeeping," and she would scurry into the cracked-open closet, out of the way, until the maid had gone.

Mother, now dressed in her favorite emerald green velour top and slacks, held out a hand to me.

"What's this?" I asked, taking the silver object she offered.

"A rape whistle, dear."

"Oh-kay . . . I'm not wearing that."

"Then keep it in your pocket." She had hers around her neck on a silver chain.

"No, I don't think so."

Mother shrugged. "Suit yourself. But we're in the *Naked City* now, where there are eight million stories, few with happy endings."

She had conveniently forgotten that I'd lived in Chicago for ten years before my divorce.

But to placate her, I said, "I'll think about it," and set the whistle on the coffee table.

Mother stared at me with a frown. "Dear, meaning no offense and not intending in any way to redraw battle lines, but . . . you do look a fright. I hope you're going to freshen up before we go to the reception."

There was a preconvention get-together in one of the ballrooms for the guests and professionals—artists and writers—along with staff members. Most of the pros were involved in the comics industry, but others—like Mother and me—were from related fields, like movies and books.

This was also preview night—when preregistered attendees got a three-hour "sneak" look at the vendors, before opening tomorrow to the general public. But we were skipping that.

"This is as fresh as I'm gonna get," I said grumpily.

Mother took my hand and led me to the couch, pulled me down to sit with her.

"Brandy," she began gently, "I know what's troubling you."

"You do?"

"Yes. You miss *him*."

By "*him*," I knew she meant Tony Cassato, former Serenity chief of police, with whom I had begun a romantic relationship before circumstance and fate intervened. Tony had been forced to flee into witness protection after New Jersey mobsters dispatched a contract killer to retaliate for his testimony against them.

Mother was saying, "Taking your frustration out on me won't help, dear. You've been a grouch all day. You are better than that."

She was right. About the me being a grouch part, anyway.

"I'm sorry," I said, nodding, sighing. "I'll try to be better."
Mother patted my knee. "There's my sweet, good girl."
So I washed my face, combed my hair, reapplied makeup,
and put on a Max and Cleo geometric-print dress, little
Juicy Couture cardigan, and short tan Frye boots.

Mother had once again locked herself to the briefcase
and, after we'd pinned on our convention badges for the
reception, we headed out.

The reception, held in one of the smaller ballrooms—
PennTop North on the eighteenth floor, with a spectacular
view of the city—was in full swing as we arrived, the guest
professionals and staff talking and laughing, competing
with a disc jockey in one corner who was playing loud
dance music. That disco beat never seemed to go out of
style in NYC.

I was both disappointed and kind of relieved that there
was nary a costumed superhero in sight—they were lined
up in the lower lobby, outside the huge Globetrotter Ballroom where the booths were set up, waiting to get in. And
their presence would increase on the day of the costume
ball and contest.

While Mother stood in the doorway—whether expecting to be noticed, planning her next move, or choosing a
new victim to befriend—I made a beeline for the buffet,
where I filled up my small plate to overflowing.

How to be a one-trip salad bar cheat—a.k.a. salad bar
hacking: First, fill a bowl with food, then lay carrot sticks
on top as a second "floor." Next, build a circular wall of
cucumbers, tomato slices, and/or oranges. Finally, fill the
tower in with other salad bar goodies. (Be careful your
tower isn't the leaning Pisa kind, because more than one
of mine has toppled all over a restaurant floor.)

Balancing my plate, utensils, napkin, and bottled water,
I surveyed the tables, looking for an empty chair, but
found none. Then I remembered passing by a little alcove

outside the ballroom, with end tables and two overstuffed chairs, and decided to go there.

Mother was across the room, flitting from person to person, inserting herself into one conversation or another, showing off her briefcase bracelet. I wanted to get her attention, to motion I would be out in the hall, but had no free hand to do it.

Which didn't matter; I wouldn't be missed.

Finding the alcove empty, I settled into one of the comfy chairs. The food on my plate looked yummy, but admittedly at this stage of my long day, I would have found cardboard a feast. I was in the process of removing juicy bits of meat and vegetable from a skewer when an altercation between two men outside the alcove interrupted.

One of the pair I immediately recognized: our host, Tommy Bufford. The other was tall, slender, with wavy dark hair and an angular face; he wore a yellow polo shirt and tan slacks, a preppie alternative to train-wreck Tommy.

"You signed an *exclusivity* clause, remember?" the wavy-haired guy said angrily, poking Tommy in the chest with a hard forefinger. "You weren't supposed to operate a competing convention for five *years*, and I'm gonna sue your stinky ass."

"So sue me," Tommy said, and shrugged. "But you'll be wasting your time and money, Gino. I'm just a hired hand here."

The wavy-haired guy snorted. "That won't wash. You're *running* things—your name is being used."

Another shrug. "Just because we cofounded the Manhattan comic convention doesn't mean you have any claim to *my* name. Or do I need to sue *you* over *that*?"

Now Tommy poked the other man's chest.

"And that goes double for the Buff Awards," he added. "Buff is short for Bufford, you know. If you wanted to keep presenting those at the *old* con, then you should've included *that* in the contract."

As Tommy walked away, the guy yelled, "Sometimes I could just *kill* you, you *bleeper!*" Fill in the bleep yourself. Then he was gone, too.

I had meant to tell Mother about the scrap, but when we returned to our suite—Mother having made countless new friends, me having gone through three plates at the salad bar—I was so full and so tired, I just flopped on the couch, not bothering to unfold the bed, still in my dress and cardi.

I don't know how long I'd been asleep, when something woke me. The room was dark, as was Mother's bedroom, though I could hear her snoring behind the closed door, like a sea storm roaring behind a shut porthole. That was probably the noise I'd heard, I thought, and rolled over.

I felt around for Sushi, but she wasn't with me, having deemed a soft bed with Mother more appealing than a cramped couch with her mistress.

As I lay curled up with my head on one of the small davenport pillows, my eyes accustomed to the dark, it seemed to me as if something or someone was coming through the wall directly across the room!

I froze as a figure moved stealthily toward the bedroom.

The intruder had not seen me, apparently not expecting anyone to be camped out on the couch . . . which gave me an advantage.

I grabbed my rape whistle off the coffee table, stuck it in my mouth, and blew.

The shrill, eardrum-splitting sound startled our uninvited guest, who stumbled into the dinette set, toppling a chair.

Suddenly the door to the bedroom flew open and Mother, in red flannel pj's, came rushing out, crying,

"*Rape! Rape!*" at the top of her voice. And Sushi was not far behind, yapping for all she was worth.

The intruder fled back through the wall, which I realized held a connecting door to the next room. And there was a little "click" as it was being locked from the other side.

How had our side gotten unlocked?

"Quick, dear," she said. "We can catch him."

I shook my head. "No! I'm in no mood for a struggle. Anyway, he's gone by now. And I think you'll find that the room next door is empty."

"You're no fun," she said poutily. "But surely those whistles, our yelling, will result in help arriving unbidden!"

"You're in Manhattan," I reminded her, and a siren underscored my point. "Anyway, this is what you *get* by letting everyone under the sun know we've got that Superman drawing in our room. The first thing tomorrow, we're putting that thing in the hotel's safe!"

"I suppose you're right," Mother replied sheepishly. "But we should call security."

"In the morning. Go back to sleep. He won't be back. If it makes you feel better, I'll leave the lights on out here."

"Very well," Mother said disappointedly. "But I still think, with a little effort, we might well have caught him."

"Good *night*, Mother," I said with finality.

She shuffled into the bedroom, making a decidedly untheatrical exit. For her.

And I went back to the couch—after making doubly sure our side of the door was locked and had a chair propped under the knob.

But I didn't sleep. Couldn't.

Because there was something I hadn't told Mother about our intruder—and the reason I didn't want us running after him.

When she had opened the door coming to my rescue,

the light from the bathroom caught the glint of metal in his hand.

In the shape of what seemed to be a knife.

A Trash 'n' Treasures Tip

Comics conventions are not just about selling or buying funny books. You'll find at these fun functions a wide array of pop-culture memorabilia and collectibles: cartoon figurines, autographed photos, original comic artwork, and even clothing. I'm looking for a set of Shmoo salt and pepper shakers, because I think they're so darn cute! The Shmoo was a famous critter in the *Li'l Abner* comic strip. But Mother finds them repellent, insisting they are "phallic symbols with eyes, dear."

Chapter Three

Con Seat

The following morning, a cool, overcast Thursday, judging by the view from our suite, Mother and I left Sushi behind and headed to the security office to report last night's break-in.

Mother was once again handcuffed to the briefcase—the Superman drawing safely within—but this time I did not make light of her precautionary measure. I didn't even suggest that she leave the drawing behind in our little room safe, which wasn't all *that* safe—according to the Internet (where things are sort of true), most hotel-room safes can be forced open with a screwdriver. Those not bolted down can even be carried out the door.

Mother, in her lavender Breckenridge slacks and sweater outfit, looked rested and lovely—no dark circles under *her* eyes. I was a different story—my bags had bags. While I had stayed awake in case our intruder returned, Mother had snored contentedly away in the next room, as if a hotel break-in were just some typical big city fun arranged to show a couple of tourists a good time.

Even Sushi had abandoned me for the comfort of Mother's comforter, albeit burrowing her head in the latter to cut down on the sounds of sawing lumber.

Today, I was wearing the same clothes I'd had on for the past twenty-four hours, lacking the will and the energy to change; next to me, Tommy Bufford would look natty.

And now, in the light of day, as our elevator reached the lobby floor, I wondered if the whole nightmarish episode hadn't been a simple misunderstanding; someone occupying the room next door, possibly a little tipsy after a festive night out, may have mistaken our connecting door for their bathroom.

I was even starting to question whether I'd really seen a knife in the intruder's hand. The room had been dark, and that glint could have been any number of things—a silver pen or cigarette lighter (or rape whistle).

The security office, according to a sign with pointing arrow, was located down a short hallway beyond the registration desk. I hesitated, wondering if we should first speak with a hotel employee, the concierge perhaps, before barging into the security office. But the two check-in clerks were busy checking out guests, and the concierge desk was vacant. Besides, Mother had already barreled forward.

"Now, let me do the talking, dear," she instructed, hand gripping the doorknob of the security office. "I have much more experience with this kind of thing."

"Having your hotel room broken into?"

"Dealing with New Yorkers. I lived here for a time, you know."

"I lived in Chicago."

"Different animal. Entirely different animal. You'll follow my lead, dear?"

There was another option?

I dutifully nodded, and we entered.

The room was as richly appointed as an office furniture showroom—ornate, mahogany desk with padded burgundy leather chair, two Deco-print visitors' chairs angled in front, the mandatory standing fern plant in one corner, poised as if to take notes.

On the wall behind the desk was a display of gold-framed photos, featuring the hotel's interior and exterior at various times over its long history. On an adjacent wall, pictures of modern-day police officers—one grouping before a sign reading MIDTOWN PRECINCT SOUTH—hinted as to the manager's previous occupation.

Yes, over the course of these investigations, I have become a trained sleuth.

We approached the desk, where a nameplate resting on its edge read ROBERT SIPCOWSKI, SECURITY MANAGER. The swivel chair was empty.

"Not here," Mother observed.

Also a trained sleuth.

"I suppose we might have phoned ahead," she said a little irritably. Mother feels that everyone should be at her beck and call at all times.

"We could leave a note," I suggested, gesturing toward a pad and pen by the phone on the otherwise uncluttered desk.

A door to our right suddenly opened, startling us both, and a man strode in.

For a brief moment, before the door shut again, we got a peek into the adjoining room: the nerve center of the hotel's security operation, where several dark-suited employees were monitoring a wall of security screens.

"I'm Robert Sipcowski, head of security," the man said, businesslike but friendly, offering a hand first to Mother, then to me. He seemed not at all offended that we'd invaded his space. "You're guests at the hotel?"

We nodded.

He smiled—again, businesslike. Though his eyes never

seemed to leave our faces, he somehow seemed aware of that briefcase dangling from Mother's wrist like bizarre goth bling. "How may I help you, ladies?"

At my tender age, I wasn't crazy about being called a "lady," but he meant well. A man can't call a woman of thirty "a girl" without getting in trouble. On the other hand, a man can call a woman over forty a girl and get a smile for it. As these pointless thoughts threaded through my brain, I was noting Sipcowski's presence in the various police photos on the wall.

The ex-officer was of average height, in his mid- to late fifties, his stark white hair conservatively cut, as was his navy suit, the white shirt and striped shades of blue tie almost a uniform. Years on the NYPD had given his oval face a well-grooved, weathered look but his brown eyes remained alert.

Mother, taking an immediate shine to the middle-aged man, said coquettishly, "We had a teensy-weensy little problem last night."

At least she wasn't speaking in her fake Brit accent.

"Oh?" His eyebrows went up, but the alert eyes became half hooded. "What kind of problem?" He gestured toward the visitors' chairs. "Please, please, ladies, sit."

And he moved behind his desk and into his chair, leaning forward, fingers tented, ready to calm any guest's concern or irksome ire, his manner conveying that he took seriously whatever that concern or ire might be.

And at a hotel like this one, he could encounter a lot of screwballs with wacky concerns and ires. For example, right now he was about to deal with Vivian Borne.

Mother placed the briefcase on the floor beside her, handcuffed arm dangling down as if wounded.

"Mr. Sipcowski," Mother began, "you may have noticed my briefcase."

"Please, call me Robert. And, yes, I did."

Mother nodded. "Very well, Robert. And please take the liberty of calling me Vivian."

I closed my eyes. I tried to keep my groan interior.

Mother was gesturing toward me with her free hand. "And this is my daughter, Brandy—oh! I guess I should say, technically, she's my *granddaughter*. Peggy Sue—that's my real daughter, that is, I mean to say, my natural daughter, not that little Brandy is *unnatural* in any way...." And here she giggled girlishly. "... Well, Peggy Sue had Brandy on the other side of the blanket, as folks were wont to say back in the day, but of course Brandy didn't *know* about that until last year."

Robert's smile had frozen, the alert eyes glazing over. This happened fairly often to people meeting Mother for the first time.

I said, "We had an intruder in our room last night."

Mother frowned in my direction, as if I'd spoken in a most inappropriate manner. "I thought we agreed that *I* was to do the explaining, dear."

"Well, you explained quite a bit, and now I'll just fill in what you left out."

"I *was* getting around to it, dear."

"I'm sure, but, uh, Mr. Sipcowski might be interested in how the story of our lives pertains to his hotel. So I cut to the chase."

"Dear, there was no chase. The intruder simply scurried out when you blew that rape whistle."

This perked Robert up. "Well, that's a start—you've cleared up the source of the shrill whistle that awoke several guests on the fifteenth floor last night."

I said, "We're in fifteen thirty-seven. Although we may be registered in fourteen-twenty-one."

Robert cleared his throat. "Ladies . . . perhaps we *could* back up and start at the beginning."

Vivian, whose chin was up defensively, said, "I thought that's what I was doing."

I said, "Not that far back, Mother."

The security chief said, "Could we get to the pertinent information? Vivian, would you like to try again?"

Back in the game, Mother batted her long eyelashes, a feminine "perk" of her glaucoma medication. "Certainly, Robert."

And she hauled the briefcase up, slapping it on the desk, like a fisherman landing a mackerel on a boat deck.

"Someone," she said with melodrama that might have been better saved for the Serenity Community Playhouse, "was after *this*."

Robert seemed less impressed than Mother might have liked. "What is it?"

Mother smiled slyly. "I'll show you—as soon as I rid myself of these handcuffs." She gave me a look usually reserved for magicians' assistants. "Brandy? The key please."

I sighed. "I don't have it, Mother."

Mother's smile continued on, fairly regal now. "No, dear, I'm sure I gave the key to you."

"No. You didn't."

Déjà vu. And gesundheit.

Mother sighed. She gave Robert a smile of girlish embarrassment. "Well, it's of no great import. I'll just open the case."

With her free hand, she began fiddling with the little four-tumbler lock. "Let's see, I just changed the combination this morning. . . ."

"Zero, zero, zero, zero," I suggested.

"That was yesterday."

"One, two, three, four."

"The day before."

"Try the year you *claim* you were born."

She shot me a nasty look, and I admit that had been a

low blow. "You're not *helping*, dear." Then, "I remember!
It's our room number." She turned to me. "*What's* our
room number again?"

But Robert beat me to it: "Fifteen thirty-seven."

Mother raised a forefinger. "I'll try *that*."

She did, and the briefcase snapped open. Mother
twirled it around on the desk, and Robert leaned forward
for a look.

"A drawing of Superman," he said flatly, sounding a little surprised but mostly disappointed, perhaps having en-
visioned diamonds or cash.

Mother, unfazed by his lackluster reaction, gushed,
"Not just *any* Superman drawing, my dear man."

"Really."

She nodded vigorously, and for a moment I thought
something in her head rattled, but it was only the handcuffs.

"It's *extremely* rare," Mother explained. "Drawn by the
creators of Superman, who are dead." The latter was delivered as if very good news. "That simple drawing is
worth a small fortune."

Robert frowned. "How small? Or should I say, how big?"

"That's part of why we're attending the comic book
convention here. It's going to be auctioned off, and this
drawing is a real draw." She smiled at her delightful play
on words.

Robert was still frowning at her. "And you've been carrying it around with you?"

Mother shrugged. "Well . . . yes. But it was in this
locked case."

Robert again sat forward. "Ma'am," he said sternly, almost crossly, using a term ladies of all ages hate to hear,
"you've been very foolish, not putting that valuable drawing in the hotel's safe. And it was reckless that you didn't
call us *immediately* after the break-in."

Mother, looking crestfallen by the reprimand, was at a rare loss for words.

I said, "We apologize for our inaction—I guess we forgot we're not in Kansas anymore."

Mother's magnified eyes blinked at me. "Don't you mean we're not in Iowa, dear? You'll have to forgive her, Robert, she's most flummoxed this morning, after our close call last night."

"*Wizard of Oz* reference, Mother? Hello?" I asked Robert, "Could we please leave the drawing with you? You'll see that it's put into the hotel's safe?"

"Of course," he said, nodding. "I'll get the necessary papers for you to sign. But first, let's take things back a few steps, okay? Not all the way to the wrong side of the blanket, if you don't mind."

I smiled. Maybe I blushed.

"Dear," Mother said, "I think Robert would like you to stop going down these side roads, and tell him about the break-in."

I did, with Mother pitching in when necessary, and pretty much behaving as she did so.

"*Was* it a knife?" Robert asked, very concerned.

"Honestly, I don't know now," I said. "It could have been almost anything reflective. I'm afraid it may just have been my imagination."

"But what if it wasn't? What if someone with a knife really did break into your room?"

"Well, he scared off awfully easily. I just blew that whistle. I mean, it's shrill, but if he was somebody dangerous with a knife, he could have come over and . . . and silenced me."

Robert appeared troubled.

Mother asked, "Do you have security cameras everywhere around the hotel?"

Robert shook his head. "Not *everywhere*, no. In the lobby, in front of the ballrooms—the more public places.

Not on the floors of the guest rooms, with the exception of the elevator areas. It's just not possible to monitor that many cameras in a building as large as this, with our limited staff-to-guest ratio. We concentrate on areas of high security risk."

I asked, "So there's no way to tell who may have come and gone in the room next to ours?"

Robert rocked back in his chair, shaking his head glumly. "No. Brandy, if you think that your intruder was armed, we should call the police in on this."

"I'm not sure. Can we avoid that?"

All I could think of was the NYPD checking with the Serenity PD about us and getting back a most interesting "rap sheet" for their trouble.

A short time later, after entrusting the drawing to Robert's care, we emerged from the security office, heading toward the lobby.

"I feel so much better about our safety now," Mother said. "Don't you, dear?" She still had the empty briefcase handcuffed to her wrist. "Now that Superman is locked away in the hotel safe."

I nodded. "But it wouldn't hurt for word to get around that we don't have the drawing with us anymore."

"I'll see what I can do," she said. Then, "Robert was nice, don't you think?" Apparently, his reprimand of our behavior had been forgotten.

"Yeah," I said, steering Mother through the lobby traffic. "Nice man." Considering what we'd thrown at him, anyway. . . .

"Of course, you noticed that he was flirting just *shamelessly* with me."

"No. Afraid I missed that."

"Oh, toward the end of the interview, it became quite obvious he was attracted to me. A girl can tell such things."

See what I mean about women over forty liking that term "girl"? Way over forty, in this case.

I grunted. "Then I guess it's a lucky thing you have your rape whistle handy."

Mother halted and frowned at me. "Dear, it's not nice to joke about such things."

No, it wasn't. I'd had a close call myself once, back in the Windy City, which I'd foiled by way of a small can of mace. But Mother didn't need to know about that.

"Brandy, dear?"

"Yes?"

"Please don't take offense, but . . ."

No sentence in the history of man that began in that fashion went anywhere good.

". . . you desperately need a shower. I'm afraid you have that pungent quality so common to some of these comic book aficionados."

"Then I'll fit right in, won't I? Anyway, I don't care."

"Have you no pride, dear? No shame?"

"Not when I'm starving, I don't. I need food, but not just *any* food. I want *New York* food."

"Well, all food served in New York is by definition New York food, isn't it?"

"No. I want *real* New York food. I want lox and bagels for breakfast!"

I was raised a Methodist, but my stomach was born Jewish.

"All right, dear, calm down, calm down." She cocked her head. "You *have* been taking your Prozac, haven't you, sweets? We have a pact, you know . . . I stay on *my* medicine if *you* stay on yours—even though I obviously don't need mine."

Mother is bipolar, and she definitely needs hers, while I was merely stressed out (and definitely needed mine).

She was saying, "Here's a suggestion for your approval,

as Rod Serling used to say on *Twilight Zone*. Since I *have to* go back to the room to get these cuffs off, you may as well have a nice hot shower. *Then* we'll find a deli, I promise."

I frowned like the child she could so easily turn me into. "I'm holding you to that, lady."

We made our way through the crowded lobby to the even more crowded elevators, finally squeezing into one, standing between two Star Wars troopers, as if being taken prisoner. Also on board was a rather lumpy-looking Batman, and a white-faced, green-haired Joker whose garish lipstick smile reminded me just a little too much of Mother.

In the suite, Sushi greeted us, then trotted back to Mother's unmade bed, while I headed off to the shower.

Half an hour later, refreshed, hair blown dry, makeup applied, I emerged in a hotel white robe, smelling better than anybody you might encounter on an elevator during a comic book convention. Mother, I saw, was free of her handcuffs and the briefcase that had been at her side like a clunky purse for so very long.

I put on a pair of dark denim DKNY jeans, and a purple cashmere sweater (well worth the money, unless you have moths in your closet), and slipped into a pair of black sparkly UGGs (gotta have *some* glitter in this life).

We shared the elevator down with some cute Japanese girls (of an age when that word was neither an insult nor a compliment) who were dressed as anime characters in short skirts, with kitten ears and shaggy tails.

Once again we battled our way through the lobby (where was a lightsaber when you needed one?) and, as we approached the Eighth Avenue doors, I could see the beckoning sign of the Stage Door Deli across the street. That was when someone took my arm from behind.

I turned, startled, as New Yorkers are known for a lot

of things, but touchy-feely isn't one of them. Not in a good way, that is.

"Excuse me," the young blond man said in a second tenor caressed by a charming Scandinavian accent. "That was rude, but I did not want to lose you."

I didn't know why he wanted to find us in the first place, but whether he'd been rude or not, or just simply impulsive, I wasn't sure I minded.

In his midtwenties, he had light blue eyes behind wire-framed glasses, a straight nose, and sensual mouth. He wore a colorful sweater in a zigzag pattern, dark jeans, and sneakers.

"May I speak to you both, please? You are the Bornes?"

"We're the Bornes who were just leaving for breakfast," I said, in halfhearted protest. "Can this wait until after we've eaten?"

But Mother chimed in, "Unless, young man, you'd like to join us. You look like you, too, are a stranger in a strange land."

He smiled at that, but I wouldn't bet two cents that he understood what she meant.

I was less eager, no matter how cute our new Nordic friend might be. I can be as sociable as the next gal, but the sight of me scarfing down deli food was nothing I wanted to subject myself or a friendly stranger to.

"I would love to join you for coffee," he said, and revealed a wealth of perfect white teeth as blinding as sun reflecting off icy blue waters. (I was going to add *of a fjord*, but that seemed a little much.)

The Stage Door Deli, on the corner of Thirty-third and Eighth, catered to the business and tourist crowd around Madison Square Garden. Some delis, like Canter's in LA, haven't changed since the dawn of time, or anyway since *I Love Lucy*'s first season. Here the decor was modern and upscale, with cream-colored walls, soft lighting, and cherrywood tables and chairs. But the food—piles of meat and cheese and fish and desserts displayed behind long glassed-in counters for takeout—looked just as tempting as the funkiest deli on either coast.

The restaurant was bustling, but we managed to find a table for four in a far corner, and settled in.

"I am Eric Johansson," our guest announced. "And you are the Bornes. I am a fan. I have read you."

Immediately, Mother asked, "Is your first name spelled with a *c* or a *k*?"

Was she starting *that* again?

"A *c*."

"And your last . . . two *s*'s or one?"

I kicked her under the table. Did she have any idea how expensive mailing her thick Christmas letter overseas would be?

Mother frowned in my direction. "Dear, I realize you're peckish, but let's not be beastly."

Good lord, was the British accent coming?

"Two *s*'s, Mrs. Borne," Eric answered with an amused smile.

"Where are you from?" I asked, trying not to be beastly.

"Denmark," Eric replied.

Mother chirped, "Why, what a wonderful coincidence! *We're* Danish, too—well, Danish extraction, second and third generation. Brandy and I are big fans of TV shows from your country and its Nordic neighbors. We just *love* your TV series *The Killing*."

"Ah, yes," Eric nodded. "In my country, it is called *Forbrydelsen*."

Mother seemed about to try repeating that, then thought better of it.

A waiter appeared, efficient and a New York mix of friendly and surly, and Mother and I both ordered lox and bagels. Eric had black coffee.

When the waiter left, Mother asked, "Eric, what was it you want to talk to us about? Our last book? Our *next* book?"

Eric removed a monogrammed white-and-blue-striped handkerchief from his pocket. "When I saw you in the lobby," he said, cleaning his lenses, "I had just come from the security office. I spoke to this man Sipcowski there. You see, I have the room next to yours."

"Ah!" Mother's eyes narrowed. "Go on."

Eric returned the handkerchief to his pocket, and replaced his glasses. "I went to report that my room keycard had been stolen—or, at least, I could not find it this morning."

"This morning?" I asked. "If you don't mind my asking, why didn't you miss it last night?"

Before our break-in.

"That is a logical question . . . you see—this is a bit awkward—I did not spend last night in my own room." He shifted in his chair. "Anyway, the security manager, Sipcowski, told me someone had broken into your room, entering through mine. Most alarming! And I wanted you to know that it was *not* me."

"Because," Mother said, "you spent the night with Violet."

Eric's mouth dropped open. Mine, too. It was like Sherlock Holmes looking at your shoes and deducing where you went to college.

His forehead frowned but his mouth smiled, those wonderful teeth again on display. "How . . . how did you know?"

Mother smiled slyly. "I saw the way you two were looking at each other last evening, during the reception."

Eric's cheeks reddened, and he said quietly, "We do not want anyone to know. I would appreciate your discretion. You both."

"Why a need for discretion?" I asked.

He leaned forward, said quietly, "Because Violet is in charge of the awards. And I am a nominee for best writer."

So he wrote comic books. I wondered if his characters all spoke with Scandinavian accents and avoided contractions.

"So?" Mother pooh-poohed. "Violet doesn't pick the winners, does she? I didn't think so. As I understand the process, that's already been done by the comic book store owners, who were mailed ballots months ago."

"That is true," Eric said. "But you know how people talk." He shrugged. "I do not know why I am so concerned—Harlan Thompson is almost certainly going to win best writer."

Thompson, a veteran comic book writer who had toiled for years in near obscurity, recently had a property of his made into a movie. I was no expert on comics, but what Eric said made sense.

Eric was saying, "But it is an honor to be nominated, and to get my work in front of American audiences. And someday I *will* have that pen."

"Pen?" I asked.

He nodded and flashed the smile again, a little embarrassed. "Forgive my ego. It is the award given for writers—a gold pen with your name inscribed upon it."

"I wouldn't mind winning that," Mother mused, adding ridiculously, "I can always use another good pen."

Our food arrived, and Mother and I dug in, Eric finishing his coffee, which had already been served.

"You know, I really should be going," Eric said, checking his watch. "The opening ceremony will be starting soon. Will you two nice ladies be attending?"

Ladies again. Rats!

"Wouldn't miss it for the world," Mother said, dabbing

daintily at her mouth with a napkin. "But *you* go ahead, Eric—we'll see you there." And she reached for his check on the table. "And *I'll* take care of this."

I managed not to roll my eyes. All he'd had was coffee, after all.

Eric stood, giving her a dimple-cheeked smile. He was very cute, and it was a darn good thing I was in love with someone else already. But not so good that my guy was in the witness protection program, without me. . . .

"That is very kind of you, Mrs. Borne." He nodded at me. "Brandy. And thank you both for keeping my . . . se-cret."

"No problem," I answered.

But it wasn't much of a secret, now that Mother knew.

After Eric departed, Mother pronounced, "I tend to be-lieve his story. What about you?"

"For now," I said through a mouth full of bagel.

"Dear?"

"Yeah?"

"You have cream cheese on your face. It's no wonder the boy bolted."

Warned you I was a sloppy deli eater. Or maybe when a girl's boyfriend is in witness protection, she lets things slide a little. . . .

I paid both checks (*not* Mother), then we meandered back over to the hotel to catch the convention's opening ceremony.

But our moseying, while good for the digestion, proved bad for us snagging any remaining seats in the Gold Ball-room, located on level C. The chamber, with its gold walls, blue-and-red kaleidoscope–patterned rug, and multi-chandeliered ceiling, was packed with fans, some in costume, most just casually attired and ready for a good time.

Not that Mother was easily dissuaded. She marched up

the center aisle, eagle-eyeing each row of blue and gold chairs until spotting an aisle seat covered by a coat.

"Is that seat taken?" she asked a young woman dressed in a Catwoman black leather outfit that looked painted on. (Good thing she had the body for it.)

"I'm saving it for my boyfriend," Catwoman said.

"Dear," Mother said patronizingly sweetly, "if we fail to follow the convention's rule of not saving seats, we shall descend into chaos, and anarchy will soon follow."

And Mother picked up the coat, handed it over to Catwoman—who was thinking that speech over—and plopped herself down.

That seemed risky to me, considering Catwoman looked like a refugee from an S&M bar (not that we have any in Serenity), but Mother had her own claws and could take care of herself.

I was on my own. Toward the back, I discovered a chair devoid of person or garment, beside a heavyset man, the chair already half taken by his bulk. Maybe it was still available because nobody wanted to sit next to the Incredible Hulk, sort of a surprise in this crowd. And he didn't smell any worse than I had earlier, so I squeezed in.

Violet was taking the podium on a little raised platform, having slipped out from behind the gold curtains. Dressed in another sexy, formfitting dress—white with red cherries, this time—she looked radiant. Perhaps spending the night with Eric had agreed with her. Anyway, I could sure see what he saw in her.

"Welcome to the first Bufford Con!" she said into the microphone.

The crowd clapped and cheered and hooted and whistled.

"Are we having fun yet?"

"*Yeah!*"

"Are we having fun yet?"

"*YEAH!*"

"We're going to have a *fantastic* weekend," she went on, her smile lovely and enthusiastic. "Tonight is Preview Night—doors open at five, so make sure you have your badges. Early panels will start today on the sixth floor, so consult your program booklets. Friday night, the awards ceremony is in the Skytop Room on the eighteenth floor, where the costume ball will be held on Saturday night. That's just the broad strokes, so keep your program booklets handy. You don't want to miss any of the action."

Violet paused, glancing at her notes.

And Mother took advantage of the silence to pop up from her chair like burnt toast in a toaster.

"*My daughter and I do not have possession of the Superman drawing anymore!*" she announced, using her best back-of-the-theater projection.

As all eyes went to her, I shrank in my seat. Or as much as I could shrink in half a seat.

"*It's in the hotel safe!*" Mother added. "*So if you're not a safe cracker, my advice would be* fuh-geddaboutit!"

Violet, temporarily thrown by this guest speaker, said, "Uh, okay, Mrs. Borne. That's Vivian Borne, one of our honored guests, half of the Antiques mystery-writing team. Good to know . . . I think."

Scattered, confused applause followed.

Encouraged, Mother went on, "*So no one need accost us!*"

Violet said, "Ah . . . Mrs. Borne?"

"Yes, dear?"

"I believe you've made your point. Sit down, please?"

"Carry on!" Mother said, and sat.

Next to me, the Hulk asked, "Who was *that?*"

"I have no idea," I said.

"What's an 'antiques mystery,' anyway?"

"Not a clue."

Violet, addressing the crowd again, was saying, "And now I'd like to turn the ceremony over to Bufford Con's creator—one of the true pioneers in the comics convention world . . . *Tommy Bufford*!"

Above the cheers, Tommy shouted into the microphone, "Thank you . . . thank you, for that warm welcome! If it weren't for you, the fans, this convention would not have been possible."

More cheers, and some hooting, a number of attendees getting back on their feet to holler encouragement.

"But you believed in me, and my retro vision of a smaller comics convention—where anyone who wanted to attend a panel could. Where security was here not to hinder, but to help the fans. And where the bottom line was not about making money, but having eff-you-enn, *fun*."

A whoop went up from the audience, some still on their feet.

Despite the noise, my lack of sleep, coupled with the heaviness of the meal, made me nod off. A while later, something jolted me awake, and I found I'd rested my head against Hulk's pudgy shoulder, using it as a soft pillow.

"Oh," I said, embarrassed. "Sorry."

He smiled sideways at me, shyly. "Huh . . . that's okay, miss."

Miss. So much better than "lady."

Tommy had been replaced at the podium. "Who's that?" I asked the Hulk.

"That's the Fan Guest. These cons almost always showcase some fan who's made a name for himself. That's Brad Webster."

This particular honored guest was rail thin, in superhero t-shirt, jeans, and sandals, with uncombed brown hair, and a case of acne I could see from my back-row seat.

I asked, "How does a fan make a name for himself?"

"Well . . . be somebody special, I guess. Webster runs a really popular website devoted to comics fandom—Webbie on the Web."

Actually, I had heard of it, from my geek pal Joe Lange. Webster was going on, but you couldn't understand him, a mix of talking too softly and eating the microphone. Something about taking fandom back for the fans seemed to be the gist, though from whom they were taking it, I couldn't tell you.

"He's about done," Hulk said after a while.

"Good—'cause you may have noticed, I need some serious naptime."

But it was another ten minutes before Webbie on the Web would relinquish his moment in the spotlight. The applause he got was a little halfhearted.

As the crowd dispersed, I stayed put, waiting for Mother to find me. When she did, I asked, "Do you think that was wise? Spouting off like that?"

Mother looked surprised. "Dear, what better way to get the word around?"

"Well, passing out leaflets wouldn't have been quite so embarrassing. Posting notices on bulletin boards and on the walls, maybe."

"Perhaps you would rather have me shout it from the observation deck of the Empire State Building."

"Good idea. That'll be me, standing right behind you. Giving you support."

"Dear, that smirk will become a permanent fixture on your face—just look at what it did to Bruce Willis."

"Made him a kazillionaire?" I sighed, "I'm sorry, Mother, if I seem hard to get along with. But I just *have to* catch a nap. I hardly slept at all, after our incident last night."

Mother cocked her head like Sushi trying to understand me talking on the phone to somebody. "You *do* look a trifle white around the gills, dear. But, I'm afraid, with everyone heading to the elevators, it will be a while before we get to our room—unless you want to use the stairs."

I did not. Not fifteen floors of them, anyway. "Let's look for a service elevator," I said.

"Good thinking, dear. Perhaps behind that curtain. . . ."

Behind the curtain was a storage room of tables and chairs and linens. A door marked EXIT led to a back hallway, down which was, indeed, a service elevator.

Mother, punching the UP button, said, "You know, dear, we're going to need costumes for the masquerade ball." She put a finger on a cheek. "I wonder if that nice *Vikki* would loan us some costumes from *Wicked*."

"Oh, no. Anything but that. Promise me you won't call her. You can't think that we could borrow costumes from a Broadway—"

The elevator door slid open, and we both gasped.

On the elevator floor lay Tommy Bufford, pioneer comic con organizer, on his back. He had been presented one final award: a gold pen, stuck in his chest.

A Trash 'n' Treasures Tip

Wear comfortable shoes when attending a comics convention. Besides standing in long lines, you'll be walking all day. Mother thought her moose slippers might be just the thing, but I talked her out of it. Maybe that was a mistake, as she just might have won the costume contest.

Chapter Four

Con Found

While Mother stood guard over Tommy's body in the service elevator, I hurried back along the vacant hallway, then through the Gold Ballroom, on my way down to the security office to alert Robert Sipcowski of the murder.

I knew full well Mother would be making her own preliminary investigation. Why? Because she'd said, "Take your time, dear. The poor man can't be helped now."

"Don't touch anything, Mother," I'd said.

"Of course not, Brandy. This isn't my first time at the rodeo."

"Well, it's your first time at a rodeo in Madison Square Garden, so cool it. At least...don't leave any fingerprints."

"I can do all the necessary touching with my eyes."

That would have been a disturbing image even if she hadn't been widening her baby blues behind those thick-lensed glasses.

I had no desire to hang around the corpse of our host. While Mother could remain calm and even clinical at the sight of a dead body, I couldn't—not even on Prozac. And when I arrived at the security office, I was out of breath and probably as wild eyed as a charging boar.

Robert looked up from his desk, eyes alert, his response clipped: "What's happened?"

"Service elevator behind the Gold Ballroom." I swallowed, still catching my breath. "Looks like murder."

He frowned. "Hell, you say! Who?"

"Tommy Bufford. My mother's there."

He was on his feet. "What makes it look like murder?"

"The gold thing stuck in his chest. It's a pen, some kind of award from the convention."

"Lord. Anyone else know?"

I shook my head. "Mother and I found him. We were avoiding the main elevators because of the mob."

He frowned, taken aback. "The mob?"

"Not the Mafia Mob. The comic book–fan mob."

"I'm not sure which is more frightening," Sipcowski said, before disappearing into the control room.

In moments he reappeared, two men in security uniforms on his heels. They hurried by me and through the office door. I followed, but couldn't keep up, my knees feeling weak, arms growing numb. I had tears in my eyes.

Why did that thoughtless Tommy Bufford have to go and get himself killed before I had my nap!

And before very long, I had lost them in the crowded lobby.

My mind rushed past my own childish need for a nappy-poo in the face of a terrible and unexpected tragedy. What would happen to the convention once the word got out? Would it be cancelled? How would that affect the fans, and the vendors, and the already planned events, from the costume party to the awards show? And what about the auction, where Mother and I counted on selling our drawing?

If the convention was cancelled, we'd be out money we

couldn't afford to lose. Our cross-country trip had been fi-
nanced on the promise of a nice payday from our disposal
locker find of that vintage Superman drawing.

But what if the convention went on? I could only imagine the kind of pall that would drape itself over the rest of
the proceedings. Would this be the first *and* last Bufford
Con, now that Tommy was gone?

As I moved by the hotel's open-walled bar, I saw that it
was crammed with fans of drinking age, loud, boisterous,
and blithely unaware that a murderer was among them,
perhaps in their midst right now.

Her cherry-festooned white dress exchanged for a more
businesslike dark pants suit, Violet was seated at one of
the little tables; with her was a woman in jeans and a gold
t-shirt boldly labelled in black: STAFF. Tommy's assistant, a
tablet computer before her on the table, appeared to be
giving the staff member instructions.

I paused in the bar's entry area, biting my lip. Surely Violet, as Tommy's right-hand "man," should be informed
about his death. But was it my place to do it? As I pon-
dered that, the staffer got up, said something with a tight
smile, and quickly left, with the purposeful gait of an un-
derling dispatched to duty.

I shrugged to myself and approached Violet.

The tall goth girl with the Bettie Page hair and pink lips
looked up blankly. I might have been a waitress whose
presence hadn't been requested.

Just a little cross, she said, "Yes?" Then recognition
spread across her face, and the crossness left, though nothing particularly friendly replaced it.

I said, "We met yesterday. I'm—"

"Brandy. Brandy Borne. One of our honored guests."
She smiled mechanically. Then her features softened. "If
you're here to apologize for your mother's outbursts at the
opening ceremony, don't bother. Actually, I've had very

good feedback about that. Eccentricity is valued in these circles."

"Well, that's nice to hear, but this isn't about that. It's—"

She raised a red-nailed hand. "Mr. Sipcowski told me that someone entered your room last night, and the convention is very sorry about that. But these things happen in the city."

"It's not that, either," I said. "There's something that you should—"

Her violet eyes flashed with alarm. "You *have* put the drawing in the hotel's safe?"

"Yes." I sat down. She was making it hard, with all her efficiency, for me not to just blurt out the terrible news about her friend.

She sighed. "Good . . . because it would be awful if anything happened to it—it's the centerpiece of the auction."

For a moment there, I actually thought she might be concerned about Mother and me.

I said, "This isn't about my mother or the drawing. It's about your friend—Tommy."

Her heavy eyebrows rose. "What about Tommy?" She put the tablet aside, and pushed back her chair. "Make it quick, would you? You can't imagine how busy I am."

"I'm afraid you're about to get a whole lot busier."

Violet's eyes narrowed, as she sensed the disaster in my voice. "God, what is it?"

The time for blurting had come: "Tommy's dead."

She smiled briefly in disbelief, but then could see I wasn't kidding, her expression darkening. "That's impossible. I just saw him. *You* just saw him."

She was already punching the speed dial of her cell phone. Listening, she frowned. "Tommy never lets it go to voice mail. . . ."

"He *is* dead, Violet. My mother and I found him."

The dark eyes flashed. "Where?"

"Service elevator behind the Gold Ballroom. I'm on my way back there. I just alerted Mr. Sipcowski. You should probably come with me."

Her eyes got moist and a quaver entered her voice. "How . . . how did he . . . ?"

"I'll tell you what I know on the way."

I did so.

As Violet and I stepped off the elevator on level C, we were approached by one of the uniformed hotel guards.

"Mr. Sipcowski says you can go into the ballroom, but no farther."

I asked, "Where's my mother?"

"Is your mother the, uh . . . talkative older woman?"

"That's her, all right."

He gestured with his head and, as a tribute to his professionalism, did not roll his eyes. "She's in there now."

The guard opened a ballroom door, and Violet and I entered, while he maintained his post.

The huge room seemed somber now—all the former fun and joy sucked out of it. Mother, in a middle front-row seat, craned her neck at the sound of the door clicking closed again.

"That ungrateful so-and-so Robert threw me out, dear," her unhappy voice echoed back. "But not before Vivian Borne had herself a good, long look at the crime scene. Why, hello, Violet . . . sorry we had to be the bearer of such bad tidings."

I sat next to Mother, while Violet, cheeks mascara-streaked now, took the chair next to me. Then we were just sitting there, staring at the small stage, where only a short time earlier an ebullient Tommy had given his opening address to an adoring audience, basking in their praise for his pioneering status in their four-color world.

Mother dug in her fanny pack and produced a tissue, and, reaching over me, handed it to a sniffling Violet.

Violet, wiping her eyes, said, "I don't understand it . . . I don't understand it. . . ."

Leaning forward, Mother asked, "*What* don't you understand, dear?"

She blew her nose, a surprisingly unfeminine honk coming from the attractive young woman. "Who would want to kill a sweet soul like Tommy?"

"Well, obviously *someone*," Mother said matter-of-factly, causing me to give her a sharp look, her seeming callousness prompting Violet to sob.

Mother was not actually unkind, but had long since developed a pragmatic acceptance of the second half of the life-and-death dynamic.

The gold curtain parted as Robert Sipcowski came through, like an actor taking the stage for a one-man show. Maybe he was about to present one.

He looked at Violet, then the brown eyes in the weathered face turned disapprovingly on me. "Is there anyone *else* you've told?"

I squirmed in the chair, a kid called to the principal's office. "No, sir. I just thought Violet should know. After all, she's Tommy's assistant, and—"

"I'm more than that," Violet snapped through a sniffle. She looked toward the security chief. "I manage our office. A convention is a business, you know."

"I understand," Sipcowski said, his voice softening. "But this event has to be contained until the police arrive."

Is that what Tommy's murder was? An event?

Robert's walkie-talkie squawked on his belt and he retrieved it. "Yes?"

"*The police are here.*"

"Good. Escort them by the stairs—I don't want the guests alarmed. Who's in charge?"

"*Ah . . . that detective from the Fourteenth—Cassato.*"

I looked sharply at Mother, our eyes asking the same question. Could Tony be out of witness protection, and back on the force?

And if so, why hadn't he told me?

Mother whispered, "A lot of Cassatos in a city this size, dear."

"*Cop* Cassatos?"

"Why, certainly. It's a name as common as Johnson or Smith."

"More like as common as Sipcowski."

Who, not having heard any of that, told us, "You three will need to stay here until the police interview you—I'll keep you posted as to when. They'll want to see the body first."

And the security chief left us alone again.

Violet turned to me. "You said Tommy was murdered. That he was stabbed. With a . . . knife?"

"No. He was stabbed in the chest. With a pen."

Her eyes grew large. "A *pen?*"

"Yes, dear," Mother responded, leaning forward to see past me. "A *gold* pen. Rather expensive looking, and probably fountain style, as that sharp tip would be helpful in performing the act. It's one of your awards, isn't it?"

Violet's hands flew to her mouth. "Oh, my God," she said through splayed fingers.

Mother's lack of tact had been a tactic. Everybody was a suspect now, except Mother and me. And Tommy.

Mother asked Violet, "You were *missing* one of the awards, weren't you, dear?"

The woman nodded slowly. "Yes, one was stolen. The writer's award. And it *is* a pen. Tommy was looking into the theft."

Mother shrugged. "It would appear he found it."

"*Mother!*"

Violet stood, took a step toward Mother, and, eyes flashing, looked down at her. "How *dare* you treat Tommy's murder so . . . so *lightly!*"

I reached out and took the young woman's forearm. "Violet . . . my mother doesn't mean any offense, really. It's just her way of dealing with death. Tommy's death."

Mother said gently, "I am sorry, my dear. I was very fond of Tommy. We had many a lively conversation on Skype. And you needn't worry—I'm going to do everything within my power to bring his killer to justice!"

Violet, returning to the chair, said archly, "You're kidding, right?"

"I don't kid about murder. I may not go into hysterics when I encounter a dead body, child . . . but about *murder*, I do not kid."

"Isn't investigating this . . . this *crime* the job of the police?"

"It has been my experience," Mother returned, "that the boys in blue are extremely efficient when it comes to parking tickets, speed traps, and school presentations on the dangers of drugs. Murder investigation requires a more expert touch."

"Mother," I said quietly, "this is not Serenity. And the NYPD isn't the Serenity police department, either. We should leave this to the professionals."

"I'll take that under advisement, dear."

"Advisement? Whose?"

"Why, my own, of course."

Once again, Robert came through the curtain, told us that the forensics team had arrived, and that Detective Cassato would be with us shortly. *That name again.* And he went back out.

I whispered to Mother, "*Could* it be Tony? Could it?"

Mother whispered back, "Courage, dear."

How that was supposed to help, I had no idea.

It had been two months since I'd heard from Tony—he'd been calling from a pay phone (talk about antiques!) at some undisclosed location, maybe left over from when Dick Cheney was vice president.

I sat on the edge of my chair, eyes fixed on the gold curtain, anxiously awaiting . . . *would Tony appear?*

And when he did, when it *was* him, I sprang to my feet, my heart jumping to my throat and pounding like a triphammer.

Then I froze.

Frowned.

Squinted.

The man looked like Tony, but *different*—younger, not as barrel-chested, his hair more pepper than salt. He was neither in uniform nor the business suit of a plainclothes officer, rather in a navy NYPD jacket, unzipped to reveal a blue shirt and navy tie. Black slacks and black shoes completed his ensemble.

But he spoke in the same clipped New York accent as Tony, in a voice that might have been Tony's.

"I'm Detective Cassato," he said, looking the three of us over.

I was still standing there taking in this almost-Tony when Mother asked, "By any chance, Detective, are you related to one Anthony Cassato, a.k.a. Tony?"

Detective Cassato's eyes narrowed. "Why do you ask?"

"Because, dear boy, *I* am Vivian Borne and this is Brandy Borne. If you are a close relative of the former chief of the Serenity police, those names may be meaningful to you. You may already know that Tony used to date my daughter back in Iowa before he had to go into—" She halted, and lowered her voice—both in loudness and register. "*You-know-where.*"

Then she mouthed: *wit-ness pro-tec-tion*.

Now she brightened. "Perhaps he *mentioned* us, from time to time?"

"From time to time . . . he did."

Mother beamed. "Many was the instance when my daughter and I used our detecting skills to help Tony out in collaring perps—murderers in particular. But we never took credit, and were happy merely to have our efforts enhance the chief's career."

I glanced upward to see if lightning might strike in the ballroom.

Detective Cassato, with a little smirk, said, "So *you're* the legendary Vivian Borne."

"Yes, but I assure you, my legend was not 'born,' but *made*, by myself . . . and my daughter. And you will, I am sure, be delighted and relieved to know that, in this instance, we are at your service."

And she gave him a salute.

I've seen sillier things, but not without paying at the door for it.

"That right?" he said.

"Yes indeedy." Then she added, "Diddy do."

You know what I hate about ballrooms? No windows to jump out of.

The detective stepped closer, hands on hips, and loomed over Mother. "Let's get one thing straight, Mrs. Borne . . . I'm *not* my brother."

"Oh, is Tony your *brother*? Well, *of course* you're not your brother. I'm sure you're very much your own man! And if I might say—"

"No. You might not say. You will listen as I inform you that I will *not* put up with your small-town, busybody meddling." He pointed a finger at her like a gun, a gun he wished were loaded. "You stick your nose into this investigation, Mrs. Borne, and you'll find your fanny in stir. Understood?"

She nodded, but her smile only reminded me that that particular threat never worked on her. Mother likes her occasional soirees in jail—she meets the most interesting people there.

Mother put one hand to her chest. "My dear man, I wouldn't *think* of usurping the authority of the NYPD. We are guests of your fair city, here on holiday—and we have left our deerstalker caps at home." She turned to me. "Haven't we, Brandy?"

"Sure. The cape-coat thingies, too."

"Ulsters, dear," Mother corrected. "I only mean to say, Detective, that we are available to you in any supportive fashion that might prove of help. We are witnesses, after all, or at least we found the body."

Cassato grunted, "Yeah."

I said, "Tony mentioned a brother on the East Coast. Nothing very specific, but . . . are you Salvatore?"

He nodded. "Sal to my friends. You two can call me Detective Cassato."

Mother said, "What a wonderful sense of humor! Just like your brother."

But I didn't figure Detective Cassato was kidding.

Violet spoke up. "Detective Cassato, I'm Tommy's second-in-command. I run the convention office."

"The murder victim? Thomas Bufford?"

She nodded. "Yes. Which means, I guess I'm in charge of the convention now. And, frankly, I need to know where we go from here. There's a lot of money—*other* people's money—tied up in this convention. Fans pay to attend, the dealers pay for their booths, and so on. It would be *disastrous* if we had to shut things down and send everyone home."

Sal Cassato considered the dilemma for a few moments. "You three are the only ones connected to the convention who know about this?"

"Yes," I said. "Mother and I found Tommy, and I went straight to the security office. On the way back here, I told Violet what had happened, because I thought she needed to know."

He was nodding. "All right. It is possible that the convention could continue, more or less as planned, *if* we call this a 'suspicious death' and not a murder."

Mother said, "I suppose he could have fallen on that pen. Mightier than the sword, you know!"

Sal closed his eyes. Then he opened them. "Just for now—for *cosmetic* purposes—we'll term this a 'suspicious death.' Understood, ladies?"

The odious "ladies" again.

Violet nodded, and so did I, and so did Mother, after I elbowed her.

The detective continued: "Not revealing the exact circumstances would be of help to us in the interview process." He looked at Violet. "How you want to handle the news of the 'suspicious death' is up to you—press release, announcements at your various events. But it should be done soon, before any rumors get going."

And he looked directly at Mother.

"What?" she said. "What are you *implying* with that glower, young man?"

The detective said, "It's just that I've heard a lot about you from my brother."

"Well, then, we'll just have to sit down sometime over the weekend, Detective Cassato, and have a chat, so I can straighten you out on what's true and what's false."

Violet, ignoring that, said to the detective, "Thank you, Detective. I know Tommy would have wanted the convention to go on as planned. We'll make it a . . . a *tribute* to his memory. A monument to everything he accomplished."

The detective, clearly not giving a damn about any of that, merely grunted again.

"Is it all right with you if I go?" Violet asked. "I'd like to put the announcements in motion, and there are press releases to write, and . . . ?"

The detective nodded. "I can interview you later. Neither one of us is going anywhere for a while."

Violet stood. "Thank you."

As the dark-haired young woman left the ballroom, moving quickly despite the burden of the tough assignment she'd just been handed, Sal Cassato returned his attention to us.

"Now," he asked, hands on hips, "how is it that you two just *happened* to find the body?"

Mother stiffened in her chair. "My dear man, I *do* hope you are not implying anything specious, much less suspicious, by that remark. We were innocent bystanders in this."

Bystanders, yes. Innocent, no . . . particularly if Mother had compromised the crime scene while I'd gone for help.

The detective smirked. "Why, *of course* you're innocent bystanders. It's just that I've heard the accounts of your past 'investigations' from my brother, and if I may be frank . . . ?"

"Certainly," Mother said, wide-eyed and eager.

"It strains all credulity that you two could 'innocently' stumble onto corpses and generally get involved in murder. If you'd done that on my beat, I'd have called in the FBI to mark you as a suspected serial killer, Mrs. Borne."

Mother frowned in a way that indicated she was not sure whether to feel offended or complimented.

Then she said, "First of all, Detective Cassato, my

daughter and I never allow 'credulity' to stand in our way. That's for the dull among us. As for you thinking I might be a serial killer . . . thank you! The organizational skills that involves are always indicative of a high degree of intelligence. You and I will have to share a good meal and discuss this more, perhaps over fava beans, liver, and Chianti."

He was just looking at her now, agape, like a clubbed baby seal.

I said, "Detective Cassato . . . and if I might—Sal? We have a little dog back in our room that's in need of her insulin shot. Might we go tend to that?"

"Of course," he said, then cleared his throat. "Tony told me about that little mutt. Rocky's favorite playmate."

Rocky was Tony's police dog.

His brother was saying, "Anyway, this is just a preliminary interview. We can make it brief. Just tell me in your own words how you discovered the body."

I let Mother recount the unpleasant event first, which she did with relish. With horseradish, actually. Then I had my turn, adding very little. Not even catsup.

"Thank you," Sal sighed. "You girls can go—but I may want to talk to you again."

Not sure how I felt about that particular use of "girls," I told the detective that we'd be available through the weekend.

Mother, her hands clasped before her, assumed her most helpful air. "If I might point one detail out, Detective Cassato, relating to the pen used to kill Tommy?"

He frowned. "It's not a pen, really, is it? It's an award, right?"

"Well, I believe it's a working pen, but gold-plated, as part of the writer's award. Normally it's not stuck in a person, but in a marble base, I understand. No sign of that base, incidentally?"

"No. What's your point?"

"My 'point' is the point of that pen," she said, rather too proud of herself. "I allowed myself a fairly close look at the wound and the instrument of death, before your arrival."

"I'll just bet you did."

"The name of the winner was engraved on the pen, although, because of its rather forceful insertion into the late victim's chest, all you could make out was 's-o-n.' "

I blurted, "That could be Eric Johansson! He's one of the nominees."

Mother said, "So is a writer named Thompson, Harlan Thompson. So you may have a suspect. Which name was on that pen, Detective?"

He gave her a nasty look. "I think it was 'Bic.' "

"More likely Montblanc, but I refer of course to the name of the *winner* engraved there. Whose name was it, Detective?"

"That, Mrs. Borne, is none of your business."

Mother's expression was aghast. If not her business, then *whose*? But I could see her wheels turning.

As we were about to leave, she said, "Detective Cassato . . . Salvatore. I'm afraid you and I have rather gotten off on the wrong foot. My enthusiasm can be intimidating, and my judgment poor. Might I make amends?"

"What did you have in mind, Mrs. Borne?"

"Do make it *Vivian*, please. Why, I feel I've known you forever."

"It feels that way to me, too, Vivian."

She leaned in, in a confidential manner. "I'm sure you'll be needing to conduct other interviews here in the hotel."

"Obviously."

"But I'm afraid that you'll find all of the rooms are taken, with meeting rooms unavailable due to the ongoing panels. Even this ballroom has other events scheduled. And the security area is rather small."

"True."

"Might I suggest you use our suite for your sessions? The outer area is quite large—offering such amenities as coffee and a comfortable couch—plus the setting might have a calming effect on those being interviewed."

Detective Cassato was frowning. So was I—I didn't want to give up our room! And what the heck was Mother up to, anyway?

"And don't worry," Mother rushed on. "We won't be there during the day. Why, Brandy and I have so much to do, what with the convention, sightseeing, shopping. . . ."

By the way, whenever Mother says, "Don't worry," that's your cue. To worry.

"What about Sushi?" I protested.

"Why, we'll take the little doggie with us—she must be tired of being cooped up. We have plastic baggies for her poo poo. One must curb one's dog in the Big Apple!"

One must curb her mouth, if she says things like "poo poo."

Still, it was clear now that Mother was up to something, so I'd best play along.

"All right," the detective said. "I'll take you up on that offer, which is quite generous of you, and I thank you, and the city of New York thanks you. Or, we will as long as you stay out of my way while I'm interviewing."

"But of course," Mother replied sweetly.

"You *can't* sit in, Vivian."

"I understand. I do understand."

"And I'll only use the room for the rest of this afternoon. After that, I'll make other arrangements."

After this victory (*what* was *she up to?*), Mother hurried off to get an extra room keycard for the detective, leaving me alone with him.

"Detective Cassato," I asked, "have you heard from Tony?"

He shook his head. "Make it 'Sal.' No, Brandy, I haven't. Not since he went into WITSEC—too damn dangerous. And you?"

I sighed, and nodded. "Briefly, a few months ago. I . . . I wish I knew how he was doing."

"Tell me about it."

"It's so unfair. Doesn't the Mob usually leave police officers alone? I thought it was their code where law enforcement personnel were concerned."

Sal sighed. "New York, maybe. But this is *New Jersey* wiseguys that Tony testified against . . . and they've got a whole other way of doing things."

Like sending a hit man to my hometown, after finding out Tony had moved there.

The detective was saying, "They do things by their own rule book, ya know? Only, their rule book don't have any rules in it that I know of."

"Detective? Sal?"

"Yes?"

"Not meaning to overstep, but . . . you might like to know that Tommy *did* have at least one enemy."

"When you share what you know, Brandy, that's not called overstepping. It's called cooperating."

I told him about the heated confrontation I'd overheard yesterday evening between Bufford and his ex-partner, Gino, admitting that I didn't even know the man's last name.

He thanked me for the information. "You know, I can see why Tony likes you."

"Thanks."

"I can also see why your mother drives him bananas."

Then he went back through the gold curtain to the crime scene.

Since Mother would probably be a while getting another keycard, I returned to our room, where I found Sushi sleeping soundly on the freshly made bed. Lucky her.

"Any problems to report?" I asked.

She opened one eye, then another, finally yawning by way of an answer, then rolling over on her back for a tummy scratch.

After a minute of that, I padded over to the minibar to select something to eat—vanilla cream–filled cookies, for only five times their going rate back in Serenity—of which I shared a few bites with Soosh, getting crumbs on the coverlet.

I went back for a bag of four-dollar chips, and got even more crumbs on the bed—maybe on purpose, peeved as I was with Mother for getting us involved in yet another murder. I hoped Sal Cassato had been kidding about fingering us to the FBI.

And here I had been looking forward to a fun-filled vacation in New York, with the only detective work in our plans being that of searching the countryside for Aunt Olive.

Spitefully, I reached over, picked up the mattress remote control from the nightstand, and pumped the gage up to one hundred, making the bed hard as a rock.

Let Goldilocks sleep on *that.*

With my malaise lifting a little, I got out my cell and saw that I had just missed a call from Joe Lange. I had wanted to check in with him anyway, because he was running our antiques shop back in Serenity while we were away.

Joe, a friend since my community college days, an avid collector of Star Trek memorabilia, was pretty knowledgeable about antiques in general. He had wanted to come along to the convention—excited about Tommy Bufford starting a retro-style con at a smaller venue—but found himself short of funds.

Or maybe the pre-con search for Aunt Olive had discouraged him.

He answered on the first ring. "Trash 'n' Treasures, Joseph Lange speaking."

At least he'd left off his rank and serial number.

"Joe," I said, "everything cool at the shop?"

"Affirmative."

Something else you need to know about Joe: he still talked in Marine-speak, even though he'd been discharged ten years ago.

I asked, "You doin' okay, dude?"

"For a first civ-div."

Translation: a former Marine in the civilian world (I had gotten pretty good at deciphering his dialect).

"And the shop? All's well?"

"Affirmative."

Less than thirty seconds into the call and he was repeating himself already. Conversations with Joe went that way a lot.

"You must've called for a reason, Joe," I prodded.

"Saw the buzz on the Net that Bufford's a casualty."

Yikes! Violet's press release was out already?

Joe was saying, "And that PR bilge about a suspicious death? Bum scoop. My gut? Bufford was deep-sixed."

"You think so?"

"Affirmative."

"Who by?"

"Best guess? Gino Moretti—Bufford's former partner. Bad blood there after he forced Tommy out of Manhattan Con."

"You may be right, Joe. I saw them arguing the night before."

"Then he's your man." Pause. "I assume you and Big Mama are on the case."

"I hope not. But probably, yeah."

"Brandy? You do any recon on Moretti, take care."

"Oh?"

"Guy's mobbed up, big-time."

I thanked Joe and ended the call.

What a warm feeling a girl got, calling home from the big city. . . .

Then I heard Mother yelping out, "Yoo-hoo, Brandy! Are you here, dear?"

"In the bedroom, Todd." That's a reference to an old Bob and Ray radio show running gag. If you got it, you're smiling right now. If not, probably just irritated. Sorry.

She rushed into the bedroom, out of breath, face flushed, eyelashes aflutter. "I gave Detective Cassato an extra room keycard—and he'd like to use it right away. So we must vacate, toot aysap."

"I want my nap!"

"Well, you don't get it."

She crossed to the dresser and yanked open a drawer. "Now *where* did I put that thing?"

I got off the bed. "All right, okay, spill it, lady . . . what are you *up* to? You didn't offer up our suite out of the goodness of your heart."

Mother turned to gaze at me, a child who'd asked a really dumb question. "Well, of course not, dear. Do I look like a fool?"

"Is that a trick question?"

She returned to rummaging around in the drawer.

"Ah . . . *here* it is!" Mother held up a key-chain.

Only it was not just *any* key-chain, rather a recording device she'd recently ordered from a spy-gear website. Attached to the ring was a round leather fob—the recording

part—about an inch in diameter. The gizmo was voice ac-
tivated, would record up to three and a half hours, and
had a sound file that could be transferred to a computer by
using it as a flash drive (for you computer-savvy folks). To
the ring, Mother had added a couple of our old house
keys, by way of deceptive trimmings.

Oh, and just so you know? That gizmo wasn't cheap—
about three hundred smackers. Which might help to
explain why Mother couldn't afford a new handcuffed
briefcase.

And, no, I didn't bother asking her if she intended to
record Detective Sal Cassato's interviews. Some things between mother and daughter are just understood.

Mother headed into the other room as I followed.

"Let's see," she said, eyeing the furnishings. "Where to
put it? Where to *put* it?"

"Out in the open of course."

Mother crossed to an end table by the couch and set the
key ring down.

"Bring me my purse, dear."

I did.

She dug through it, pulled out a few other items—some
change, a pen (not the murder weapon, though), match-
book, and tube of lipstick—which she arranged around
the recording device.

I nodded in approval. "Just looks like a bunch of harm-
less stuff."

Mother, satisfied, even pleased with herself, said,
"Now! Let's gather the little doggie and go, dear."

I went to the closet to get Sushi's harness bag, then
began strapping it to my chest. Soosh, hearing the velcro
strips pulling apart, began to go bananas, dancing at my
feet, barking, thrilled to be leaving with us.

I picked up the wiggling mutt, then placed her in the
bag, facing forward.

And the Three Musketeers left. One for all and all for . . . Mother.

"You know," Mother said, as we walked down the gold-and-blue-patterned hall carpet toward the elevators, "Tommy's murder changes everything."

"It does?"

Mother nodded. "Hasn't it occurred to you yet, dear? Our intruder was not after our Superman drawing, after all."

"He wasn't?"

"No, dear. Remember—we were not supposed to be in that suite—*Tommy* was."

I stopped to look at her. "Our intruder intended to kill Tommy, right then and there?"

"As opposed to later in the service elevator? Perhaps. Worth consideration, at any rate." She smiled cheerfully. "So I guess we may have been lucky girls last night, since it seems we likely had a murderer in our room."

A Trash 'n' Treasures Tip

When attending a comics convention, be sure to bring the right tools. That's different for everyone, but some standard items would include a list of things you seek, a comic book price guide, and a spiral notebook with pen (or a tablet computer). Usually the convention gives out a free bag for carrying purchases, but at Bufford Con, the giveaway tote clashed with Mother's outfit and she substituted a shopping bag from the Stage Door Deli.

Chapter Five

Con Traption

After vacating our suite to allow Detective Cassato to use it for interviews—and for Mother's electronic eavesdropping—we decided to spend the rest of the afternoon getting the feel of the convention by way of the dealers' room. (And by "we," I don't just mean Mother and me, but Sushi as well, tucked away in her baby-style in-front carrier.) As much as fans might enjoy the panels and various special events, it was the chance to pick up collectibles that made the Globetrotter Ballroom on the lower level the hub of the con.

But first, we had to get past a quartet of staff members in red t-shirts who were paired off on either side of the open double doors. A hefty, dark-haired woman in her twenties with a nose-piercing stopped us with an upraised palm.

"No entry without badges," she said curtly.

I'd forgotten about those. The plastic name tags provided by the late Tommy Bufford himself were in Mother's purse somewhere. Of course, so were the original blueprints for Stonehenge and ticket stubs from a 1944 Frank Sinatra concert at the Aragon Ballroom, most likely.

"Stand to one side," the staffer said, almost nasty.

While searching her purse, Mother huffed and puffed, but there was no blowing this officious guard's house down.

"We are guests of the convention," Mother said, rummaging. "*Honored* guests, young lady. We don't *need* no *steenking* badges!"

This latter was, of course, a famous line from the film *Treasure of the Sierra Madre*, and a joke that might have gone over with someone from a couple of generations prior to that of the pierced-nose staffer, who only heard an old lady making a bizarre, politically incorrect remark.

"You *do* need badges," the woman insisted. "Stand aside *please*."

And just then Mother found the little plastic rectangles, and handed them to the woman as if they were tickets. The staffer scowled at this breech of protocol, but then took the opportunity to look the badges over, as if they might be counterfeit, before handing them back to Mother.

"Put them on," the staffer commanded.

As I was putting mine on, clipping it to Sushi's carrier, the staffer frowned and pointed at my chest.

"That's a dog!" she said.

"Right," I said, resisting the urge to comment on her keen powers of observation. "Why, does *she* need a badge?"

The staffer didn't know what to say to that, though the other staffer working the door with her—a redheaded woman of about thirty-five—started saying, "Ooooh, what a cutie! What a cutie-pie!"

Presumably, she was talking about Sushi, not Mother or me.

Throughout this little confrontation, other convention-goers had to squeeze past us by the other guards, and I was getting increasingly embarrassed. You might think I'd be used to Mother's antics by now, and maybe I am, but I am still capable of feeling embarrassment.

"It's a pet-friendly hotel," I told the staffer.

Who finally relented, gesturing in a sarcastic after-you manner, saying, "Go on ahead."

As we went by, Mother held her head high, throwing a comment back at the guardian of the gate: "You dishonor your late founder!"

Mother had a point. The staffer had been brusque and borderline rude, which didn't match up very well with the late Tommy's vision of a kinder, gentler convention.

"That's no way to treat honored guests," Mother harrumphed.

"Let it go, Mother. She was right."

"Well, she didn't have to be *snippy* about it."

"You're lucky that other staffer—the Hispanic one?— didn't clobber you for that 'steenking badges' remark."

"That was meant in good fun! Well, isn't *this* quite the spectacle . . . ?"

And it was, a sort of World's Fair of popular culture, wide aisles between facing rows of dealers' booths, predominantly comic book sellers with wall displays of precious rare issues ("Golden Age!" "Silver Age!") and long boxes of other comics, all plastic bagged, for fans to leaf through. Now and then a booth would offer posters or t-shirts or DVDs, and an occasional booth would center around video games. The biggest, showiest displays—so typical of a trade show—were by the major comic book companies, Marvel, DC, Dark Horse, and a few others.

What made this comic con different—and what had been a precept of Tommy Bufford's retro thinking—was a ban on Hollywood movie studios from attending. This had been an outrageous and dangerous move on Tommy's part, because Hollywood usually pumped tens of thousands of dollars into the big comic book conventions. But that emphasis on movies and TV had pushed actual comic book fans off into a ghetto-ish corner of the world they had created.

And Tommy had wanted to take a big, nostalgic step backward.

So comic books were king in the realm of the Globe-trotter Room, which was packed with fans, both in and out of costumes, creating a steady stream of nerdity flowing by us as we moved slowly, cautiously along. I had to take hold of Mother's hand so we wouldn't get separated, and we fell in step with the others, letting the crowd sweep us along, driftwood carried to no particular destination. Sushi was distracted by the various smells, the best of which came from fast-food carts, and didn't seem to realize we were engulfed in a mob.

And we had been told today would be the *slow* day. . . .

The upbeat if frantic atmosphere suggested that the news of Tommy's demise hadn't reached most attendees, and I doubted Violet would have made any announcements over the sound system. Still, her Net news releases about the tragedy would almost certainly have gone viral by now, and here and there clusters of fans stood with stunned expressions, some teary eyed, others just sad and staggered as the news spread further via word of mouth and texting.

As we walked wide-eyed, like children at their first carnival, allowing the crowd to dictate our pace, we suddenly sensed movement behind us. The crowd parted like the Red Sea as a phalanx of media moved through, on their way somewhere, anywhere.

Not just one group, either—but clusters from various networks and local TV stations. Of course, it was not unusual for local TV, even national news outlets, to cover a comic con. All that pop culture sharing space with nerds made for good visuals and cheap laughs on the five o'clock news.

I was happy to move aside as they trooped by.

Unfortunately, Mother had other ideas.

"Well, dear, I think the time has come," she said, trying to sound casual but with a manic edge to her voice, as she watched the army of microphones and HD-cams marching by. "Now that the word is out, it's best to take the bull by the horns."

And before I could think to stop her, much less try, she was knifing through the crowd and down past the media storm troopers. I pressed forward, too, not enough to catch up, but still able to see her fling herself in front of the press corps and thrust out her arms, like a desperate hitchhiker before an oncoming car.

Her theatrically schooled voice managed to cut through the dealers' room din.

"*I can give you the straight skinny on Tommy Bufford!*" Mother announced. "*I am Vivian Borne, honored guest of the convention! And I found the body!*"

So, do you see what I mean about not ever losing the ability to be embarrassed by Mother?

A thirtyish newscaster, in tan slacks and black polo shirt with a Channel 6 logo, eagerly thrust his microphone in Mother's face, as a cameraman locked onto them.

"You found the body?"

"Indeed, yes." Mother, in a relatively subdued version of her fake Brit accent, declared, "My darling daughter Brandy and I discovered Mr. Bufford's body. As to the particulars . . ."

"*Mother!*"

I had finally clawed my way close.

My stern look reminded her of the pledge to secrecy we'd made, and with nary a hint of Merry Olde England in her voice, she went on, ridiculously: ". . . I am afraid I am committed to confidentiality."

I was wishing she were "committed" period, about now.

The reporter pressed: "Is 'suspicious death' code for murder in this matter, Mrs. Borne?"

Flustered now, Mother said, "I'm afraid I can't speak to whether that term is code for matter in this murder. I can tell you only that my daughter and I are consulting with the police on this . . . matter. We are the famous Borne sleuths from Serenity, Iowa."

A blond woman, so attractive it seemed unreal, moved in with her mic: "Are you the Vivian Borne involved in a reality show pilot?"

"Why, yes. Thank you for asking. We'll be shooting it very soon, in our quaint hometown on the Mississippi. The show's called *Antiques Sleuths*, and—"

The male reporter cut in, dueling mics with the blonde. "Aren't you and your daughter the Bornes who were implicated in the Senator Clark scandal last year?"

Now all the mics and cameras were pressing in. For a moment, I thought Mother might be crushed under the weight of this media frenzy. And for a moment, I wasn't sure I minded. . . .

But when Mother glanced at me helplessly, I grabbed on to her arm, pulling her away from the closing-in newscasters. We were quickly swallowed up by the sea of fans, a tide we swam against until I was able to propel us out the door we'd come in fifteen minutes (or was it five hundred years) ago. The media horde, however, was in pursuit, the fans jumping out of their way. . . .

Getting a frown from the pierced-nose staffer at the door, we ran past her and down the carpeted corridor. All the while, a confused Sushi was thumping against my chest, before we took refuge in a ladies' room, which would at least keep the males among the newshounds at bay.

I turned on Mother. "Take the bull by the horns? More like the tail, you mean!"

Mother, out of breath, managed a weak, "*Olé?*"

"Now we're *stuck* in here," I grumbled.

Mother was still catching her breath. She had the expression of somebody in a zombie movie looking for nails to board up a window with. "It . . . it won't be long, dear, before the *females* among them make their move—and then we're done for."

There were already other females among us, con-goers and not reporters, thankfully, using the stalls, washing hands at the sink, touching up or applying makeup, particularly those in costume.

Of the latter, two young women in particular caught my eye. They stood at the far end of the ladies' room, in front of a full-length mirror, making adjustments to their look—specifically, Alice in Wonderland and the Queen of Hearts.

In the vein of the Tim Burton movie remake of a few years back, Alice wore a powder-blue dress with tight bodice and little puff sleeves, her white shoes reminiscent of Victorian button ankle boots. Innocent-sexy.

The Queen was in a red-and-black velvet floor-length gown, red hearts sprinkled across the front, gold stripes down the sleeves. While Alice's makeup was minimal, the Queen's was garish—bright blue eye shadow, rose-colored circles on each cheek, and crimson lipstick in the shape of a small heart on her lips. A tiny gold crown was perched on her head, secured by the top bun of a blood-red wig.

I approached the pair.

"Ah . . . hi," I said. "Cool costumes."

Alice said, "Thanks," and the Queen echoed her. Both were a little wary.

"How would you like to make some money?" I asked, no more hysterical than somebody who just fell out of a hot air balloon. "Both of you?"

Comics fans could always use more cash at a convention, right?

They looked at each other, then back at me.

"What do you have in mind?" asked the Queen.

"And how much money?" queried Alice. "Cute dog, by the way."

"Thanks!"

And I explained our predicament with the press, and outlined my plan. Then we negotiated the price for a temporary rental of their costumes, and their aid in applying that distinctive makeup.

"It'll be fun," I said.

"Fifty," the Queen said.

"Each," Alice said.

What I wanted to say was, "Off with your heads!"

What I did say was, "Sounds fair."

Ten minutes later, Mother—dressed (and made up) as the Queen, and myself as Alice, with Sushi still in her front pack, passing (I hoped) as the Cheshire Cat—sailed out of the bathroom and right past the milling media.

Soon we were up on level C, in the ladies' room by the Gold Ballroom, where two girls in Brandy and Mother costumes traded their clothing back to us for Alice and the Queen. I washed off the Alice makeup, but I caught Mother admiring herself as the Queen for several moments before doing the same. It did suit her.

We stood just outside the ladies' room.

A sheepish Mother said, "I'm afraid I did make a wrong decision back there, holding that impromptu press conference."

"You think?"

"Perhaps I'd better make myself scarce for a while."

"Well, you can't go back to the dealers' room," I said, adjusting Sushi in the baby sling, "and our suite is off-limits till four p.m. Maybe you could slip into a panel and just sit there. And mind your own business?"

Mother's eyes were moving behind the magnifying lenses, rolling around like somebody trying out a new pair of glass eyes. "No, I think I'll go off by myself, if you don't mind. If you can get along without me for the rest of the day."

"I'll try."

"This might be just the opportunity to look up some old thespian pals from my theater days."

"Lucky them."

"There you go again, Debbie Downer. I'll be happy to take a break from that bad attitude of yours!"

"I *still* need a nap, and you turned our room into an interrogation booth."

"Find yourself a quiet corner, dear, and just rest a while. Take a cue from Sushi—she can sleep anywhere."

Something told me I shouldn't let her go off by herself—whether that was concern or apprehension, I couldn't tell you. "What if I need to get in touch with you?"

"Call my cell."

"You don't have a coat—it's pretty cold out."

"Why, I'll just whip up a hot flash, dear."

She still had them at her age. Which meant I probably had that to look forward to.

Lucky me.

"Toodles," Mother said, heading toward the elevators.

And then, there among costumed comic book fans and nerds of every variety, the world seemed suddenly less strange, and considerably less interesting.

"Well, Soosh," I said, scratching her furry head, "what shall *we* do with ourselves, without Mother to entertain us?"

I couldn't risk going back to the dealers' room, either—I'd been seen with Mother, and I'd had some notoriety of my own in that mess surrounding Peggy Sue and Senator Clark (my father, by the way) (do try to keep up)—nor did I feel like sitting through any of the ongoing panels in meeting rooms on the sixth floor. The evolving nature of the supporting cast of *Wolverine* and the deeper meanings of *The Dark Knight Trilogy* were not topics to which I cared to subject my brain.

But there was a hospitality room somewhere on the top floor, an oasis where honored guests (and presumably their dogs) could hang out and take advantage of the free drinks and snacks. Maybe a girl could even catch a nap.

I was directed to the eighteenth floor, where I wandered around for a while until spotting a handwritten sign taped to the door of PennTop North, and went in.

Though a smaller banquet room, PennTop North was no less elegantly appointed, the sun casting in golden rays through floor-to-ceiling windows to burnish the room. Maybe a dozen guests—men and a few women, mostly in their later twenties and thirties, dressed casually but better than the fans—were seated here and there at the linen-clothed tables. They partook of bottled water, cans of soda, and cups of coffee, procured from a staff-supervised banquet table offering those freebies as well as such snacks as pretzels, chips, and M&M's.

Though putting my hoped-for nap at risk, I helped my-self to some coffee, as well as a bottled water and extra cup for Sushi.

I was heading to an empty table with a window view, when I noticed Brad Webster, Webbie on the Web himself, sitting alone at another table, a can of Diet Coke in one hand. He wore a green, white, and black plaid shirt and chinos.

I strolled over to the Fan Guest of Honor, whose slender, acned face seemed rather puffy.

"Excuse me," I said. "Hi."

"Hi," he muttered, staring at the Coke can.

"I just wanted to say that was a very nice speech you gave at the opening ceremony."

"Thanks."

"I'm Brandy, by the way. Brandy Borne."

He looked up, eyes red rimmed. "Oh . . . right. You and your mother brought the Superman drawing."

"We're also writers. Or anyway, I am."

"Mysteries, right?"

"Yeah, uh, with antiquing and collecting as a sort of backdrop."

"You ran across that Siegel and Shuster drawing in a disposal unit, somebody said. Some find."

"Yes, we're auctioning it off on Sunday. But you probably know all about that. You're always gathering info for your web show, right?"

"Right." Brad's eyes drifted away.

"Mind if I join you?"

He shrugged. "Sure. Cute dog. Weird eyes."

"She's blind. Sushi's her name, very nice animal. She only *looks* like she's possessed by the devil."

I set my drinks on the table, sat down, and removed Sushi from her pouch, putting her on my lap.

Watching this, Brad said, "You and your mother were invited by Tommy, right?"

"Yes."

"You've . . . heard about that?"

I nodded glumly. "If you mean his death, yes. So awfully sad. Mother liked him a lot. They were Internet buddies."

"Sometimes it's easier making friends on the Net than in real life."

"Isn't the Net real life?" I opened the bottled water, poured some into the cup, put it under Soosh's nose, and she began lapping it up.

"I guess," he said. "Just not real enough."

"Quite an honor."

"What?"

"Being chosen Fan Guest."

He nodded.

I went on, "Not surprising, considering your website. I mean, it's major."

He looked at me. My remark seemed to surprise him, coming from a grown female who was not in an anime costume. "You've heard of it?" he asked.

"Webbie on the Web?" I gushed. "Who *hasn't*?"

Brad offered a small smile, but at least I'd pleased him.

I continued. "A friend turned me on to your website. I think he posts comments sometimes—Joe Lange?"

"He wouldn't post that way. He'd use a screen name."

"So now I get all my comics fandom news from your site." If I'd been wearing a Pinocchio costume, would its nose be growing?

"Thank you, uh . . . Brandy."

I took a sip of my coffee. "Horrible about Tommy. Did you know him well?"

Brad stared at his Coke can, as if something were hidden there. "We met a few years ago, when he was running Manhattan Con. We hit it off. Common interests. Even shared an apartment in the city for a while. Till I got my website up and running."

"Were you friends with his partner, who ran Manhattan Con with him? What's his name—Gino Moretti?"

He winced; I might have slapped him. "That bastard. He's no friend of mine. Anyway, not since he forced Tommy out of Manhattan Con. Don't get me wrong, Tommy had his ruthless side, too . . . and he could be really, well . . . *insensitive*."

His emphasis made me wonder if he and Tommy had been more than friends.

Brad tore his eyes away from that fascinating Coke can to look at me. "There's a rumor that you and your mother found the body."

News travelled fast in these circles.

"That's true. But the police asked us not to advertise it."

"Do you know how he died?"

I shrugged. "He died in that service elevator."

How evasive was that?

He was squinting at me, trying to bring me into focus. "An accident, you mean? Like . . . the doors malfunctioned, or there was an electrical-system fire? Dear God, tell me Tommy didn't step into an empty shaft!" His red-rimmed eyes grew large in horror.

"All I can say is that the police are calling it a suspicious death."

"But you *did* find the body. You and your mother."

"We found him on the floor of the elevator and ran for help. We were just two of a lot of people who were interviewed, who happened to be around the service elevator behind the Gold Ballroom around that time."

Brad sneered. "I bet that *wasn't* any accident. Whatever happened, I will *bet* you that Gino Moretti had something to do with it."

"What makes you think that?"

He shrugged forcefully. "First of all, because of their history. But, mostly? Because I saw that son of a bitch hanging around while Tommy was at the podium, waiting there for him."

"To talk to Tommy?"

"Confront him is more like it."

"And *did* Moretti confront Tommy?"

Brad shrugged, not so forceful now, and sighed. "I don't know, because, after that, I was giving my speech, and when I finished . . . they were both gone."

I sat forward. "You'll need to tell this to the police. There's a detective named Cassato you need to talk to."

Brad snorted. "Well, I wish New York's finest a lotta

luck finding Gino. You can bet he's scurried back to Jersey, where his Mafia buddies are keeping him safely under wraps."

"Still," I said, "the police need to know what you've seen, and what you know—really, I'm surprised they haven't interviewed you yet."

He gestured around him. "I've been up here in the hospitality suite since I heard about it—just couldn't face anyone, you know?" His eyes were beginning to tear.

"Yeah. I know. It's hard to lose somebody you're close to, and even harder in circumstances like these. I'm sorry you lost your friend, Brad."

He swallowed, and dabbed his eyes with a knuckle. "This Detective Cassato—is he still around?"

"Yes," I said, and gave him our room number.

Outside the PennTop North, I was retrieving my lip gloss from my fanny pack when I came across two room keycards in there. Did I have Mother's?

Then I recalled seeing Mother take her card, which meant I should have only one.

And it occurred to me that when we'd exchanged rooms with Tommy, we must have given him only *one* of our two cards.

And this extra card was to our original room.

In order to test my theory, I took the elevator down to the fourteenth floor, then proceeded down the hallway toward 1421.

Halfway there, I stopped short.

Coming out of that room was Robert Sipcowski.

Which didn't arouse my suspicion, exactly; the security chief would quite naturally want to secure Tommy's room for the police investigation. Nor did I question his wearing latex gloves, an understandable precaution—he wouldn't want to mix his prints with any others left behind.

What *did* arouse my suspicion, though, was the security chief's nervous manner, as he sneaked out of the room, including furtive glances to the left and right.

One of those glances almost caught me, but I ducked into a vending machine alcove, where I pretended to get a snack, until the man had walked by. Sushi looked up at me irritably—this herky-jerky journey I was taking her on was starting to be no fun.

Then I approached our old room, and tried the keycard. It was possible the lock had been changed by now.

But no—I was able to open the door.

The lights were off and the curtains closed—dark but for some sunlight bleed around the window edges. Using my elbow on a wall switch, I turned on a lamp, illuminating the room, which was one unholy mess.

I had a hunch that while the stereotype of comic book fans as notorious slobs might have a certain basis in fact, this case was different: drawers opened, their contents strewn; sheets torn from the bed; suitcases dumped upside down. Someone had been looking for something.

As they said in the old detective movies, somebody had tossed the joint.

Had Robert Sipcowski done this? Or had he discovered the room this way?

Stepping over one of Tommy's discarded Hawaiian shirts, I crossed to the closet, its door yawning open, revealing more tropical shirts puddled on the floor, having been pulled rudely off hangers.

The room safe was open, with nothing inside.

My stomach grumbled, and I wondered if any of the fruit I'd left behind in the small refrigerator would still be there. After all, it *was* ours, and certainly wouldn't be of any interest in the investigation. And, anyway, when did anybody ever get busted for eating evidence?

I opened the fridge. The apples and oranges and grapes were just as I'd left them on a little tray.

But something else had been added: a file folder, beneath that tray.

I withdrew the folder, and was about to look inside, when I heard the front door lock click.

Shoving the thing up in my blouse, behind Sushi's carrier, I dashed to the closet and closed the door.

Sushi whined and I shushed her.

She was a good little girl and stayed shushed.

I could hear someone moving around out there and wished I'd left the door open a crack so I could see who it was.

And that was when Sushi sneezed.

After which somebody opened the closet door.

And Detective Cassato glared at me.

And I smiled weakly. "Just looking for skeletons," I said cheerfully.

But he was not amused.

A Trash 'n' Treasures Tip

Don't buy anything but an ironclad steal on the first day of a comic book convention. Many dealers discount their items with each passing day. Of course, if you wait too long, what you want may already be gone. Or, you could be standing in line when the convention's final bell rings, as happened to Mother, waiting to buy a Munchkin doll for a little-person pal of hers, only to get turned away empty-handed. Even when she protested that the doll in question was for "a personal friend of Billy Barty," no exception had been made.

Chapter Six

Con Nected

You are in luck!

This chapter is penned by none other than myself, Vivian Borne, about to regale you, dear reader, with the amazing adventure that transpired after I took my leave of Brandy and Sushi, following a certain unfortunate truncated press conference, a debacle for which I can only say: my bad.

The tale you are about to hear (read) is one I might not believe myself, had I not experienced it. This is the case even though I've had many (adventures) and told many (tales) (I do hope you appreciate a creative use of parentheses), and perhaps I risk building up your expectations too much—like the trolley stories I've shared in previous volumes. But I must first make use of my unfortunately limited space herein to bring up a few issues and/or set the record straight.

Firstly, several readers (not many—two or three) (well, perhaps four or five) (six tops) wrote to complain about my most recent Serenity trolley story. The delightful anecdote in question concerns a spinster who dressed her pet chimpanzee as Goldilocks in order to sneak it onto the gas-powered trolley, after which an elderly man with cataracts mistook the animal for a little girl, affectionately pinched its cheek, and got his finger bitten off. This relative handful of readers felt my account to be more grotesque than amusing, though, in my defense, I must point out that I didn't claim that the story was funny.

This was not one of those "you had to be there" instances, because I *was* there and it actually was fairly grotesque. Amusement came later, upon reflection. And besides, the bitten-off digit was found, immersed in ice water, and sewn back onto the poor fellow, good as new. No charges were pressed, perhaps because chimps aren't subject to any law but that of nature, or possibly because the elderly gentleman felt he did not wish to risk ridicule in court. He had already been subjected to a certain amount of joshing from his peers, who made such tasteless remarks as, "When you're at the market, Homer, does that finger quiver near bananas?" and "Why, you old monkey masher, you."

Where was I?

Ah! *Secondly!*

Secondly, my sincere thanks to those of you who have written to our editor to request that my literary contributions to these nonfiction accounts be expanded. Brandy has consented to make it at least two chapters, and our editor (such a lovely woman!) has agreed, though placing certain limitations on word length (not the length of individual words, but the length of words strung together) that require me to stay on point and avoid needless digression. So I am holding a tight rein on things, my dear ones, and if you keep the pressure on my editor, you may see me advance to three chapters per book!

Fingers crossed.

Thirdly, I have a correction to make in the material written by Brandy that you've read thus far. Truth be told,

I could make many corrections, but I am holding myself to a single particularly troubling blunder of hers. Let it be known that in my all-too-short career some years ago as a thespian trodding the Broadway boards (Broadway in the loosest sense, I grant you), I *never* played Hoboken, despite what Brandy said. Newark, yes. Hoboken, no.

And now, back to our regularly scheduled mystery.

My first stop after leaving the Hotel Pennsylvania was Coppola's restaurant, which I reached by cab. There I ordered a large to-go order consisting of baked ziti, linguine with clams, chicken Parmesan, veal piccata, garlic bread, and desserts of cannoli and tiramisu. This took a while, because they make all their delicious foods fresh.

A nice waiter packed the food compactly in a box, then hailed me another cab, and helped me into the backseat with my order.

"Where to?" the cabbie asked in a rather charming Middle Eastern accent.

I could only see the back of his head, but his I.D. with photo (why would such a nice-looking young man not get a closer shave before having his picture taken?) had a name that I feared was a typographical error.

"The Badda-Bing!" I instructed, then corrected myself. "I *should* say, the Badda-Boom."

He showed me his profile—he was frowning, rather in irritation or confusion, I could not say.

"Madam, do you know what this place is?"

"I believe it's a nightclub, but I understand it's open during the day as well."

"That's what you call a strip joint, madam."

"Of course, young man," I said. He was in his midthirties, but it never hurts to flatter a person in service. "Never fear. I am on a sociological expedition to the outer reaches."

He frowned, shook his head as if to clear it, then sighed

as if he were Atlas with the globe on his slight shoulders—
or the Big Apple, anyway. "Badda-Boom strip club is not
in Manhattan, madam."

"Of course not. It's in New Jersey. That's what I meant
by outer reaches."

"I drive over there, I won't get return fare. Madam, I
take you to bus station, instead. Cheaper."

I leaned forward and gave him my most charming smile.
"What if you, I believe the expression is, leave your flag
up? And we negotiate a flat rate?"

"Possible. This is possible."

"I assure you, I have the funds."

"Madam, dangerous in this city to carry too much
money in your purse."

"I feel safe with you, young man." Anyway, I kept the
bulk of my paper money pinned inside my brassiere. "And
I'm a good tipper, to boot—if you don't drive recklessly or
too fast."

"Madam, you got a deal."

He swung out into traffic, and I settled back to enjoy
the ride.

The cab turned right onto West Thirty-first Street, heading for the Lincoln Tunnel, where we found traffic busy
but not rush-hour crushing. The trip—most of it on the
New Jersey Turnpike and finally good old Interstate 80—
took under half an hour, during which the delicious aro-
mas of the boxed food kept me company, though they did
clash somewhat with a certain incense fragrance in the vehicle. The final leg of our journey was Route 17, taking us
to Lodi.

The cab pulled into the parking lot of a large building
with white siding, where a tall black stand-alone sign bore
bold red letters reading BADDA-BOOM GO-GO GIRLS, the *i*
in Girls dotted with a star. Good touch.

I paid the nice cabbie—there was enough in my purse to

take care of it, no need to dip into the bra bank—and he said, "Good luck, madam. You may need."

That was thoughtful, though I confess it struck me a real gentleman would have helped me in with the box of food. Instead, he left rather quickly, the cab's tires kicking up gravel.

Struggling against a chill wind, I managed to make it to the club's entrance, where I stood, flummoxed on how to open the door while laden down with that food box.

Then a rather brawny-looking biker wheeled in, got off his motorcycle, and came to my rescue.

"Let me help you with that, ma'am," he said politely.

He was bald and had a colorful snake tattoo across his face, one of the snake's eyes his own; he wore torn blue jeans and a black leather jacket, chains hanging from the shoulders. Quite colorful.

Then, taking my box, he balanced it in one hand while opening the door with his other.

"It's nice to know," I said, "that there are a few real gentlemen left in this crazy old world."

"Hey, no problem. I was a Boy Scout once."

"And I was a Girl Scout! What a lovely coincidence."

We were just two strangers, sharing a quiet moment of bonding.

Let that be a lesson to you, gentle reader: don't judge a book by its cover. Here's another one: when in the presence of colorful individuals, keep your rape whistle handy. That goes for you, too, fellas.

As I stepped inside, loud electronic dance music assaulted me—a *thump, thump, thump* reverberating off the walls. The lighting was minimal and for theatrical effect, but sunlight filtered in through several high windows, allowing me to take a good gander at the place.

The room was large, its periphery dotted with small tables and chairs, glowing beer signs hanging on the walls.

In the center was an elevated, rectangular stage surrounded by the bar, a sort of moat swimming with burly bartenders (at the moment, only two) positioned to protect the girls (one dancer presently) from any patron's unwanted attention.

About a half-dozen male customers with bored expressions perched on the stools around the rectangular counter, appearing more interested in their beers than the charms of the suspiciously busty woman dancing just a few feet away. Her hair was a long mane a shade of red that you might find in Sherwin-Williams, if not in nature, and she had excellent muscle tone. Little of that tone was concealed—her panties were scant, but I'm afraid so was her sense of rhythm. Of course, it would be difficult to dance well in those spiked heels. Her breasts were bare and gravity defying, and she was working a pole like a fireman reluctant to slide down and answer an alarm.

I set the heavy box down on the bar, and watched as she hung upside down, the red mane swaying, her legs in the air, *V* for victory. *V* for something!

"*Dear!*" I called out over the music. "*Less is more! Don't give away the store! Do leave* something *to the imagination!*"

It's all been downhill since the bikini was invented.

The dancer responded, but the music drowned it out, though I am fairly sure it was a negative reaction, judging by her facial expression. Still, she was hanging upside down at the time, and with my chronic earwax buildup, I'm afraid I couldn't be sure.

Well, if my constructive criticism was going to be ignored, I might as well get to it. I collected my food box and headed back to a pair of swinging doors.

Behind me, a bartender yelled, "Hey, you! *Lady!* You can't go in there!"

But he was too far away, and rather trapped within his

own fortress, and not quick enough to keep me from entering the back room, pushing through like Matt Dillon entering the Long Branch Saloon.

Once through the swinging doors, I froze, the way a perp does on TV when a cop yells, "Freeze!"

Four guns were trained on me.

Four guns brandished (isn't that a wonderful word?) by a quartet of tough-looking men, who had simultaneously jumped to their feet from an oversize wooden card table, where carefully arranged stacks of poker chips went tumbling over.

I hauled out my most dazzling smile. "Good afternoon, gentlemen! I'm Vivian Borne, and I've come all the way from Iowa to bring you some delicious Italian food."

The men, guns still on me, exchanged puzzled looks.

"Don't worry," I said, almost giddily. "I didn't bring the food with me *from* Iowa. It was prepared by one of the finest bistros in Manhattan."

Now, before I go any further, dear reader, I will not be using these gentlemen's real names, in an effort to protect the innocent (*moi*). But I will assure you that their real, actual names are prominently featured in FBI documentation of racketeering in New Jersey. And for that reason I will not describe them in detail, either, although I will admit that I was rather astounded by their resemblance to a number of major players on that old HBO series *The Sopranos*. Why, they could have been stand-ins for the actors portraying characters on that excellent if violent program.

I wish I could just nickname these individuals by the names of those characters, but—like the elderly gent whose finger was bitten off by a chimp on the Serenity trolley—I would prefer not to go to court.

So I'll just call them Johnny Contralto, Fabio, Petey Pecans, and Big Kitty.

Now, you may think I was intimidated by such dangerous company. And perhaps I would have been, had I not watched all six seasons of *The Sopranos* and felt I was among old, dear friends, not to mention knowing quite a lot about the Mafia in New Jersey. Television can be so educational!

Behind me, the beefy bartender, who had somehow found his way out of his self-imposed barricade, pushed through the swinging doors, letting in briefly the thumping music.

"I tried to stop the old bat, boss," he said apologetically. "Want me to throw her ass out?"

"*Really!*" I said. "That kind of talk is most uncalled for! 'Bat' indeed."

Smiling, his gun in hand at half-mast, Johnny Contralto said, "That's okay, Vinnie. We got this. You go back to work."

(I'm going to risk using Vinnie's real first name, since I don't know his last name, and also he didn't remind me of anybody in particular on any TV show.)

Vinnie shrugged and left, taking the music with him.

Petey Pecans turned his bullet-hard eyes on me; he had weird white streaks in his carefully coiffed hair, reminiscent of Elsa Lanchester in *The Bride of Frankenstein*.

Petey demanded, "Now, why should you wanna bring us food?" He wore dark slacks and a short-sleeved black-and-gray-striped bowling shirt.

I said, "This box is awfully heavy—may I set it down on the table? Can you boys make room?"

Johnny Contralto made a quick gesture with his gun. "Yeah, okay, lady," he said, adding, "But make it slow."

I placed the box in the middle of the table—they must have been between hands, because no money was piled there—careful not to disturb their cards (it was too late for the poker chips).

And, as I had anticipated, the tantalizing aroma of the

food wafting toward the men caused them to lower their guard, and their weapons.

"Do you have a microwave?" I asked. "It was a half-hour ride here from the city, and you may wish to heat this up a skosh. But the box still feels warm."

Big Kitty, his shark eyes seeing a potential meal, stepped toward the box. "What did ya bring us, honey?" He had on sweatpants and a too-tight baseball jacket.

Fabio, under a dizzying pompadour, said, "Take it easy, Kitty. This might be the craziest hit that ever went down— she might have hardware in there." He was wearing a black leather jacket unzipped over a white t-shirt, a gold chain around his neck.

Petey Pecans said, "Or it could be fulla rat poison! But, uh . . . what *is* it, anyway?"

Like a mother informing her four strapping, mischievous sons what was for dinner, I said, "Linguine with clams, veal piccata, and chicken Parmesan. And for dessert, cannoli and tiramisu. Oh, and garlic bread, *naturalmente.*"

Fabio's lower lip extended into a pout. "What, no baked ziti?"

"Oh, that's in there, too. Just an oversight in reporting my inventory."

It would have been disastrous to have forgotten baked ziti! Seemed like on *The Sopranos* Tony's wife, Carmella, served that dish whenever she wanted something, which she then usually got.

Petey Pecans asked, "Where's it from?"

"Coppola's," I said.

Fabio, licking his lips, said, "They got some good gravy, over at Coppola's."

For those of you with basic cable: "gravy" is Italian for marinara sauce.

"*And* they got truly righteous cannoli," Big Kitty added, then made a kissing gesture with his mouth and fingers.

Johnny Contralto was holding back his culinary approval, studying me with sharp, tiny eyes. "You ain't answered us yet, lady. . . ."

"Call me Vivian, please."

"Okay, Vivian. Nice to meet you, Vivian. Thanks for wheelin' in the meal wagon, Vivian. But *why* are you doin' us this generous thing? We ain't never seen you before. Which makes me think there's something that you want from us."

"Very perceptive, sir. I can see why you're in charge. . . . You *are* in charge?"

Johnny Contralto nodded. He was studying me shrewdly.

I continued: "But why don't we talk about that while we eat? The food will get cold. Strike now while the takeout is hot! And we won't even have to fire up the ol' microwave."

Johnny Contralto was still studying me.

"If you're worried it's been poisoned," I said with a dismissive shrug, "I'll be happy to taste everything first. But, please, for gracious' sakes . . . let's eat already! I've had to smell this wonderful feast all the way here in a taxi."

Big Kitty looked woefully at Johnny Contralto. "Boss, cut us a break, will ya? I'm starvin'! I ain't had a bite since lunch. You need a taste-tester, I'm your man. Heck, hand me a darn spoon and I'll dig into the gosh-darn stuff."

(Something else I should mention—I will be substituting the saltier language with less offensive alternates, so as not to offend you, gentle reader. Not to mention Walmart. I wonder if they will *ever* carry our books.)

Johnny Contralto shrugged. "Fair enough, Kitty. Let's put on the flippin' feedbag. *Then* we'll talk, capeesh?" To the others, he ordered, "Get some dishes."

And faster than the St. Valentine's Day massacre, the table was cleared, plates and utensils were brought, and cold beer was fetched from a fridge. Then we passed the dishes around and dug in, just one happy family (get it?).

In between bites, I filled my new friends in on a little background, chiefly that I live in a small town called Serenity.

"Never heard of it," said Big Kitty through a mouthful of linguine. "Where is dat, anyway?"

"As I said, I'm from Iowa, and our little jewel of a town is nestled along the banks of the majestic Mississippi."

"What's it like, living there?" Fabio asked.

"Have you ever seen a Frank Capra movie? *It's a Wonderful Life? Mr. Deeds Goes to Town?*"

There were nods all around. Capra was one of theirs, after all.

"Well," I said, "like that, but . . . not as well directed."

"Aw, that's a make-believe world," Petey Pecans grunted, a red dot of gravy on his pug nose. "No such thing nowhere."

"*Au contraire*. There are plenty of good jobs, a wonderful public education system, and everyone looks out for everybody else."

Johnny Contralto, chewing, said, "I don't believe it. A river town? That close to Chicago? You got crime. Don't tell me different."

"Well, yes, but practically none. Of course, we've had the occasional murder . . ."

Johnny Contralto smiled smugly and nodded, spooning pasta.

". . . but those were crimes of passion. And what *other* crime there was in sleepy Serenity, some gang violence, for example, has disappeared in recent years. All thanks to one man."

"The mayor?" Big Kitty wondered, a kid in class who hoped he'd stumbled onto the right answer.

I risked a healthy swig of beer—not really advisable on

my medication, but, in this instance, needed to bolster my nerve.

"No, dear," I said. "I'm speaking of our former police chief—a fine public servant who shares your colorful ethnic heritage."

"Yeah?" Petey Pecans asked. "Who? Maybe I heard of the guy."

"Maybe you have," I said casually. "His name is Anthony Cassato. Tony?"

Forks on the way to mouths froze in midair. As if a cop on a TV show had said, "Freeze!" Oh. I used that one already. Sorry . . .

Johnny Contralto asked, "This visit of yours today? It's about Tony Cassato?"

I nodded. "I came here to urge you to remove the, uh, I believe the term is *contract* that, uh, certain associates of yours appear to have taken out on him."

Johnny Contralto sat back, smug again. "And that's how you think it's done, huh, lady?"

"Vivian, please. Vivian."

"You just waltz in with some pasta and gravy, and we ask you what you want in return? That it?"

"The food was meant as a . . . peace offering. An icebreaker. Friends break bread together, and—"

"We break a lot of things," Fabio said.

"Fellas. Boys." I held up a peacekeeping palm. "I can well understand that when Tony was working in your province, he was probably in your hair. . . ." I glanced at the balding Johnny Contralto and added, "Figuratively speaking. . . . But what harm might he do you when he has relocated to the faraway Midwest?"

The four looked at me. It would have been quite sinister had they not all had gravy on their faces.

I continued: "Serenity needs Tony back. The town depends on him. Otherwise, Old Man Potter will take over

Bedford Falls!" I was still working the Capra angle, if a little desperately.

"Look, Vivian," Johnny Contralto said, his manner calm, his voice almost friendly now, "even if I *wanted* to cancel that supposed contract you mention . . . I couldn't."

I frowned. "Why not? Aren't you the head of the New Jersey family?" That's what the Internet had said, anyway.

He shook his head. "Vito Corleone is still the Don."

(Again, I am protecting myself by substituting a fictitious name, which I'm borrowing from *The Godfather*, an excellent book and even better movie!)

"I thought he was retired," I said. (Internet again.)

"He is what you call semiretired," Johnny Contralto said. "But he's still chairman of the board."

I thought Frank Sinatra was chairman of the board, but maybe Vito had taken over after Frank's passing.

Shifting in my chair, I asked, "Can you arrange for me to have a meeting with him?"

"Ain't likely," Fabio said, shaking his head vigorously, though not a lock of that pompadour was able to make a break for it. "The Don's in a old folks home in Teaneck, and he sees nobody but his son."

I sighed, disappointed. "Well, that's that, I guess."

Petey Pecans said, "Sorry you come all this way for nothin'. But the food was a nice gesture, Viv. Okay I call you Viv, doll?"

"I feel honored, Petey." (Again, not his real name.) "But perhaps I could ask another favor? Or I should say, a different one?"

Johnny Contralto said, "You want we should call a cab for you?"

"No, I want you should call Gino Moretti for me."

"Who?"

I smiled. "Please, we're friends. Friends don't insult each other."

Fabio said, "Not without risk, they don't."

I ignored that, and kept my eyes on Johnny Contralto's interesting face. "We all know that Gino is part of the Jersey family."

I knew this not from the Net, but from eavesdropping on Sal Cassato talking with one of his men, when I'd gone back to the crime scene to give the detective a keycard to our suite.

I continued. "Obviously Gino isn't here. Perhaps you've got him squirreled away somewhere. Holed up?"

Johnny Contralto smirked. "And why would we do that, Vivian?"

"To keep him from being questioned in the death of Tommy Bufford."

Petey Pecans asked menacingly, "Who *are* you, lady?"

I shrugged. "I'm an honored guest of the Bufford Con . . . *and* the one who found Tommy's body. And I'm someone else, too. . . ."

Fabio said, "And who would that be, Viv?"

"Why, the only one who can *clear* Gino."

The men exchanged looks that were equal parts confusion and skepticism.

I went on: "The police know Gino had an argument with Tommy, and that Gino threatened to kill him. That puts Gino on the top of their suspect list."

I paused, then asked, "By the way, do you know who's in charge of the Bufford investigation?" Not waiting for an answer, I said, "Sal Cassato—Tony's *brother*. Now, I ask you, how fair a shake do you think Gino will get?"

A few seconds passed as the men sat there as frozen as . . . custard? Make that an Italian ice.

Then Johnny Contralto withdrew his cell phone from a pocket and punched in some numbers.

For about an hour, I joined my new friends in a game of poker ($5 white chips, $10 reds, $25 blues). It was dealer's choice and I opted for Chicago (high spade in the hole splits the pot) and the game caught on, everybody dealing it for a while. I had just won my sixth pot when someone new pushed through the swinging doors to join our little get-together.

Johnny Contralto gave me a nod that said, *Gino*.

This was my first look at Bufford's ex-partner, who wore a black jacket unzipped over a white shirt, blue jeans, and black boots. He had dark wavy hair, a large nose, and small eyes; but his sensuous mouth and cleft chin threw him into the "handsome" column.

"Cash me out, boys," I said. I was up two Cs (that's two hundred dollars). "Is there somewhere we can talk?"

"Right here is fine," Johnny Contralto said. "We'll just take a break and grab a few brews. Out at the bar."

They did.

With Gino to myself, I gestured to the chair next to me and he sat, slouched, eyes hooded. "What do you want, lady? I wouldn't be here if—"

"If Mr. Contralto hadn't told you to get your behind over to the Badda-Boom?"

He shrugged sullenly.

"And what I *want*," I said, "is to help you avoid the hangman's noose. But that attitude of yours isn't helping."

Of course nobody got hung anymore (actually, *hanged*), but I had no doubt a New York jury would give him a stiff sentence.

"Besides which," I went on helpfully, "bad posture will only make you old before your time."

He smirked and snorted a sort of laugh.

"Well, I'm glad I'm a source of amusement, anyway." I pushed back from the table and stood. "Very well, I'll take my leave," I said, adding, "It is well-known that Vivian Borne never stays where she's unwanted." (Not precisely true. . . .)

Suddenly, Gino straightened. "No, no, I'm curious—let's hear what you got to say." But his smirk remained. (I might have lectured him on the dangers of smirking, as I had recently done with Brandy; but smirking suited Gino's face, and, anyway, if you're a man, what's wrong with looking like Bruce Willis?)

I sat down and folded my hands in my lap. "First, let me assure you most sincerely that I do *not* believe you killed Tommy Bufford."

A fib—actually, Gino was my number one suspect. But all's fair in love, war, and murder investigations.

I continued: "But you were seen arguing with him on the evening of the reception . . . even using the incriminating phrase, 'I could kill you.' "

"Come on, lady, you know that's a—what? A figure of speech!"

"Such a figure of speech can get you landed right smack in the slammer, young man—haven't you ever seen *Perry Mason*?"

"Harry who?"

Don't you think it's just a travesty that these younger generations ignore our wonderful old TV shows? But I restrained myself from berating him.

"I understand," I said, "that you and the late Mr. Bufford were quite close—even best of friends. And in spite of your acrimonious parting, would I be right in assuming that you still held him in high regard? Perhaps even loved him like a brother?"

Yes, that was a bushel of Iowa corn, but it brought the desired result.

Gino's smirk disappeared, the defiant eyes softened, and the sensuous lips quivered just a little.

"I . . . do," he admitted. "I *did*."

"Then, dear," I said gently, "why don't you tell me about it?"

"Who are you? Why do you want to know these things?"

"I am an independent investigator," I said, liking the sound of that, "who happens to have the ear of the detective in charge of the case. Detective Sal Cassato? I can *help* you."

"All right." He sighed deeply. "Tommy and me, we went to the same private school, but we didn't hit it off right away." He shook his head. "Two of us couldn't have been more different—Tommy was a geek, and me, I was a jock—quarterback. Darn good one, too."

Here Gino paused, enjoying the memory.

Then he went on, "We got thrown together in a math class where I was right on the verge, you know, of flunking out. And Tommy, he offered to help me . . . so I wouldn't get thrown off the team. That's when we found out that we both loved superhero comic books—you might say I was a closet comics fan all my young life. Anyway, we heard about the San Diego convention—the biggest one in the world—and made plans to go that summer together and share expenses."

"An exciting destination for a pair of young comics fans."

"Oh, it was a blast. But it was way the hell across the country, so Tommy and me began talking about starting our *own* convention. And there were things we didn't like about San Diego—like how big it had got, and how un-user friendly it was for people attending."

"Like the Manhattan convention quickly became?" I asked gently.

I was referring to the convention that Gino and Tommy had created together.

Gino smiled and shook his head. "You're right. And the irony is *not* lost on me, lady."

I switched gears. "Starting up a new convention takes capital—it's a massive enterprise. Am I right in assuming you had an angel? That someone staked you boys at the outset?"

Gino nodded. "That's the funny thing—and I don't mean funny *haha*. It's something else Tommy and me had in common . . . we both came from . . . families—you know the kind of 'family' I mean, right?"

Did he really need to ask this, in back of the Badda-Boom? He was saying, "Me, Jersey—Tommy, New York. And we got each of our two 'families' to put up the money to start the convention." He laughed dryly. "It's the only time I know of that those two families weren't feuding. But *now*. . . ."

I nodded. "You're afraid of a war. And that's why you've been lying low."

"Yeah. I'm afraid that New York thinks Jersey had Tommy killed."

"Jersey *did* force Tommy out of Manhattan Con."

Gino shrugged. "He got a good financial settlement." He spread his hands. "Hey, you saw how Tommy looked—even . . . smelled. I mean, he was a good guy, but he'd become an embarrassment. Not who you want as the face of a big event. And it wasn't just *Jersey* who expected high profits from their investment."

"You're saying New York wanted him gone, as well?"

"Some factions, yes. The younger ones. They saw future earnings being hurt. Tommy was the past, when comics conventions were about comics. The future of cons, hell, the *present*, is Hollywood."

I was nodding. "Then Tommy starts his *rival* convention—that must have made everyone nervous."

Gino waved that off. "He was no threat—his convention would always be small."

I shook my head. "Perhaps, at first . . . but you're forgetting the prestigious Buff Awards that gave his convention credibility. And from a little acorn a mighty oak may grow."

Gino shrugged, nodded. "I suppose. And I know he and that girl Violet were looking into taking his con to half a dozen other cities in the U.S.A., and four or five overseas. So, yeah, the Bufford Con thing could chip away at the Manhattan Con."

"Are you aware of how Tommy died?"

He shook his head. "Just that it's being called a suspicious death."

"I was there. I found the body. And I can tell you the details if you like."

He winced, but said, "Yes. Please."

And I told him.

By the time I'd finished, his face had gone ashen. "Oh, my God," he said slowly. "I was *afraid* it might be murder. Lady, I have to get out of here. If I don't lay low. . . ."

"That the murder weapon was a Buff Award is not helpful, is it?"

"No. Looks like somebody leaving a message."

"A message signed by you?"

"Or Jersey, anyway. This is bad. This is awful."

"Do you have an alibi?"

"No . . . and I'm afraid it's even worse than that."

"Go on."

"I was there," he said, "at the opening ceremony— backstage. I felt bad for what I'd said to Tommy the night before, and wanted to apologize, and wish him the best for the convention."

Apologize, perhaps, but I couldn't believe Gino could be magnanimous enough to wish him good luck. But I didn't see any merit in pressing.

I asked, "Did you speak with him?"

He shook his head. "I didn't have a chance. Tommy was

busy talking to Violet—he seemed upset about something, and she was trying to calm him down—and then he got into an argument with Brad Webster. So I just left."

"Really? Tommy had words with his Fan Guest of Honor?"

"Yeah. Quite the flare-up."

"Do you know what they might have argued about?"

Gino shook his head.

Again, I wasn't sure I believed him. But what good would browbeating him do?

Instead I said, "I can understand tension between Tommy and Violet—both under a great deal of pressure to make the convention a success. But I thought Tommy and Brad were good friends."

Gino's smirk returned. "Maybe once upon a time. But lately? Tommy couldn't *stand* that jerk."

Did I detect a note of jealousy?

"Then why did Tommy choose him as Fan Guest?"

Gino seemed to be considering his answer. After a few moments, he said, "Look, Brad had a thing for Tommy— but Tommy was straight. They were roommates, and there was a bad scene at some point, and . . . words got exchanged that couldn't be taken back."

"Ah."

"And I think Tommy was kind of, you know, trying to make it up to Brad, by giving him that honor. But then Brad took it wrong. Like maybe Tommy meant it as a sign that . . . well, anyway. That's what I think their argument was about—Tommy rebuffing him."

"I see."

Gino shifted in his chair. "You gonna tell the police you located me through the club?"

I reached over and patted his knee. "Of course not, dear. Why have *them* bumbling around?"

And messing up my chance of solving this case.

"Besides," I went on, "I'm sure if I could figure out that you could be located through the Badda-Boom, they can do that, too. They are not *that* incompetent. But it will take them a while to extradite you for questioning, and by that time? I'll have solved Tommy's murder." I stood. "In the meantime, do stay out of trouble. Stay in and read some funny books, why don't you?"

Gino said he thought that was a good idea, and said I could keep in touch with him through the Boom.

After he left, I boxed up the leftover food, and I went out into the bar.

My four new friends were seated at the counter, beers in front of them, and I asked Johnny Contralto to call me a cab so I could return to Manhattan.

But I didn't go back to the city.

I needed to pay my respects to someone in a Teaneck nursing home.

Mother's Trash 'n' Treasures Tip

Don't be afraid to haggle at a comics convention. If someone is resistant to lowering their price, say you saw the same item at another dealer for a lot less (even if you're fibbing). It isn't exactly a lie if you're just making something up, is it?

Chapter Seven

Con Tact

A peeved Sal Cassato reached into the closet, latched on to an arm of mine, and pulled me out like a garment bag. While I wouldn't say the detective was rough, exactly, he moved fast enough to get a growl out of Sushi, who let him know in no uncertain terms that she didn't approve of manhandling.

And neither did I.

"Hey!" I said. "Let go of me! You break it, you bought it."

His eyes flared, but there was embarrassment on his face for having gotten physical. He released me, asking gruffly, "How the hell did *you* get in here?"

"The closet or the room?" I asked, rubbing my arm.

The almost-Tony's face frowned. "I think I can figure out how you got in the closet. I *am* a trained detective."

"Good to hear."

He let out a sigh that sounded like steam escaping. "How . . . did . . . you . . . get . . . *in* . . . here?"

"The room, you mean?"

"You *know* what I mean!"

Okay, I was vamping for time. Trying to work up a story, thoughts careening off the inside of my head like a spirited game of racquetball.

Finally I said brightly, "I lost a ring?"

"Is that a question?"

"No. I mean, I lost a *ring*—thought it might be here. You remember—this used to be our room, Mother's and mine, before we traded with Tommy? I told you all about that."

That seemed to relax him, but his look of distrust only deepened. "Right. But presumably you swapped keycards with the late Mr. Bufford. *How* did you get in?"

I shrugged. "Still had a keycard left over. Found it in my purse. No harm, no foul . . . right?"

He held out a paw. "Gimme."

I gimmied.

We walked a few steps away from the closet into the torn-up room.

He said, "Please tell me you didn't make this mess. You know, looking for that imaginary ring?"

"Who says it's imaginary? And I haven't made a room this messy since high school. But it does seem like somebody else was looking for something, too."

He was glancing around at the destruction. "And not a ring."

"Probably not a ring."

Now he looked at me again. "If you had to guess, what would you say this somebody was after?"

"If we knew that," I said cheerfully, "we might be getting somewhere in this investigation."

He formed a fist and shook it—at me, or maybe at God. "I *told* you and your mother to stay *out* of this case!"

I stuck my chin out, as if daring him to use that fist. "You mean a trained detective like yourself hasn't figured out yet that that's *not* going to happen?"

Startled, Sal Cassato backed up a step.

So I took a step forward. "You've been around my mother long enough to know she's not going to quit. You've talked to your brother about the cases we've solved, yes, *solved*, and you probably know all about his own frustrations with Mother."

"She's *your* mother. Can't you control her?"

"How many children can control their parents? It's an even smaller number than the parents who can control their children."

"You could try."

"I *have* tried. Often, I've tried. Do you know the definition of insanity? It's performing the same task again and again, and always getting the same outcome, and then trying once more, thinking you might get a new one. No, I can't stop her. But there's one thing I *can* do."

He was starting to look plain tired. "And what, Ms. Borne, would that be?"

"I can help her get this murder solved as quickly as possible."

That remark gave him renewed energy. "And I can throw her rear end in jail! And yours."

"Go ahead! She'd *love* it. And I've been there, too. It'll be a big step up from our jail back home—a feather in her cap. Next time she's in the Serenity clink, she'll have bragging rights. What's the charge, by the way?"

"I'll jug you girls as material witnesses."

"Just like in Nero Wolfe! Mother will be ecstatic. Oh— and while we're inside, waiting for bail? I guarantee you there's not a guard or a dispatcher she won't be able to transform into her personal informant. Trust me, the only place for the police to have Mother that's worse than outside is inside."

Cassato was scrutinizing my face as if working on a scientific study on the subject of whether mental illness could be passed on via heredity. Then he sighed again, and it didn't sound like steam escaping this time. More like his soul leaving him to float to some safer, saner place.

Then he asked, "Why do I think you have a suggestion?"

"Because I have one. And here it is: join forces."

Cassato gave the kind of look a bartender gives a kid who just handed him terrible fake I.D.

I asked, "Why, are you already close to making an arrest? And don't need any more help?"

". . . I can't comment on that."

"I'll take that as a 'no.' Then perhaps I could offer you some information that might prove helpful."

His eyes narrowed. "If you know something, lady, you better tell me right now."

Earlier, I'd been a "girl," and I much preferred that to "lady."

But, nonetheless, I told him about Robert Sipcowski having been in this very room just before I arrived.

Cassato's expression existed in that no man's land between a smirk and a sneer. "Surely you don't think *he's* involved?"

I folded my arms like a particularly smug Barbara Eden in *I Dream of Jeannie*. "I'm going to take a wild guess that he didn't walk away from a pension at the NYPD for a chance to work hotel security."

"You can make a pretty fair living in the hotel security field." There was something defensive, even evasive in the detective's tone.

I shook my head. "No sale. I've seen the photos in his office—he's proud of his career. It's written all over him—he'd give anything to still be on the job."

Something flickered in the detective's eyes.

I asked, "What aren't you telling me?"

He said nothing.

"Your *brother* would tell me," I said.

"I'm not my brother."

I was starting to realize that.

I asked, "Was Sipcowski forced out?"

". . . More or less."

"Why?"

He glanced around, a ridiculous search for privacy in an upended room where the only other inhabitants were myself and a blind shih tzu.

"I didn't tell you this," he said.

"You haven't told me anything yet."

"There were cases of his where a certain New York family were involved that didn't turn out the way they should have . . . is all I can say."

But of course I pressed on: "You're saying the hotel's security chief has ties to a New York crime family? I mean, when you said 'certain New York family,' you didn't mean the Rockefellers."

"Not the Rockefellers, no."

I frowned at him. "Have these Mob ties been substantiated?"

"Let me put it this way—and you never heard this from me—but Robert Sipcowski was given a choice between resigning or sticking around for a full-scale investigation into those suspected mishandled cases. And that's all I'm willing to say about it."

He'd said plenty.

Then he added, "But you and that doggie're barkin' up the wrong tree with Sipcowski. I don't see this as having anything to do with that murder."

"Are you sure? Sipcowski certainly had the opportunity to kill Tommy—as security chief, he can go anywhere in the hotel, at any time, without rousing suspicion. And he's got access to the security-cam footage."

"And what's his motive?"

"What, do I have to do everything?"

He winced, as if I were causing him physical pain.

"Look, Detective," I said, "I have a six o'clock dinner

appointment, and I have barely enough time to freshen up. If you want me, a trained detective shouldn't have trouble finding me. You know what room I'm in. You were in it most of the afternoon."

"Go, go," he said.

Leaving Cassato to ponder Sipcowski as a possible suspect, I returned to our suite. I took a few minutes to have at least a cursory look inside that thick file I'd found in Tommy's little fridge. Inside was a stack of filled-out Buff Awards ballot sheets.

Had Tommy purposefully hidden them? Or absentmindedly stuck them in the fridge? The latter seemed highly unlikely, even for a healthy eater, so these pages *must* have had some significance.

I just had no idea what. . . .

I returned the papers to the file, then set the folder on the end table next to Mother's pile of trinkets, noting with satisfaction that Detective Cassato had apparently not discovered her little recording device. The key-chain bug didn't appear to have been touched.

My shower was quick enough to rate a world record, and my quick do-over at the mirror would have been a candidate for the same. After giving Sushi a kiss—she was nestled now among the pillows on the bed—I said, "I'll be back soon, sweetie," and slipped out.

Located just off the lobby, Lindy's (its *i* dotted with a star) was one of the hotel's four restaurants.

Eclectically decorated in a mixture of vintage signs and sports memorabilia, the eatery (so famous for its cheesecake) also had an entrance on Seventh Avenue, attracting a clientele beyond just hotel guests.

But Ashley had beaten me there, having snagged one of the few booths across from the central bar, and she waved to get my attention.

I realize some of you are asking, *Who's Ashley? And why are we meeting her halfway through the book?*

Ashley is my niece. Correction—she's my half sister. She *was* my niece until last year, when I found out that my birth mother wasn't Mother (who had raised me), but rather my much older sister, Peggy Sue. (Mother had blurted some of this to Robert Sipcowski, as you may recall.) At the time of my conception, Peggy Sue was having an affair with then-state-senate hopeful Edward Clark; she was newly eighteen and unmarried, working on his campaign. He was also unmarried and working on his campaign, but should have known better. Fortunately he didn't, or you wouldn't be reading this. Because I wouldn't be here.

Sorry to throw this at you Trash 'n' Treasures newbies, but trust me—whichever book you start with, you are going to be at least a *little* confused. And if you started with this book, or you're a loyalist who just needed a refresher, the above paragraph was a necessary evil . . . that is, if you want to follow the conversation that Ashley and I are about to have in the next few pages.

Oh, and Ashley? When she first heard the stuff in that paragraph before the last one . . . *brother* (or maybe *sister*), was *she* furious! Furious with Peggy Sue for this deception, enough so as to quit college and flee to New York. To my knowledge, Ash hasn't spoken to her mother since.

And while Ashley hadn't been as furious with me as she had been with Peggy Sue, she was still put out with me. We were close, and I should have told her. But, frankly, I didn't find out about all that soap-opera craziness myself until a few months before she did.

So now you know that Aunt Olive and the Superman drawing weren't the only things on my agenda. Going to New York was my opportunity to try to reconnect with my niece. Sister. Half sister.

"How are you, Ash?" I asked.

I can tell you how she was: stunning. I say that without family pride, just the realization one woman has when she sees another woman who's better looking.

In fact, Ash was even more beautiful than Peggy Sue had been at that age, with the same silken auburn hair, porcelain complexion, perfect features, and startlingly green eyes. She always knew just what to wear—today, that was gray jeans, a black sweater, and a colorful Hermes silk scarf around her neck; on the seat next to her was a burgundy tweed coat, a silver Coach purse at her side.

I bent, gave her a hug—she hugged back, which was a relief—then slid into the booth opposite her.

Ashley smiled, showing perfect white teeth. "I'm doing *great*, Bran," she said, a little too cheerfully. "And you?"

"I'm on a trip with your grandmother," I said. "How do you think I'm doing?"

She laughed. "I was hoping Grandma would join us. It seems like a century since I saw her."

"Actually, I haven't seen her since late this afternoon." I reached for a menu. "She was heading to her theatrical haunts to look up old pals. Thought she'd be back by now, but don't worry, you'll see her before we leave town. *Yikes!* Nineteen bucks for a turkey sandwich?"

"Welcome to Manhattan."

"Wanna split one?"

She shook her head, arcs of auburn hair swaying. "Afraid I only do salads these days—have to stay thin if I want to work in print ads."

Far as I was concerned, she was verging on too thin, but I kept that to myself.

"I'm glad you're having some success," I said. "That's a tough trade."

This was the first I'd heard that she was modeling. We'd had very little contact—not that I hadn't tried.

Ashley was saying, "Not exactly on the cover of *Elle* yet. Still waiting tables in the Village. It's what I think they call eking out an existence."

"Eek, period."

"No, Bran, it's great. I love this city. So vital. Just nothing like it. Everything you hear about it is true."

Muggings in Central Park, aggressive homeless people, Wall Street sharks . . .

I set the menu aside. "I can't help myself. I feel an attack of advice coming on. Afraid I still think of myself as your aunt."

"Maybe, but we were always more like sisters."

"Sweet of you to say, but . . . I can't help but wish you hadn't left college."

She shrugged. "Never too late to go back."

"Why'd you do it?"

She didn't reply, just looked down at the white plastic tablecloth, traced its maze-type pattern with a finger.

I tried again. "Okay, I know *why*—but I still don't understand it. Hurting yourself doesn't get back at your mother. And, anyway, you always had a great life. I'm the injured party here, if there is one—I'm the foundling who grew up with Vivian Borne as a mother."

I hadn't meant that as a joke, but we both found ourselves laughing at it.

But the mirth was fleeting, and she said quite seriously, "It was just the final straw with Mom. I love her, but her social-climbing ways, all that status-seeking nonsense . . . *ick*! It's a bitter pill, realizing that you don't like somebody you love."

Nothing there I could argue with.

She went on, "But I was injured, too. Denied the experience, the fun we would have had, growing up as sisters together."

"Oh, Ash," I said, shaking my head, smiling gently, "we

wouldn't have grown up together—too many years separated us."

"I know, but—"

"If your mother had claimed me, and grown up with an
illegitimate child back in those days . . . ? What a hard,
rough life she would have had. She and your father may
not have gotten together. And you might never have been
born. Which is the kind of 'what if' you can drive yourself
crazy thinking about."

I should know, because I'd already dealt with such issues with my therapist.

She was thinking about all that.

I touched her hand and gave her half a smile, which
seemed plenty. "And I wasn't such a bad aunt, was I?"

She gave me the other half of the smile. "No. Not a bad
aunt at all. You've been fun, so much fun. But *you*
could've been happier. Aren't you even mad at her?"

"At Peggy Sue? No." Maybe a little. "I've been plenty
happy in my life. And any unhappiness has been my own
doing. Besides, living with your grandmother has been an
experience in tolerance."

Now her smile turned ornery. "An experience in tolerance, or an intolerable experience?"

"Six of one, sweetie. Six of one."

We fell silent for a moment.

"Ash, will you do something for your former-aunt-now-
half-sister? It would mean a lot to me."

"You want me to call Mom. In D.C., where she lives
with that man."

After the unexpected death of Ashley's father, Peggy Sue
had reconnected with Senator Clark, after a mere thirty
years, and moved to Washington to be the perfect political
wife. But for this fairy tale to have its requisite happy ending, I would have to get Ashley to give her mother a second chance.

" 'That man' is *her* husband and my *father*," I said. "The senator has paid for his sins in the media. And he's a decent, a truly decent man, Ash. Call her."

"Brandy, I just don't know. . . ."

"I'd really appreciate it."

She sighed. She laughed silently, shook her head, as all the things we descendants of Vivian Borne had been through together were rushing through her mind at once.

"All right," she said finally. "I will do it—if it'll make you happy."

"It will. And you know what? It just might make you happy, too."

She rolled her pretty eyes. "And for all those years, I thought you were such a cool aunt. Now it turns out you're just my cornball older sister from Iowa."

"Growing up is such a disappointment, don't you think?"

"Absolutely."

"Now, where's a waitress?" I groused. "I'm *starving*—nineteen dollars for a turkey sandwich is starting to sound like a bargain."

In between bites of food, we talked, falling back into our old comfortable relationship, exchanging excessively detailed accounts of what we each had been doing since we'd been out of touch. Ashley was in the middle of a funny story about her roommate, a Cyndi Lauper look-alike, when I noticed Violet and Eric coming into the restaurant through the hotel access.

Violet looked voluptuous in a black-and-white check-ered formfitting dress with a wide black patent belt, black heels stark against her bare, pale legs. But the stress of holding the convention together was starting to show in her face, cracking her heavy makeup.

Eric seemed chipper, though, looking very Nordic in an

Alpine gray-and-red ski sweater, black jeans, and black boots.

The two took stools at the bar, then ordered drinks from the bartender. I tried to listen in on their conversation, but the pair had their backs to me and kept their voices low, heads together. At one point, Eric slipped an arm around Violet's shoulders—the gesture seemed consoling, not sexual.

"Are you okay, Bran?" Ashley asked.

She'd been talking, and I must have seemed distracted.

"Uh, yeah. Some people I know at the bar is all. You were saying?"

"I was *saying*," Ashley said with a wry smile, "that I probably should be leaving. Movie date tonight."

Now she had all my attention. "Serious?"

Ashley smiled coyly. "Early days, but . . . yeah. Pretty serious. I hope you and Grandma get to meet him before you go home—he works on Wall Street."

Well, she'd been raised by Peggy Sue, after all. Quitting college hadn't lowered her standards.

I raised my eyebrows. "Think he's ready for us?" Meaning Mother and me.

"Well, it's not like you and Grandma get to New York every other Tuesday. Better take advantage of your presence here to find out if he can take it."

"Does he drink?"

"Well, yes. I mean, nothing that's—"

"He'll need to." I reached for the check. "I'll get this."

"Thanks, Brandy." A young woman eking out an existence in New York didn't have the luxury of fighting over a check. She gathered her purse and coat. "It's been wonderful seeing you. I feel . . . I feel better about things."

"You and me both, honey."

We kissed each other's cheeks.

Then she asked, "Is Sushi along?"

"She's not *along*. She's *in charge*."

"How cool! Can't wait to kiss her fuzzy little head."

I watched my niece/half sister leave through the Seventh Avenue revolving door, chill air reaching me a few seconds later, making me shiver.

But I wasn't going, not just yet. Not until I'd had Lindy's cheesecake—even if it was nine bucks a slice.

I had just dipped my fork into the creamy mass of goodness when Brad Webster entered from the lobby.

He strode purposefully toward Violet.

Like Hercule Poirot, I had learned that eavesdropping was a key aspect in the art of detection.

Brad was saying angrily to Violet, "I can't believe you're going on with the convention! It's . . . it's *ghoulish*."

Violet turned to look at him, her gaze withering. "Could we not talk about this here? In public?"

"It's all about the *money*, isn't it? The money and *him*." Brad gave Eric's shoulder a little shove.

Eric hopped off the bar stool and pushed Brad back, the Fan Guest of Honor bumping into a passing waitress, who dropped her order. At these prices, that was fifty bucks that hit the floor.

Then the bartender was shouting for the three to leave, and Violet did so, her anger keeping back the tears, Eric running after her, followed by a disgruntled Brad.

I considered tossing some money on the table and pursuing the trio—if the confrontation continued in the lobby, I might really learn something. But that cheesecake was calling to me, and you just don't walk away from nine-dollar cheesecake, not where I come from.

What is it about New York that makes all Midwesterners feel like they're bit players in a bus-and-truck company of *Annie Get Your Gun*?

A little while later, I returned to the suite, bringing some leftover turkey for Sushi, and found no sign of Mother.

Which struck me as rather odd. Normally, I wouldn't

have been concerned, as she often lost track of time when she was shopping, sightseeing, or sleuthing.

But this was not serene Serenity, this was the big bad city, and a little spike of worry shot through me. *Better safe than silly*, I thought, and called her cell phone.

And immediately heard Mother's custom ringtone for the trip ("New York, New York") emanate from a closed bureau drawer.

Apparently, I thought, irritated and afraid, *her vagabond shoes were longing to stray*.

She had a bad habit of intentionally leaving her cell behind should she not want to be reached. Not enough to just ignore a call like the rest of us rational folk—she had to be (as she put it) "well and truly out of pocket, dear."

Once, when the vet put a little tracker chip in Sushi's neck, so I could find the precious creature should she wander away, I had asked if he could do the same to Mother. He thought I was kidding.

Sushi was pawing at me, halfway up my legs, not in concern for Mother's absence, not hardly—she wanted that Lindy's turkey. So I fed her, then gave the little mutt an injection of insulin, followed by a bone treat for taking the shot like a trooper.

I retrieved the little recording device, and spent the next half hour at my computer in the outer room, downloading its contents, so that it could be heard through the speaker.

But I didn't bother listening to the recording, because even if I took copious notes, Mother would *still* want to hear it herself. This assumed that Mother had not been shanghaied on a boat to China nor decided to join the Foreign Legion. She was a trifle too old for the white slavers.

I was about to turn on the TV and do some channel-surfing when a knock came at the door. My first thought was Mother, but surely she wouldn't have left her keycard behind, too. Well, that would have been *really* out of pocket. . . .

I crossed over and looked through the peephole, seeing what appeared to be Detective Cassato's face via fisheye distortion. I opened the door.

Sal must have given my suspicions about Sipcowski some thought and decided that my opinions had some merit, after all. Smiling smugly to myself, I opened the door.

But the man standing in front of me in a blue NYPD windbreaker wasn't Sal Cassato. Oh, it was a Cassato, all right, just not Sal.

Tony!

And I flew into his arms, and he took me in his, but walked me backward into the room, the door closing behind us.

We kissed. Several times.

Finally, I came up for air and blurted, "What are you doing here, you great big beautiful fool? You're putting yourself in danger!"

He cupped my face in his hands. "Not as much danger as you're getting into . . . you beautiful little fool."

So he'd been talking to his brother. I guessed they were in closer contact than Sal had admitted.

We walked hand in hand into the living room area and sat together on the sofa.

"Brandy," he said, his dark eyes locked on me, two of his hands holding one of mine, "you have *got* to stop looking into this Bufford murder. You're going to upset some powerful *not*-nice people."

"You mean . . . not-nice people in New Jersey?"

He nodded. "The same Mob crew who are after me. And I don't have to tell you that they're ruthless."

I had been with him when the hit men they sent found Tony in Serenity. We had both barely gotten through that horror alive (*Antiques Knock-Off*).

I asked, "You think the same people killed Tommy?"

"*Had* him killed, yes."

"By Gino Moretti, maybe?"

He let go of my hands, his eyes wide. "Are you pumping me for information?"

"Well, uh, not exactly, I . . ."

"Brandy! Stay out of this investigation or you will get seriously hurt—and that goes for Vivian, too."

"I'm glad to hear you care so much about Mother."

"I care about her because *you* care about her. Otherwise, I would be happy to see her get what she deserves for her busybody b.s."

Their relationship in the past was . . . less than warm. At least on Tony's side.

He went on, "There could even be a shooting war between Jersey and New York factions, and the last thing I want is you caught in the crossfire. Why can't you and your Mother just come to New York and see *Wicked* like everybody else?"

"It's in our plans," I said lamely.

He took my hand again and squeezed it. "You've *got* to *promise* me that you will lay off this investigation."

"Okay . . . I will."

"I mean *promise*."

"Girl Scout's honor."

He shook his head, glanced around. "Where *is* Serenity's answer to Jessica Fletcher, anyway?"

"Out and about."

"Out where? About where?"

"Visiting some old friends."

"She has friends here?"

"Her theatrical pursuits brought her to the Big Apple, once upon a time."

"And that's what she's up to? That's *all* she's up to?"

"Yes." I hoped.

He sighed. "Well, do your best to keep her out of trouble, will you? I wouldn't put it past that woman not to just waltz blithely into some Mob stronghold, all by her lonesome."

"She wouldn't do that."

"Oh?"

"She's not *that* crazy."

On the other hand, she had done more than her share of waltzing blithely into dangerous situations.

Mother, where are you?

He laughed dryly. "Not that those bastards in Jersey don't deserve a strong dose of Vivian's medicine."

Sushi, who of course remembered Tony, had been pawing at his pantlegs since he'd come in. He reached down and picked her up, and let her settle in his lap.

"Where are you living?" I asked, tucking my legs beneath me.

Tony, scratching Sushi's neck, said, "You know I can't tell you that."

"Is it someplace . . . nice?"

"Not particularly."

"Is there room for one more there?"

"What, and have your mother come track us down? No, Brandy, this is no life for you."

"It's not much of a life now. Without you in it."

"I'm in it. Never doubt that for a moment. I'm in it."

He leaned over and gave me a quick kiss.

"I miss you so," I said. And, yes, my eyes were tearing up. Even tough-guy Tony's eyes seemed a little moist.

"I miss you, too," he said. "But, I'm afraid this visit has to be a onetime affair."

I moved closer. "Then . . . can we *make* it that? An affair, I mean?"

Later, after we'd exchanged good-byes as melancholy as they were sweet, I wandered back into the suite with only a blind dog to keep me company. I crawled into the real bed, unable to sleep, torn up by the thought of a future apart from a man I loved, and who loved me. And worry for Mother was in there, too.

Where are *you, Mother?*

Nearly two in the morning, and no sign of her. Should I call the other Cassato for help? Or 9-1-1? Contact the hospitals, maybe?

I didn't know what to do.

So I did the only thing a young woman far away from home, denied the man she loved, beside herself over the whereabouts of her missing elderly mother, could do.

I phoned room service to bring me another piece of Lindy's cheesecake.

A Trash 'n' Treasures Tip

Before buying a valuable comic book, examine it carefully for damage, removing it from its Mylar bag to do so; be on the lookout for missing pages, scribbling, tears, and wear on the spine. But always do this with the permission (and under the supervision) of a booth (or comic book shop) employee. Comics dealers do their best to pick up their wares at trash prices, but then view them as the pop-culture treasures they are.

Chapter Eight

Con Game

I have very good news for you! You need not distress your-self wondering what misfortunes may have befallen Vivian Borne on her New Jersey adventure, because Vivian Borne herself survived to tell the tale. And I am she (or is that *her*?), here to tell you.

I mean, it's heartwarming knowing that Brandy was concerned about my welfare and whereabouts, but let's not kid ourselves, shall we? Neither Brandy nor I am likely to meet any fate worse than injury or imprisonment in a book that we are writing ourselves, after the fact. I mean, really. Think about it.

Still, that's not to say that things weren't touch and go on the second half of my Joisey adventure. I was, after all, on foreign turf, wading into strange waters—or is that a mixed metaphor? Surely not—you have to have turf so that waters have a place to run through, strangely or other-wise, and, after all, there's such a thing as surf and turf, isn't there?

But I digress.

That lovely Johnny Contralto summoned a cab for me, and it arrived promptly, no longer than it took for me to throw down a drink at the bar with the boys. Let me tell you, they make a mean Shirley Temple at the Boom. A different dancer was on, a blonde with no surgical enhancements but several unfortunate tattoos. I had hoped on her break that I might counsel her to resist the urge for additional "body art," as they call it, but she was still climbing her pole when my ride arrived.

Getting in back of the cab with my Coppola's leftovers, I addressed the driver, a hobbity-looking fellow in an Ivy League cap who did not appear to be an immigrant (at least not a recent one).

"Good evening!" I said. "What's the most exclusive nursing home in Teaneck?"

I deduced that someone as important as a Mafia Don would almost certainly spend his declining years at the best.

But the cabbie gave me a look as if I'd posed a strange question.

I explained in more detail: "What I call a nursing home, you may call an assisted living facility or perhaps a convalescent hospital. I suppose some people still use 'old folks home,' or perhaps 'rest home,' even possibly 'retirement home,' but you know, when you get right down to it, political correctness aside, 'nursing home' is still the most accurate, because there are nurses on duty twenty-four/seven, in case you need help getting to the bathroom."

The squat middle-aged cabbie, Frodo with a crewcut and prizefighter's nose, shrugged. "Top-dollar nursing home? Easy peazy, lady. Royal Care."

"That does sound promising."

"Oh, yeah. If you're scopin' out facilities for some ancient relative, and wanna find someplace that don't stink on ice, Royal Care's as good a place as any to start. I mean, I figure that's what you're up to. You're way too young to need that kind of joint yourself."

What a shameless flirt he was (not to mention loquacious). Still, it's nice to be appreciated. I bestowed a smile upon him and said, "You obviously know what you're talking about, kind sir. Royal Care it is!"

And I gestured as if sending a coachman off to the castle.

And Royal Care *was* a sort of castle, albeit of a modern geometric variety, a baker's dozen of redbrick stories set back from the street on a well-manicured lawn, surrounded by trees that were just beginning to bud.

As I paid the cabbie, I said, "Why, this looks like an upscale apartment building!"

"Yeah, but me, I ain't anxious for *that* kinda condo."

"Oh, I don't know. If that's a nursing home, sign me up!"

"Not for a while yet, lady. Not for a while. Here's my card—if I can't come pick you up, somebody else from the company will."

And he gave me a wink and roared off, the charmer.

With my Lancelot gone, it was up to Guinevere to storm the castle alone (by Guinevere, I mean me), but at least there wasn't a moat. I marched up the main walk with my box of leftovers, only to find the double glass doors in front locked.

Not a surprise, whether for a nursing home or an exclusive apartment complex. At left was an intercom with a little button, which I pushed, and soon a tinny-sounding female voice asked my name and who I had come to call upon. No matter how high class a facility, intercoms always sound just a little worse than two paper cups and a string.

"Vivian Borne," I said. "Visiting . . . ah, my aunt Olive."

(By the by, I pronounce "aunt" like one of those pesky insects that are so bothersome at picnics—not the affected "ahhhnt" way that some folks do. And the *Webster Handy College Dictionary* agrees with me. You can look it up. Never too late to correct a bad habit!)

Immediately, I regretted not telling the intercom, "Aunt Mary," as certainly *some* Mary or other would be residing within. The only other Olive I knew, other than my late aunt the paperweight, was in the Popeye cartoons.

But either I got lucky or at least one Olive dwelled within, because the door buzzed, and I shouldered my way inside, takeout box in hand.

The reception area was a vast space of gray-and-tan stone walls and beige carpeting under a cherrywood ceiling with recessed lighting. An assortment of comfortable-looking couches and chairs, plus end table with magazines, were provided in what seemed to be an area designed for residents to chat with visitors, as opposed to a doctor's waiting room.

The attractive space was empty, perhaps because this was dinnertime. The latter I deduced (without much taxing of my sleuth skills) from the bouquet of cafeteria food mixed with a whiff of disinfectant. No matter how upscale a nursing home this might be, institutional food and cleaning products were as inevitable as death and taxes.

Not very far down the hall was an open office area with a counter, behind which nurses in light blue moved, if in no particular hurry. Here was presumably where one might check in or sign in or whatever procedure was required. Of course, I wanted none of that.

So I strode off in the opposite direction, in search of an elevator, again deducing that someone as important as a Mob boss must be on the top floor with the best view—the nursing home equivalent of the penthouse.

Anyway, I didn't feel that checking in at a nurse's station to say I was here to visit Don Corleone was wise. The Don's visitors' list was no doubt restricted, and a phone call might be made that could have unfortunate consequences for yours truly.

So down the hall I went, wearing the confident air of one who knows where she is going, strolling by an aerobics room, a movie theater, and a music area with a baby grand—no sign of anyone, not even a nurse or an orderly.

Then, next to a hair salon (closed for the day), I came to an elevator, pressed the button, and stepped into a space large enough to accommodate a gurney or two and any number of attendants (this *was* a nursing home, after all, not a high-rise condo), and took it up, stepping off on the top floor—fourteen.

Actually, fourteen was the thirteenth floor, but there was no thirteenth floor at Royal Care, a cosmetic touch with which I wholeheartedly agreed. The last thing a person wants at that stage of life is bad luck.

While the beige carpeting and gray-and-tan stone walls of reception had struck me as high tone for a nursing home, what I encountered here could only be described as posh— rich floral carpet, brocade wallpaper, and a sculpted plaster ceiling with small chandeliers. Positioned between numbered doors were petite Louis XIV tables with floral arrangements, and a few matching straight-back chairs.

I might have been in a five-star hotel.

But those numbered doors lacked the usual hospital-type identifying cards-in-slots, and I was left with no way to discern which suite might belong to the Don. That was when a male nurse, wearing light blue scrubs, exited a door at the far end, and came toward me, riding to my rescue. He just didn't *know* he was.

As he drew nearer, I feared my visiting-aunt cover story might not hold up—the odds of finding an Aunt Olive on the fourteenth floor seemed about as likely as finding an Uncle Bluto—so I invented a new ruse, improvisation being merely one of the actors' arts I've mastered.

"Special takeout meal for Don Corleone," I told him with the proper unabashed air of authority. If one needed a pass of some kind to carry out such a mission, I would soon be in deep do-do. Of course, in a place like this, I wouldn't be alone.

(Just a gentle reminder that I am not using the Don's real name herein—with apologies and thanks to the late Mario Puzo. Also, I will continue to censor any particularly inappropriate language, for the sake of propriety. And Walmart.)

But the male nurse merely gave me a nod and a small smile, saying, "Last door on the right," and walked on.

It occurred to me that the young man may have taken me for a high-priced concubine, as the Don might from time to time bring in such floozies for recreational purposes.

Wondering whether to feel insulted or complimented, I stopped at the door of the Don's apartment, collected my thoughts, and was about to knock, when the door swung open, and I was suddenly standing there, staring at the Don himself!

He was a fireplug of a man, in his eighties, with a lumpy liver-spotted face and thinning silver hair, and yet there was something commanding, even towering about his presence. He wore a navy nylon tracksuit, at odds with the cane on which he leaned. (And, that, dear reader, is all the description I dare give you. I have no desire to spend *my* declining years in witness protection.)

"Well?" he snapped irritably. "What the fudge took ya so long?"

Good Lord, *had* he been expecting a takeout delivery? Well, I always say it's better to be lucky than smart.

He took a few steps back and waved repeatedly toward himself. "Come in, come in, come in."

My, he *was* hungry!

I stepped past the man and into a black-and-white marble-floored foyer with mirrored walls.

"Vivian, isn't it?" he asked gruffly, closing the door.

Whoopsy.

My mouth dropped open, the box nearly tumbling from my hands. I'd been made! My cover blown! Next stop: a building site in Hackensack, waiting for the cornerstone of a new Olive Garden to be set on top of me (Olive again!). *Not* what I had in mind for a final resting place. . . .

I was speechless, or at least as close as I get to that condition. "Ah . . . yes. I am Vivian Borne. How did you . . . ?"

"Come on, come on, come on . . . get that food in the kitchen before it gets even colder. God, I ain't had decent Italian in a month of Sundays."

Then he turned abruptly and hobbled down the hallway, the cane a third leg.

Intimidated into silence and submission, I followed.

In the kitchen—really a kitchenette, small compared to what else I'd glimpsed of the suite—I set the box on the stove and turned to face him.

"How is it, sir, that you know my name?"

He shrugged. "Aw, my boys at the Boom called. They figured you might have the cojones to show up."

(I have left in "cojones" so as not to completely strip the Don of his colorful mode of speech; and, anyway, the word *has* become fairly mainstream.)

He was saying, "I made sure the front desk would let you in. And I asked Franco—he looks out for me—to tell you where I was."

My disappointment at not locating the Don on my own steam must have shown on my face. Also, it meant I had not been mistaken for a high-class call girl, which was a little disappointing.

The Don spread his arms wide. Oddly, his smile seemed both threatening and good-natured. "*What?* You think just *anybody* has access to my premises? Hey, Vivian, I got my teeth, and I still got my enemies. . . . Okay I call you Vivian?"

"Please," I said. "May I call you 'Don'?"

"Naw, make it Vito."

"Vito it is. And you're right. I'm afraid I *was* naive, thinking I could just sneak or barge or somehow get in to see you. Of *course*, you have enemies. Probably more than your share!"

"You're darn tootin' I do."

Of course, he put that more colorfully, if in an unrepeatable fashion. He was referencing the act of sexual union, followed by the first letter of the alphabet.

(**Note to Vivian from Editor:** I think it best that you simply continue your inoffensive substitutions for offensive language, without describing that language in a fashion that enables the reader to figure out what has been omitted.)

(**Note to Editor from Vivian:** But this language is such a vital part of the man's personality—I don't want to castrate him completely . . . of course, castration is inherently complete, isn't it, although perhaps not when used in a figurative manner. Or is "castrate" itself offensive? Anyway, I thought you put a moratorium on interrupting our narrative with these notes, after a reviewer took us to the woodshed over them. Hello?)

The Don peered inside the box, lifting a few container lids. "Where's the linguine with clams?"

"Your Boom boys ate it all."

"Gosh darn it! Them pesky selfish lads!" He looked murderous. And he sure as heck didn't say "pesky" or "lads."

I waved off his irritation. "Those clams don't hold up

over time, anyway. But there's baked ziti and chicken Parmesan." Then I added placatingly, "And fresh tiramisu! I believe it made the ride just fine."

"Any ganool?"

Thanks to *The Sopranos*, I knew that he meant cannoli. "There's one left. It's got your name on it!"

Better than a bullet.

He grunted. "Sloppy seconds'll have to do. Anyway, it's way the heck better than the junk they feed me here."

I would likely have agreed, if the dining-room food tasted anything like the way it smelled.

The Don pointed at me with a sausage of a finger. "You set the table—the one by the front windows. Meanwhile, I'll heat this up with the microwave. You'll join me, of course, right, Vivian?"

I wasn't about to say no to the Godfather.

He showed me where the utensils and dishes were, and I gathered up place settings for two.

The living room, unlike the opulent corridor outside or even the foyer within, was a male domain, decorated in brown, tan, and green. A comfy-looking leather couch and matching easy chair—the latter a recliner that lifted its occupant up and out—faced a large flat-screen TV. By the bank of windows offering a stunning postcard view of Manhattan across the Hudson River, lights of the city twinkling in the dusk, was a square oak table with two chairs, a game of Scrabble in progress. (I wondered who he had been playing it with. His son, who was said to be his only visitor? The male nurse? Or, sadly, himself?)

I moved the board game—careful not to disturb the pieces—to the couch, then set the table.

A microwave dinged, and I returned to the kitchen to help with the food.

As we sat opposite each other, and the Don started to

reach for the baked ziti, I asked, "Uh-uh-uh! Don't you think we should have a prayer, first?"

If movies and TV could be believed, these Italian Mafia types had an odd respect for religion, or maybe it was fear. But I wanted to put him in a forgiving mood (you'll see why) and this seemed a good start. Yes, I had once been a stickler about saying grace with little Brandy, until she started spouting, "Good food, good meat, good God, let's eat!"

"Yeah, yeah, why not?" he grumbled. "But *you* say it."

I bowed my head and closed my eyes—I can't tell you whether he did or not, because it's not polite to peek—and entoned my favorite Danish prayer: "Lord, bless this food which now we take and make us thine for Jesus's sake. Amen."

As I unfolded my napkin, the Don frowned at me. "You call *that* a prayer? You Protestants kill me. Let me show ya how's done." He bowed his head. "We give you thanks from grateful hearts for this meal, for your love, for those who prepared this wonderful meal for us. . . ." He looked up at me, eyebrows raised. "Was it *you*, Vivian?"

"No. Coppola's."

"All the way from the city?"

I nodded.

He continued, "Lord, help us to remember that you are with us around the table and may our hearts and words be a blessing to you in return. Let's eat."

We did, the Don piling up his plate, me not so much, as I was already stuffed to the gills.

While we dined on the wonderful food, sipping white wine, my gracious host (and he really was gracious) asked me to tell him about myself, my family, my hometown, my hobbies. And so I did, although I avoided using the name "Serenity," for reasons that will become clear.

Not that I believed he was really interested—I figured he was just a typical older person who wanted someone talking while he ate, keeping him from having another lonely meal alone.

Then, to my surprise, the Don began reminiscing about his own life—his beloved deceased wife, a son he adored, and several grandchildren, beaming with the pride of any patriarch, never mind what line of work he might be in. Vito seemed to get a special charge talking about the now-vintage cars he had collected over the years—Caddies, Mercedes, DeLoreans—which he had bought right off the assembly line to put into storage, knowing that one day they would be extremely valuable.

But he kept any mention of his "business" out of the conversation—for which I was thankful, as it prevented me from having to cover my ears and hum.

"That's why I'm in this glorified rat hole," he said, while we were having dessert. "I ain't really sick in no major way. It's just . . . I didn't want to be no burden to my son."

That made me feel so thankful that I was in no way a burden to Brandy.

Then, emboldened by wine that I shouldn't have had in the first place (meds), I asked, "May I ask you a personal question?"

He'd had some wine, too. And we were old friends by now. "Sure, Viv. Shoot."

Well, I didn't particularly like the way he'd put that, but I took him at his word and asked, "Why did you put Tony Cassato on the spot?"

Suddenly, the Don's genial manner disappeared. "That's a very old way of puttin' it—'on the spot.' Goes back to the twenties, Vivian."

"Well, I thought it might be rude for me to say, 'Why

did you take a contract out on Tony Cassato?' I mean, you've been such a lovely host, and I don't want to offend."

"What the heck do you know about that Cassato thing, anyhow?"

And I told him: That the Serenity chief of police was my daughter's beau. About the attempt on Tony's life in Serenity by two hit men, and how Brandy had been with him at the time.

The Don pushed back in his chair, shrugged facially. "You gotta understand—I reached out to your Tony, and asked him to give a relative of mine a pass on some minor thing. I didn't insult him with no offer of money. I didn't threaten him—just asked him to show me some respect. We come from the old neighborhood, you know. His family at one time was in the same business as mine."

"Really?"

"Yeah, Vivian, really. But he turned me down, and he embarrassed me, made me lose face with my crew . . . and I had to do somethin' about that. Cop or no cop."

"My daughter could have been killed, over some silly grudge of yours! You have a son, Vito. You know what that means to a parent."

His response seemed sincere: "My apologies."

"I thought your crowd had a hands-off policy when it came to police officers."

"Usually, we do."

I waited for the explanation that this seemed to promise, but none came.

"Please tell me, Vito. I need to know. I won't repeat anything you share with me. I promise."

He sighed. "It was my nephew, Carlo. Tony Cassato put him away. Cassato led the investigation, he made the arrest, he gave the key testimony."

I said, "Sounds like an officer of the law just doing his

job. Was there already bad blood between him and your people?"

"No." The Don tossed his napkin on the table. "Makes no difference! I promised my wife, before she passed, that I'd look after that kid. Carlo was her favorite—although God knows why. He's a mope, he really is, that kid."

"What did Carlo do that got him arrested?"

"Well, he wasn't working for me. My wife made me promise that I wouldn't hire the kid, that I'd help him go straight. But he's no good. I get him into college, he drops out. He got to taking dope, and that's something, by the way, that my family has never done business in."

"What did he do, Vito?"

The Don shrugged, shook his head in disgust. "He and some pals busted into a jewelry store, stole a bunch of Rolexes. They sold the things one at a time, mostly to pawn shops, and one of those guys dropped the dime."

He meant a legitimate pawn shop dealer had called the police after checking the "hot" sheet of stolen items. I knew this from watching *Pawn Stars*. (By the way, for those of you too young to know, or too old to remember, a dime is what a phone call used to cost. Back when there *were* public phones.)

"Carlo sounds like a real *gavone*," I said.

For a tense moment, I didn't know how the Don would react to me calling his nephew an idiot.

Then he laughed. "You got that right, Vivian! A first class *jamook*!"

"Oh well. Perhaps Carlo will learn something from his time in prison."

I always find incarceration instructive.

The Don was nodding. "He can start with, 'Don't get caught.' " The old boy sighed and sat back. "Well, at least the kid *is* outta my hair for a while."

I smiled and raised my wine glass. "Dark cloud, silver lining."

We clinked glasses.

Then the Don shook his head, his expression glum. "Only, now I got another problem with *another* relative—distant though he may be."

"You mean Gino, and the Bufford killing? *He* called you, too, didn't he?"

The Don studied me for a moment, his eyes dark and hard. Then he nodded.

"Tell you what, Vito. I'll make you an offer you can't refuse." You just knew I'd go there, didn't you? "If I clear Gino of Tommy Bufford's murder, *you* drop the contract on Tony."

Gentle reader, you've no doubt realized by now that finding Aunt Olive and peddling our Superman picture were not my *only* agendas in making this East Coast journey.

"All right, Viv," he said, nodding slowly, admiration in his sly smile. "You got yourself a deal."

"Goodie! Do we need to prick our fingers and make a blood oath?"

That made him laugh. "No, I think maybe we can skip that, just this once."

Great! The Godfather and I had a deal. This was going just as I'd planned . . .

. . . just so long as Gino didn't turn out to be the killer.

The Don was saying, "That kid being suspected of that murder, it's bad for business."

"The boys did seem a little jumpy," I said, referring to the four-gun salute that had greeted me at the Badda-Boom.

The Don nodded. "Things been good between Jersey and New York for some while—oh, we have our little territorial squabbles from time to time. But I'm afraid if

Gino's not cleared, we could have a real war on our hands."

"Well, we can't have that, can we?"

My left hand had been resting on the table, and he placed his on top of it. "There *is* something *else* you can do for me, Vivian. . . ."

This was a little early for the Don to be calling in his marker.

"What is it?" I asked.

His voice was strangely gentle. "Stay, Viv. Don't go right back to the city. Stay tonight."

Well, dear reader, I was so flabbergasted I nearly tumbled out of my chair! On the other hand, I felt a rush of pride for being back in the high-class concubine sweepstakes. Still, I was just too conservative for such casual carnality—after all, we had just met!

Then again, sometimes a girl has to do what a girl has to do, as John Wayne said (although in a boy way).

Then the Don, reacting to my expression, threw back his head and laughed heartily, so much so that tears filled his eyes.

"My dear lady," he said, or rather coughed, at last catching his breath, "I wasn't propositioning you . . . lovely though you are. It's just that I have this terrible gosh-darn insomnia, and I would love it if you'd stay . . . and play Scrabble."

"It will be my pleasure," I said, if *that* was his pleasure.

And play Scrabble we did, well into the night.

If anything else transpired, well, you won't get it out of me.

Haven't you ever heard of the code of Omerta?

Mother's Trash 'n' Treasures Tip

When attending a comics convention, the hotel's safe is not your only option for protecting valuables. Consider leaving your collectibles with a trusted dealer in the dealers' room, where the after-hours security is high. Of course, when I asked one dealer friend of mine to guard my recently acquired autographed picture of Sonny Tufts, he merely laughed at me.

Chapter Nine

Con Grats

I was in the outer area of our suite, seated on the couch, about to put away one last bite of room-service cheesecake, when the door opened with the suddenness of a slap.

A buoyant Mother breezed in. "A moment on the lips, dear, a lifetime on the hips!"

I jumped up, relieved to see her, and went to her like a worried parent whose errant teenager had shown up well past curfew, scolding, "*Where have you* been?"

Despite her sunny disposition, Mother looked a mess—hair mussed, makeup smeared, clothes wrinkled.

"Let me catch my breath, dear," she said with a dramatic hand to her bosom. "I have *so* much to tell you."

She traipsed over to the couch, plopped down, kicked off her shoes, and clunked her nyloned, bunion-ridden feet onto the coffee table.

"Let's start with why your top is on backwards," I said, sitting back down next to her.

"Is it, dear?" She waved a hand. "I hadn't noticed. A trifling detail in a story whose broad strokes are so compelling." She peered at the plate on the coffee table. "May I have that last bite, dear?"

"What happened to 'a lifetime on the hips'?"

"At my age, that's less of a commitment." She speared the remainder of Lindy's fame with the fork.

I folded my arms and looked at her like an irritated eunuch in a harem (you'd be irritated, too). "I tried your cell phone—and guess what? You left it behind in a drawer."

"Did I, dear?" she said, savoring the morsel. "Why, I *am* getting forgetful in my golden years."

"Don't give me that! I know your devious ways. You left it on *purpose*."

"And what if I did? There are times when a woman does not want to make herself available."

"That would carry more weight if your top weren't on backwards. Anyway, you *lied* to me. I asked you, 'What if I need to get in touch with you?' and you said you'd have your cell."

"No, dear. What I said was, 'Call my cell.' You only assumed I'd have it with me. And how often have I told you? When you assume, you make an ass of you and me."

Shot down again by Mother's specificity. No woman in history had ever found more relish in fooling her daughter on technicalities.

She was saying, "And if you're going to be shrill and unpleasant, I will not share with you what I discovered and where I've been."

"*Shrill?*" I said, and realized it's impossible to deny being shrill without sounding that way. "All right. All right." I smiled. "Pleasant enough for you?"

"I suppose a forced smile is better than no smile at all."

My tone was soft, my words measured. "Mother . . . where have you been? Not visiting old thespian pals, I take it."

She gave me a smile that on the demented scale was about a seven. "You'll never guess!"

"I don't *want* to guess! Just friggin' *tell* me already!"

She drew herself up. "Dear, I won't engage in conversation with a potty-mouth. Well . . . actually, under certain circumstances, conversing with potty-mouths can be a necessity." She sighed dramatically, not that she ever sighed any other way. "I've had enough foul language in the past twelve hours to last me a lifetime!"

"Good. It can keep that bite of cheesecake company."

"Maybe we should continue this after you've had some rest. Lack of sleep makes you decidedly crabby."

I raised surrender palms. "Sorry. Sorry. Really, Mother, sorry. I was just very, very worried something had happened to you."

She patted my knee. "I understand, dear. Your concern warms the cockles. Thursday was quite a busy day, wasn't it? And yet they say it's the slow day at the convention! Is there anything else to *eat*? Perhaps we could order room service."

Defeated, I said, "If you don't want to tell me, I will just go back to bed. We can resume this in the morning."

"I need nourishment. It was a long cab ride back from New Jersey."

Okay. Now she had me. I got up, and went to the minibar, and came back and gave her a six-dollar packet of cashews. "Nuts for the nut," I said.

"Cheap shot, dear. Really. Particularly considering we are *both* on medication." She popped a few cashews, chewed, swallowed, and said, "After I left you, I took a cab to Lodi, New Jersey."

"Lodi, New Jersey?"

She pressed a finger to her cheek. "No, that's not right. *First* I went to Coppola's for a takeout order of scrumptious Italian food, *then* I took a cab to Lodi, New Jersey."

"What is in Lodi, New Jersey?"

"Why, the Badda-Boom, dear!"

"That sounds like a strip joint."

"Well, I believe they consider themselves a nightclub,

but they do have exotic dancers. You know, this surgical enhancement is getting out of hand. And the tattoos!"

"Why on earth would you go to a strip joint in New Jersey?"

"Well, none of the appropriate nightclubs are in Manhattan. I didn't want a club run by *New York* mobsters. I wanted to commune with the New Jersey variety."

"Commune with the . . . you went looking for the *New Jersey* Mafia?"

"Yes. And from the disapproval in your tone, is it any wonder I didn't invite you along?"

"How could you even know about a place called the Badda-Boom?"

"The wonders of the Internet, dear. The twenty-first-century detective's best friend!"

"And what was the takeout Italian for?"

"Isn't it obvious? A peace offering."

"Tell me you're kidding." Though she never kidded. "Tell me you aren't capable of doing something as crazy as approaching mafiosi." But of course she was.

"I thought it best to beard the lion in his den—or in this case, lions in *their* den. Anyway, I wanted to hear from the horse's mouth if they were responsible for Tommy's death—oh, dear, I'm mixing metaphors again. I think it's that horse's head in *The Godfather* that got me off track."

Suddenly, I didn't feel so good. An order of Lindy's cheesecake might be comin' right up.

"Mother," I groaned, "you're going to get us in serious trouble. I mean *real* trouble. I mean get-us-killed kind of trouble."

"Pish posh. Those men were quite cordial, once they put their guns away, and assured me they had nothing to do with Tommy's demise."

"Well, *of course* they'd say that!"

Mother stared at me. "Brandy, skepticism can stay etched in one's face, and yours is much too pretty to risk it." She tossed a few more nuts into her mouth and chewed. "You have simply *got* to shake this negativity, dear, always thinking the worst of people."

"Thinking the worst of *gangsters* isn't negativity, Mother—it's common sense." Like "common sense" was in her vocabulary.

"They were all very nice, and very helpful. Why, the boys even set up a meeting between myself and Gino."

I cocked my head. "You spoke to him? Moretti?"

Mother nodded. "He came to the club and we had a nice little tête-à-tête, during which he assured me he hadn't killed Tommy." She paused, adding, "And you know what, dear? I believe him."

Actually, that made me believe him, too—Mother had a remarkable built-in b.s. detector.

I asked, "Did Gino happen to mention that he was at the opening ceremony, waiting to talk to Tommy?"

Mother's eyes widened behind the thick lenses; it was like having a cartoon bug stare you down. "However did you know *that*, dear?"

"I got it out of Brad Webster. I wasn't completely asleep at the wheel while you went M.I.A."

"Good job!" Then she popped more nuts and chewed through them as she said, "Gino *did* inform me he went to the ceremony hoping to apologize to Tommy . . . but Tommy was too busy. Gino added that he witnessed Brad getting into an argument with Tommy backstage."

I arched an eyebrow. "Well, the Fan Guest neglected to mention that."

We fell silent for a moment.

Then I asked, "Anything else you care to share?"

I doubted Mother had been at the Badda-Boom for

twelve hours. Not unless she subbed for one of the girls, which would at least explain her backwards top.

"Anything else to share," Mother said to herself. "Let me see. . . . Well, for one thing, I can't believe how those young women can twist themselves around a pole. Limber little devils!" She tossed the empty cashew wrapper on the table. "What about you? Anything more happen while I was on safari?"

I told her about the brief confrontation involving Brad, Violet, and Eric in Lindy's, as well as my suspicion that hotel security chief Robert Sipcowski had possible ties to the New York Mob.

And I told her about my supper with Ashley, which I felt had gone well. Mother took all that in, but said nothing about wanting to make sure we saw Ash before heading home. Until this murder was behind us, she was unlikely to let anything else in.

But I *didn't* tell Mother about Tony's clandestine visit, afraid that she might let it slip, putting him in harm's way. And, really, it was none of her business. Which is why I didn't press her more on that backwards top.

Mother asked, "Did Detective Cassato discover our little recording device?"

"Apparently not. He's finished his interviews, and the room is ours again. The recording has been loaded onto my computer, so you can listen to it later."

"Later, dear? What's wrong with right now?"

"Because it's three in the morning," I said irritably, "and I went to bed bone tired but couldn't sleep because I was worried sick about you. We both need some rest, Mother. Tomorrow's going to be another big day. In fact, it already *is* tomorrow!"

"Oh, tish-tosh. Who could possibly get to sleep wondering what's on that recording?"

"Me. Like a log. As sound a sleep as Tommy Bufford's having."

"Poor taste, dear. Extremely poor taste. Well! You go off to bed, my little sleepy-time girl—just set me up out here first, with a pad and pen."

I did so.

Then, exhausted, I stumbled off to the bedroom to snuggle with Sushi, so deep in doggie dreams she hadn't even heard Mother come in.

But guess what? *I couldn't get to sleep!* No, not because my mind wouldn't shut down, but because I could hear Mother, through the closed door, talking back to the recording she was listening to, much of it repetitive, mostly calling Detective Cassato an idiot for not asking this question or that.

Even two pillows over my head didn't help, so finally, about six a.m., I rose like Dracula from his grave, only with considerably less enthusiasm, and joined Mother in the outer room.

"Well?" I asked, bleary eyed.

"How did that man ever make detective?" she fumed.

Mother stood and stretched, bending this way and that. Bones popped and she made occasional noises.

I took her vacated chair. "Never mind that—did you find out anything?"

"Nothing we didn't already know. Oh, poop doodle!"

(No, I didn't censor her. She actually said, "poop doodle." Takes more than a dumb police officer to make her use the "*s*" word—like hitting her thumb with a hammer.)

She yawned, went to the couch and stretched out, and, before you could say Rip Van Winkle, began to snore. Had we been in an old shack, the tiles on the roof would have ruffled, but the hotel held up well enough. I retrieved a blanket from the other room, covered her up, then returned to the luxury of a bed and a warm dog.

That snooze I had been looking for, since just about when this book began, finally had its way with me.

I awoke around noon, the noise of the street traffic penetrating through the wild dream I'd been having. The dream took elements of the last two murders that Mother had gotten me into and poured them into a fun house version of this hotel. I made a mental note: never again, cheesecake with a cheesecake chaser.

Mother had disappeared. But this time I wasn't worried. She'd left a note saying she'd be right back, and to help myself to the orange juice and bagels she'd gotten from the coffee shop.

I took care of Sushi first, giving her both food and insulin, then set myself up at the table, adding fresh brewed java to the Spartan breakfast. So famished was I from my busy day prior, and from that exhausting dream, that I was halfway through my second cream cheese–covered bagel when Mother called through the door.

"Mother needs a helping hand, dear! Drop that bagel and come running!"

I got up to see what sort of help she needed this time, and found her struggling in with a chalkboard easel.

"What's that?" I asked.

"What does it look like, dear? It's a chalkboard easel! Grab the other side!"

I did, saying, "Where did you buy that?"

She didn't answer, as together we hauled it over by the table.

As we set it down, I said, "Good lord! That's the menu board from the lobby coffee shop!"

This I'd brilliantly deduced, skilled amateur sleuth that I am, from the morning breakfast specials written on it.

"Mother, however did you get them to loan that to you?"

"Please. Dear. Have a little faith in my resourcefulness."

"You stole it? You stole the menu board from the hotel coffee shop?"

"Why are you looking at me like that? You know I can't solve any case without a blackboard!"

Back home, she had a much bigger not-pilfered one—an antique on rollers, once used in a one-room country schoolhouse—on which she habitually compiled her suspect list.

I said, hands on hips, "So instead of asking the hotel for one, you just stole this."

"I didn't steal it, I commandeered it. It *will* be returned." Then, in response to my continued stare, she huffed, "After all, I *did* buy bagels and orange juice from them."

As if that justified thievery.

"You can do ten to fifteen for 'commandeering' in this state," I said.

"No jury would convict me."

"*Any* jury would convict you." I shook my head. "And no one saw you carting it off?"

"Employees were very busy. Lunch rush. Everyone else assumed I knew what I was doing."

Making an ass of you and me.

I asked, "Security camera?"

"Not aimed my way. Besides, I walked with purpose, as if I were the designated chalkboard removal engineer."

I sighed, then looked at the board. "There was a French toast special? You know I love French toast. Maybe I could send down for some. . . ."

Mother, having produced an eraser and chalk from somewhere, began wiping down the slate.

"Sit down, dear," she said. "Sit."

I sat. Sushi could have learned from me.

And Mother, schoolmarm, chalk in hand, began to write, while I, her pupil, watched.

SUSPECT	OPPORTUNITY	MOTIVE
Gino Moretti	yes	business rival
Brad Webster	yes	jealous lover?
Robert Sipcowski	yes	Mob connection
Violet	yes	unknown
Eric Johansson	TBD	unknown

I questioned the addition of Eric, but Mother explained that if Violet were the murderer, Eric, as her paramour, could know that, and hence be an accessory after the fact.

Thinking that Mother was about the only person left on the planet who used the word "paramour," and possibly "hence," I asked, "Was there any mention in the recording of Eric being seen at the opening ceremony?"

"None," Mother admitted. Her eyes went to the end table. "What is that, dear? I noticed it this morning."

"Oh . . . I forgot to mention that I'd found that file in Tommy's mini-fridge."

I gave her a quick account of my encounter with Detective Sal Cassato.

"Dear, you might have mentioned this earlier. We can't afford such oversights if we want to solve Tommy's murder. And it's extremely important that we do."

"Why?"

Her expression suggested evasiveness. "What do you mean, *why*?"

"I mean, why is it important that we solve this murder? Other than we're just caught up in the momentum of it."

She gave me a condescending smile. "Has anything else happened to us lately that would make another book?"

"No."

"Then move on. And try not to leave out key matters like that folder."

"I *was* tired," I shot back. "Besides, I don't know that it's a 'key' anything—just some extra ballots."

She picked up the file, withdrew the papers, and spread them out on the table, pushing my mini-breakfast aside.

"Not *complete* ballots," Mother said. "They all seem to be the same page—there's a number two at the bottom."

"How many pages does one of these ballots consist of?"

"No idea, dear. If I could get my hands on a complete ballot, I might make sense of this clue."

"*Is* it a clue?"

"What else could it be?" She returned the papers to the folder. "In the meantime, why don't we spend the afternoon in the dealers' room—keeping our eyes and ears open."

I agreed, not having had a chance to spend time there as yet. We'd been run out of the place yesterday by that pack of press. So I refreshed Sushi's water and pee station, then snuggled her on a blanket on the couch—this was that "dog's life" you hear so much about. Badges pinned on, Mother grabbed her purse and I strapped on my fanny pack and we headed out.

But the next few hours passed uneventfully, at least as pertained to the mystery. At a booth selling vintage Hollywood photos, Mother found a signed Forrest Tucker eight by ten for fifty dollars that put her over the moon. So childish. Then I found a BARBIE FASHION #1 comic from 1991 for only twenty bucks, and could not *believe* my good luck!

On a perhaps more mature and productive note, I did manage (after asking a dozen or more vendors) to find an entire Buff Awards ballot—a comic book–shop owner who had forgotten to mail his back by the deadline had brought it along, hoping to get it in before the tabulation. But that hadn't happened, and he was happy to hand it over to me.

This may have been the only transaction not involving the exchange of money for goods that the dealers' room saw that weekend.

Around five, after taking Sushi for a walk (plastic bags handy!), Mother and I had an early dinner at the Statler Grill. The restaurant was located at the back of the hotel, off Thirty-third Street, and we both ordered the specialty, New York prime steak—mine, medium rare; hers, burnt to a crisp. The chef was probably burning, too, at such a desecration.

Then we returned to our suite to freshen up for the awards ceremony, including showers and a change of clothes— Mother into one of her Breckenridge slacks outfits (winter white), and me into black leggings and a zebra-print tunic by Juicy Couture. Eat your heart out, Fashion Barbie!

While neither of us were much interested in knowing who won what, we *were* interested in snagging good seats for what followed: a tribute to the history of Superman, which included a personal appearance by Henry Cavill, the latest actor to reprise the Man of Steel on the silver screen, Tommy Bufford's only concession to Hollywood.

Not only would the tribute be fun, but Mother and I felt our presence might enhance the sale of our drawing at the auction on Sunday. We had to finance Forrest Tucker and BARBIE FASHION somehow, didn't we?

The Buff Awards presentation was held on the eighteenth floor, in the Skytop Ballroom, the largest in the hotel. Even so, by the time Mother and I arrived, the room was jam-packed, chairs already at a premium, and a little too high-class an event for Mother to enforce the con's no-seat-saving rule.

As we stood in back, contemplating our dilemma—I certainly didn't want to be on my feet for a long presentation, and Mother (with her bunions) couldn't be—Brad

Webster threaded his way toward us through the crowd of hopeful chair-wanna-haves.

"There's a row up front reserved for special needs," he told us, adding, "I think Vivian qualifies."

Especially if that included the mentally challenged.

Mother grabbed my arm. "I'll need Brandy to steady me."

Brad shrugged. "Why not? There are plenty of seats left."

And he headed toward the front and we followed, albeit at a snail's pace.

Now, understand that Mother has severe problems with her feet. If she's on the move, she's fine. But standing can become excruciating. Just not as excruciating as what came next: Mother taking little wobbling baby steps up the center aisle, while clinging to me, in hopes of justifying that privileged seating up front.

"If you don't pick up the pace," I whispered, "there won't be any special seating left."

"I have to make it look good."

"Less is more, Mother. Less is more."

The special seating row was in the very front, the next three rows behind reserved for awards nominees and their spouses or families. We found two chairs together next to a boy of perhaps twelve in a wheelchair. I made Mother sit beside him so she would feel at least a little guilty, but I don't think she did. Between bunions and ingrown toenails, she had more of a right to sit here than I did. But with eight chairs still empty, I admit I didn't feel particularly guilty, and would have vacated if someone more deserving came along.

Settling in, I craned around to take in the room. Here, like in the Gold Ballroom, the fourteen-carat color continued, but with touches of red instead of royal blue. The carpet had a pattern like a continuous maze, chairs were cushioned and comfortable, ceiling chandeliers grand and sparkling. But there weren't many windows—just a few tall ones, draped with red velvet, which made the ball-room seem claustrophobic despite its size ... or maybe that was just due to all the people crammed within.

Speaking of which, the ballroom didn't smell wonder-ful, which was not the hotel's fault; half the audience were still in their casual clothes and sometimes elaborate, warm costumes after a long day.

While Mother chatted up the boy next to her, I had a look at the Buff Awards program booklet—not good news. I counted *twenty-four* categories, from best single issue to best continuing comic book series, from best writer/artist team to best new series, and on and on. The most prestigious awards—best artist, and best writer—would not come till the bitter end. Assuming each winner got to say a few words, the event could go on for hours.

"Are you all right, dear?" Mother asked me. "You were whimpering."

"I wish I'd brought a book to read." Something longer than BARBIE FASHION #1.

Then the audience began applauding as Violet, in a low-cut red dress the color of the curtains, took the podium on the stage.

"Welcome to the *first* Bufford Con Buff Awards!" she said, eliciting further applause, if a little less fervent. Just the utterance of the name "Bufford" cast something of a pall, and I couldn't be the only one wondering if this might be the first and last Bufford Con.

To save you, the reader, from the tedium I endured, I will skip ahead to the end of the ceremony. This is less a service to you and more an admission that all those other awards, for things and to people that were not even vaguely on my radar, became an immediate blur. Couldn't recall that stuff if I tried.

When time finally came for the presentation of the writer's award, I sat up, paying rapt attention.

"Rooting for Eric, dear?" Mother whispered.

"Yes. I know that prize means a lot to him."

"Well, he's got a fifty/fifty shot, doesn't he?"

She was right. The pen stuck in Tommy's chest had the winner's name on it, which meant either Eric Johansson or Harlan Thompson had won. The other three nominees did not share that final syllable.

And when Violet announced the nominees, the winner *was* Eric, and I got to my feet, clapping. In the first row, I was slow to realize that I was one of only a handful standing. The applause around the room seemed more polite than enthusiastic.

That Eric had not been the "audience's favorite" was confirmed by the grumbling around me.

I looked back to see one person who seemed particularly unhappy: Harlan Thompson, who had turned out *not* to be a shoo-in for the award. At sixty, his gray hair thinning, his narrow face well grooved, this revered comics veteran clearly expected his name to have been called. Many seemed to agree with him, several leaving their seats to lean in and express their condolences, as if the poor man's career had just died.

Meanwhile, an ebullient Eric rushed to the podium, where a smiling Violet handed him the award. Hearing a mild commotion, I looked back and saw what was perhaps not the most gracious move I ever witnessed, as Harlan Thompson rose, clearly disgusted. He stalked down the center aisle, the tall, thin man's face stony, as fans in aisle seats stretched out hands to pat his arm supportively as he went by.

In addition to myself and Violet—and possibly Mother, also pleased with Eric's triumph—yet another woman seemed happy, even overjoyed, at Eric's victory. After a brief thank-you speech, he left the podium with his trophy gold pen and holder. Just down off the stage, he almost ran into an attractive twentysomething blonde in a white silk blouse and a short black skirt with knee-high black boots. She had rushed to him, and threw her arms round his neck.

"*Jeg elsker dig!*" she squealed. That was a slice of Danish, meaning "I love you," that I knew well, Mother having often said as much to little Brandy.

While Eric and his Danish strudel kissed passionately, I exchanged wide-eyed looks with Mother. Then our eyes went to Violet, frozen at the podium, staring, even glaring, at Eric and the girl, as surprised as we were.

"And, uh, this concludes the awards ceremony," Violet said into the microphone, recovering. "Thank you for coming. There will be a fifteen-minute intermission before the Superman tribute."

And she abruptly left the podium, disappearing behind the platform, the slam of a backstage door audible over the crowd's chatter. Many audience members were making a dash for the bathroom.

Mother and I remained seated, watching as Eric handed the blonde his award, gold pen in marble holder, gave her a "wait here" gesture, then hurried after Violet, his jilted "paramour."

I whispered to Mother, "Wish I was a mouse following him."

"So you could listen to a *rat*," she whispered back.

I nodded. "Not as nice a boy as I thought, our Eric. Be right back. . . ."

I got up, eased through the row, and approached the pretty young blonde.

"*Hej—hvordan har du det?*" I greeted her.

Her blue-gray eyes, which had turned troubled since Eric ran off, lit up. "*Fint, tak. Taler du dansk?*"

I laughed. "Sorry! You've just heard about the extent of my Danish." I stuck out my hand. "Brandy Borne."

"Helena Nielsen." She had a lovely accent. "Borne— you're Danish, too?"

"Third generation," I replied. "But my mother speaks it pretty well." I gestured with my head. "She's over there next to the boy in the wheelchair."

But Helena kept her eyes on the backstage door, obviously hopeful for Eric's imminent return.

I asked, "Did you just arrive? Haven't seen you around the convention."

She looked back at me. "I flew in this morning. Eric didn't want me to come earlier—he said I'd be bored."

Or maybe in the way.

"He works out of home?" I asked. "In Denmark?"

"Yes. We live in Copenhagen."

"Does he write in English?"

"For this market, yes. He has American friends who help him make his work more"—she reached for the phrase—"sounding like American."

Friends like Violet. Maybe he had a *lot* of friends like Violet. . . .

I gestured toward the award, its gold pen inscribed with Eric's name. "Well, that's a wonderful honor."

She nodded. "It means much to us. The comics business in Denmark is very limited. America is *the* place."

Not "him"—*us*.

She went on: "This will make a difference. Eric will be taken serious now."

"Eric's your boyfriend?"

"Husband. I keep my own name—I have a modeling career in Copenhagen." Then, "I have seen that woman before. Violet something?"

"Oh?"

"She came to Copenhagen to talk to people about doing a convention there. Like this one."

"Yes, I heard the Bufford Conventions were hoping to break into Europe."

"Eric says she has been helpful in getting him that award."

"I think that's true."

Her mouth made a thin line. "But maybe . . . *too* helpful?"

The sleuth in me wanted to keep prying. But the decent human being (she's still in there somewhere) thought it better to give this woman her privacy. I said it was nice meeting her, she said the same about me, and I went back to Mother, taking my seat.

Quickly, I told her about my conversation with Eric's blond bride, concluding with, "His name is on his award. On that gold pen."

"Why wouldn't it be, dear?"

"They sure must have gotten a replacement quickly, because you and I saw it sticking out of Tommy's chest."

"Good point! No pun intended. . . ."

I rose. "You'll have to represent us at the Superman thingie. I'm going stir-crazy in here. Gotta get some fresh air. Only so much comic-con smell a girl can take."

"You do that. I'll be fine, dear."

I left the ballroom and took an elevator down to the lobby. On my way to the Seventh Avenue exit, I passed by the hotel's coffee shop, where a mildly distressed female waitress was talking to one of Sipcowski's staff in the doorway.

"I didn't see anyone take it," she said, gesturing with two upward palms. "Who would want a *menu* sign?"

"They'll steal anything in this town," the security guy said.

Suddenly a drink seemed more called for than fresh air,

so I turned on my heels and headed back to the Statler Grill.

At the bar, I ordered a white zinfandel. While waiting for it, I noticed a morose Harlan Thompson at the end of the long counter, hunkered over a tumbler of hard stuff. His out-of-date tweed jacket had elbow patches and his tie looked frayed. Whether this was an attempt to look writerly or a result of limited funds, I couldn't say.

I hung out at the bar, biding my time, until a stool next to him opened up, and I grabbed it.

For a while, I didn't say anything to him, just sipped my wine. But when it was time either for a refill or to vacate the seat, I swivelled toward him.

"I'm a great admirer of your work, Mr. Thompson," I said. Actually, I'd only read him once, when Joe Lange insisted I try an issue of *Batman* he'd written. I found it dark and unpleasant. Holy depressing!

"Thank you," he said with a rumpled smile.

"Like just about everybody else in that room upstairs, I thought *you* should have won. I thought you *would* win!"

He tossed back the last of the liquid in his tumbler. "That makes two of us." He caught the bartender's eye. "Again!"

"The winner," I said, "that Danish kid? He didn't get much love from the audience."

He looked at me with rheumy eyes. "What does that tell you, young lady?"

"I give up. What does it tell me?"

"That the fix was in."

The folder with those ballot pages came to mind.

He leaned toward me, a little too close. "Know why I know that?"

"No. Why?" I tried not to back away, but his breath made my eyes water.

"'cause Tommy Bufford himself *told* me I was gonna win."

"He did?"

Thompson shrugged. "As much as. After I was nominated, I called him. Explained it was a lot of money to come from California, and I really couldn't afford the trip, much as I might like to support him. Would he forgive an old man for asking for a pass on this one?"

"And?"

"And he said I needed *not* to miss this con. He said it would be a *rewarding* experience for me."

"Kind of a breach for Tommy to tell you that."

"Not as big a one as somebody else rigging it for that Danish dolt to win. Writer! He can barely speak English!"

"Are you saying you think somebody changed the results after Tommy's death?"

"Has to be . . . unless the late Mr. Bufford was playing me for a fool, just to get me to his stupid convention."

"Well . . . what do *you* think is the case?"

"What do I think? That it's a crock. Bartender! Again!"

I wondered if I was sitting next to the real winner of the best writer Buff Award.

And just about the only person I'd talked to lately who *wasn't* a worthy addition to Mother's suspect list.

A Trash 'n' Treasures Tip

Never let your purchases out of your sight—it only takes a few seconds for someone to steal your hard-found treasures. Totes and carry bags should have zippers to make pilfering harder. Warning: Once as a deterrent, Mother placed a mousetrap in her bag, but it quickly slipped her mind and she got her own fingers snapped.

Chapter Ten

Con Fur

The following day, Saturday, Mother had an errand for me to run.

Apparently, she had somehow gotten in touch with Vikki, our Hudson Parkway Samaritan, and my mission (whether I chose to accept it or not) was to be at the Gershwin Theater on West Fifty-first Street at noon. Why? Well, to pick up two spare costumes from *Wicked*, naturally, which Vikki was loaning us for this evening's masquerade ball.

You may wonder why our Good Samaritan wardrobe mistress agreed to Mother's presumptuous request. To me, it sounded risky on Vikki's part, the kind of good deed that can easily turn bad—like lose-your-wardrobe-mistress-gig bad. Well, she only consented to Vivian Borne's request on three conditions: first, that *I* pick up the clothes (not Mother); second, that the costumes be returned intact on Tuesday; and third, that she would never, ever hear from us again. This included Christmas and a free pass off Mother's Yuletide mailing list, an accomplishment that usually took death.

So risking her job was a small price to pay.

I left the hotel at eleven, on foot, with Sushi on her

leash, providing a little fresh air and exercise for both of us. The temperature had climbed to the upper forties and the sun had come out, warming the cold cement canyon of the city.

Our hike to the theater should have taken no more than half an hour, up Seventh Avenue, veering onto Broadway at Times Square, then turning left one block at West Fifty-first Street—approximately a mile. Piece of cake. (Make that cheesecake.)

Sushi was at first energetic, and thrilled with the sounds and smells that enlivened her sightless little world. But the dear only made it to Forty-second Street before stopping in her tracks, tuckered out. So I picked her up and stuck her inside the front of my coat, her furry head peeking out like that scary scene in *Alien*, minus the goop.

I, too, was pooped, not at all used to traversing these long city blocks; but a taxi seemed like an extravagance, and I didn't feel confident using the subway, with its possible perils—a native New Yorker can sniff out a tourist like Sushi could a prior pee deposit (no shortage of those in Manhattan, though not always canine). I would just have to press on—after all, we were more than halfway there.

And there was plenty to take my mind off some minor fatigue. Even in daytime, my route along Broadway, Times Square especially, was a dazzling display of vertical glamour, the kinetic energy of the crowds dizzying, all accompanied by a sound symphony of honking horns, police whistles, accelerating motors, and pedestrian chatter. To look around and realize that there were more people in view—*way* more—than lived in all of Serenity, well . . . it was staggering, exhilarating, even humbling. If I could make it here, I could make it anywhere.

And where I wanted to make it was over to the Gershwin Theater. Only a handful of such venues were located on Broadway per se, like the Marquis at Forty-sixth (play-

ing *Evita*) and the Palace at Forty-seventh (a revival of
Annie). Such big steady draws as *The Lion King*, *Phantom
of the Opera*, and *Spiderman* were playing theaters on the
cross streets.

At Forty-eighth, I ran out of steam and ducked into the
big Hershey's Store, emerging five minutes later with a
sack of candy Kisses. Sushi didn't bother whining while I
fumbled the foil off one after another; she could smell the
chocolate and knew I wouldn't give her any. Chocolate is
not good for dogs, although quite honestly I don't know
that I would have shared with her even if it were.

I rode my sugar boost over to Fifty-first and the Winter
Garden (*Mamma Mia!*) (the musical, I mean, not the expression), where I went left, walking half a block. This
took me by the Gershwin's multidoor entrance, arrayed
with large posters and placards boasting wondrous shots
of the elaborate costumes in the show, in particular, the
two witches who were central to the story. Mother's instructions had been to go to the stage door, located just
past the driveway of the theater's parking garage.

I approached black double doors, under a bold

242
GERSHWIN
STAGEDOOR

sign, found them locked, located an intercom, and rang
the buzzer.

"Yeah?" a male voice barked.

Everybody you talked to in this town sounded like you
were interrupting something more important than whatever it was you wanted. Which possibly was the case.

"Brandy Borne to see Vikki . . ." I halted, not recalling
her last name. With all the confidence I could muster, I
added, "Wardrobe."

"Hold on."

Excitement bubbled in me like carbonation. I was looking forward to going inside and seeing the inner workings of a big theatrical show—that would be incredible! It would also provide a place for me to sit down and rest my aching dogs (feet, not Sushi).

I shifted my stance—I was getting a blister on my right foot—noticing the silver metal barricades leaning against the black wall; these would be hauled to the sidewalk after the two o'clock matinee, adoring fans lining up for glimpses of stars and possibly snagging autographs.

Suddenly, the stage door opened. Our highway rescuer Vikki—in black flats, black leotards, and a purple form-fitting tunic, her blond hair pulled back—tossed a large navy gym bag at my feet. I smiled up at her, ready to thank her for her generosity. But I never got a word out.

"Rip those and you're dead," she said.

The door slammed in my face.

Mother and I make friends everywhere we go.

I picked up the bulging bag, walked back to Broadway, and hailed a cab. I was from out of town, and that's what out-of-towners do in the big city. But somehow it seemed wrong, when I realized Sushi and I had made better time on foot.

We returned to our suite to find Mother seated at the round table, munching on a room-service salad, a fork in one hand, a sheet of paper in the other. She glanced our way, her eyes glomming onto the gym bag. She pushed her plate aside.

"Put it right here, dear," she said excitedly, tapping the center of the table.

I did, letting her unzip the bag while I removed my coat, then settled Sushi on the couch. I hadn't peeked, afraid that the overstuffed contents would pop out and I'd have trouble cramming them back in. But I was pretty stoked—actual costumes from *Wicked*! I knew just who I wanted to be . . . and what role Mother would be perfect for.

Out of the bag, Mother pulled a black pointed witch's hat (typecasting?), then a full-length black lace dress with high neck and long sleeves, which I recognized from the posters at the theater as the signature costume worn by the Wicked Witch of the West. Mother held the exquisite gown up to herself—it looked like it would fit just fine—and we *oooh*ed and *ahhh*ed.

Excitedly, I dug in the now somewhat deflated bag for my costume. I assumed this would be the off-the-shoulder baby-blue sparkly bubble dress worn by the Good Witch of the North . . .

. . . only that's *not* what I found.

Instead, I pulled out a rainbow-painted leotard, a red military jacket with epaulets, a long curly tail, and two closed black umbrellas.

"I'm a *monkey*?" The tail was the tip-off, and the umbrella wings sealed it.

"Not just *any* monkey, dear," Mother said brightly. "A *flying* monkey."

"Yeah, well, I don't think they'll have the ballroom rigged for flying effects. Why didn't you get me the Good Witch's dress?"

"It wasn't available, dear. Beggars can't be choosers!"

"You call that woman back up! She was very rude to me—slammed the door in my face."

"And what would you have me tell her, dear?"

"That if the Good Witch isn't available, I want to be Dorothy!" I pointed to Sushi, snoozing on the couch. "I mean, we already have Toto, right?"

Mother put a finger to her lips. "That would be a nice touch, a real dog and all." She shrugged. "But, really,

Dorothy and Toto are barely in the musical—only *referred* to, because of copyright concerns. Anyway, being a monkey is much more colorful!"

"I suppose it's too late," I grumbled, "to find a costume shop."

"Brandy, darling . . . let's *not* be ungrateful."

"Yeah, yeah, beggars, choosers, I get it. But next time, let *me* do the negotiating. I could've gotten myself a better costume in return for that woman never having to see us again."

"Oh, but you'll look *adorable*," Mother soothed. "Besides, we shouldn't take Sushi with us tonight, anyway."

"Why not? She could be a baby monkey."

"Not without a baby monkey costume. And Toto without Dorothy is like Robin without Batman!"

"Doesn't that make *me* Batman without *Robin*?"

"Batman often goes solo, dear. Lots of fans prefer it that way. *Dark Knight Trilogy*—hello! Didn't you do *any* research before going to a comic con? Anyway, we don't need any doggie distractions. After all, we're unmasking the murderer at the ball tonight."

This news she delivered as casually as saying, "You have spinach in your teeth, dear."

I goggled at her. "You *know* who killed Tommy? Did you find something out while I was on my 'mission'?"

"More or less," Mother said. "To both your questions."

"Well? Spill!"

"Sit with me at the table, dear. And calm yourself."

I did. Well, I sat, anyway.

She retrieved the manila envelope containing the partial ballots, plus the complete one I'd obtained, then spread them out on the table. The complete ballot was three eight-and-a-half-by-eleven sheets stapled together.

Taking the chair next to me, Mother said, "I've been

comparing these, dear . . . and what we have here is a clear case of ballot tampering."

I had suspected as much, but let her go on.

She indicated the sheets I'd found in Tommy's room. "These pages were removed from the center of the mailed-in ballots, then presumably replaced with forged copies."

I nodded. "So a particular nominee would win."

"Yes. And all of these ballots are in one particular category."

I sighed, nodded. "Best writer."

"Every ballot here is a vote for Harlan Thompson. I think it's fair to assume, without risking making an ass of *anyone* except perhaps a murderer, that Harlan Thompson was indeed the real winner."

I glanced through the ballots. Under the best writer category, all the boxes next to Harlan's name had been checked. *Not* Eric Johansson.

"Quite clever, really," Mother, an admirer of creative skulduggery, was saying. "And because the first and third pages of the three-page ballot would be retained—with the comic store–owner's signature at the bottom of page three—the ballots would seem authentic."

I said, "But somehow Tommy tipped to it."

Mother nodded. "Perhaps he saw the ballots before and after tampering. Or possibly something about the replacement pages—the paper used, or a flaw in the printing, maybe mismatching folds, or a variation between the color of ink used to fill out ballots. Perhaps the restapling was inexact. Any number of things could have told him."

"Yes, and then he went looking for the original pages, in the trash, very likely."

"Possibly just in a wastebasket in the convention office. Violet would have no reason to think he was checking up on her. Because Violet is who did the tampering."

I nodded emphatically. "Absolutely! She's having an affair with Eric, and wanted her lover to win. Simple as that. But that isn't enough for her to *kill* Tommy over!"

"Possibly not," Mother said thoughtfully. "Still, she had a lot to lose, should Tommy fire her, then expose her—her job, her role in the business of Bufford Cons, and, of course, her reputation. And who knows how it might affect her relationship with Eric?"

"Was Eric part of the ballot tampering?"

"Not necessarily. She may simply have been trying to help advance the career of the man she loved."

"But, Mother . . . murder?"

"I'm afraid so, dear. Possibly premeditated, or more likely . . . crime of passion." Her eyes narrowed behind the thick lenses. "You know, I believe I can see what happened. But I need to know what *name* was on the murder pen to be sure."

My head was whirling. "The name on the *murder* pen . . . ?"

"Yes. I'm convinced it said 'Harlan Thompson' on it."

"How can you know that, Mother? And why is that significant?"

Her smile was enigmatic. "Let me tell you what I think occurred. Remember when we first arrived, and were talking to Tommy? Violet came up to him, upset, saying one of the awards was missing. I believe the missing award she spoke of was the gold pen with Eric's name engraved on it."

I shook my head. "But it's *not* missing. Eric received that award, and I saw the engraving on it myself . . . or did Violet get a *new* one made at the last minute?"

"A last-minute award *was* made, I believe . . . but by Tommy. If Detective Cassato checks with whatever firm sells the trophies, I believe he'll find that Tommy acquired a gold replacement pen, and had it engraved with Harlan Thompson's name . . . having already pulled Eric's award from those boxed up and waiting in the convention office to be presented at last night's ceremony."

I was following this. Barely, but I was. "So Eric's award *was* missing. Violet went to pick up the awards at their office and noticed that the pen wasn't in the marble base, and . . . oh, my God."

Mother smiled, proud of me. "Are you putting it together, dear?"

"Violet confronted Tommy about the missing award after the opening ceremonies—in the service elevator! And Tommy thrust the replacement award into her hands, the one with Harlan's name on it, telling her she was through, and . . ."

"And she plunged it into him and killed him, dear," she said, as if reading tomorrow's weather report from a newspaper. "Yes, exactly."

Now I was smiling, not at all enigmatically. "So it was *Violet* who broke into our suite, thinking it was Tommy's room! Looking for the *Eric* pen!"

"And for those ballot pages, seized by Tommy, yes."

"Which I found in the fridge in our *old* room, where Tommy had moved . . . a room that had been searched thoroughly."

Mother was nodding. "Enough so for Violet to have found the pen with Eric's name engraved on it. But she missed the ballots. Why do you suppose she missed those? You would think she might check the fridge."

I shrugged. "Well, the folder was under a tray of fruit. She just missed it, that's all. Mother, you've done it! You've solved the mystery."

Mother had the contented look of a cat that had just slurped down the last of a mouse; I could almost see the spaghetti-like tail getting sucked down.

She said, "I do believe I have it solved . . . *if* we can confirm that the murder pen had Harlan Thompson's name engraved on it . . . and if so, the firm selling the trophies should confirm that Tommy Bufford had that replacement pen engraved at the eleventh hour."

I frowned. "We can probably prove Violet fixed the writer's award. But that doesn't make her the killer. I mean, she has a motive, and she had opportunity, yes, but . . . what evidence do we have?"

Mother sniffed indignantly. "I can't do *everything*, dear! I'm not some plodding policeman. I merely solve the mysteries. Let the minions of law enforcement do the rest. We'll point that lesser of the two Cassato brothers toward the culprit, and let him prove us right!"

We fell silent for a moment, then it occurred to me Mother was deferring to the NYPD much too easily. Suspiciously so.

I said, "Tell me you don't intend to just walk up to Violet at the masquerade tonight and accuse her of killing Tommy."

"Nothing quite so direct."

"Mother . . ."

"But I *may* be able to wheedle it out of her. Why not try? I'll be wearing my little recording device as a necklace, to catch her words. And *her*."

"Why not *try*?" If I had opened my eyes any wider, they would have fallen out and rolled around on the floor like marbles. "Mother, if she's a murderer, who *knows* what she's capable of? Think about it—she killed Tommy, stabbed him to death, then cold-bloodedly went about the business of putting on this convention!"

"She's a resourceful girl, our Violet."

"Resourceful girl . . . Mother, why don't we share our thoughts with Detective Cassato? We could get him on the phone right now."

Her smile was Madonna-like (religious icon, not pop

star). "Because I prefer not to give that nincompoop the satisfaction, dear."

"If you're planning to confront Violet, I want no part of it."

"No, of course not, not in the state you're in."

"*What* state am I in? Besides New York, and Iowa is starting to look very good to me, by the way."

She patted my head, much as she would Sushi's. "Why, dear, you look tired. Simply pooped on your feet."

"I'm sitting."

"Why cling to details? Now, be a good little monkey and take a nap before we get ready for our big evening."

She was getting up from the table.

"What about you?" I asked. "Naptime, too?"

"Perhaps later. Right now I must pay a visit to the hotel kitchen."

"Well, bring me back some cheesecake." Hair of the dog, and I didn't mean Sushi.

"I'm not going for food, dear."

"Well, what then?"

"You'll see in due course."

What could she be after? A butcher knife for self-defense? Pepper to blow into the eyes of a crazed killer? Bananas to keep her "little monkey" in check? I wasn't sure I wanted to know.

I picked Sushi up off the couch, ignoring her half-hearted growl, and headed off to the bedroom. For a few minutes, I went over Mother's theory that Violet was our murderer, finding no flaws in it, but after that, sleep took me away from the madness of Mother on a murder hunt, and I was just a wee monkey with a little mutt curled contentedly up against my stomach.

In my dream, I was already in my flying monkey getup, actually a more elaborate costume, like the ones in the

MGM movie. But, impressive as I looked, I could not get off the ground. I ran and ran and flapped my wings and flapped them some more, but nothing happened. I was running through a field, but then I was suddenly on the roof of a high building, where I figured if I jumped off, it would jump-start my wings. So I jumped, but they *didn't* start—instead, I went straight down like a dive-bomber with that dying super-mosquito sound effect from the old Warner Bros. cartoons.

"Wake up," someone said. "Little Brandy, wake up!"

At the voice's urging, I forced myself awake moments before I'd have hit the ground and put to the test the theory that if you die in your dreams, you die in reality.

Relieved, I opened my eyes and looked into a green face.

I did what any self-composed young woman in my situation would do: I shrieked.

"It's just me!" Mother said, hovering. "Didn't mean to startle you—you were having a nightmare."

"I'm *still* having a nightmare," I said. "Your *face* is green!"

"Why, do you think I don't *know* that?"

"Wait . . . your trip to the kitchen. Green food coloring?"

Mother, other than her emerald puss, was still in her earlier attire. "It's part of my character, dear. Elphaba's skin *is* green—that's the Wicked Witch's name in the play—and I want to be *realistic*."

"Just like the real witches with green faces," I said. "What did you *do*, anyway? Smear the food coloring directly on?"

She laughed once and waved that silly notion away. "Of course not, dear . . . I stirred it into my moisturizer."

I rolled to the side of the bed and sat up. "If you've got spirit gum and monkey fur waiting for me, you can guess again." I pointed to my face. "No makeup goes on this mug but Cover Girl."

Mother's magnified blue eyes gleamed, an effect heightened by her green-tinted skin. "Why, I hadn't considered that. I wonder if I could still reach that nice Vikki at the Gershwin . . ."

"Mother . . ."

"Well, never mind. It's nearly six . . . chop chop! We'd better get into our costumes."

Which we did, Mother looking quite striking in the black lace dress and witch's hat, and, yes, her green face and hands were the perfect finishing touch. Even the recording device around her neck—attached to a long silver chain—seemed to complement her outfit.

I, on the other hand, looked ridiculous in my rainbow-colored full-body leotard intended for a male dancer, sleeves and legs too long, tight where I needed it loose, loose where I needed it tight (think about it). Plus it took Mother ten minutes to figure out how my umbrella wings attached to the back brace I had to wear beneath my organ-grinder jacket.

"How does that feel, dear?" she asked, standing back to appraise me, as if she'd just put the last brush stroke on a masterpiece painting. "Comfy?"

"I'm wearing a *back brace*—where does 'comfy' come into it?"

Actually, it was quite comfy, although I would never have admitted it to Mother. I'd had a backache since my first night sleeping on that fold-out couch, and this contraption really helped.

"Well," she said, "you won't be in that for long. But we all must suffer for our art."

"What art would that be? We're going to a costume party!"

She ignored that, tilting her head as she had another look at me. "Are you sure we couldn't apply just a smidge of facial hair to your cheeks? I could snip some fur from Sushi and, as it happens, I do always travel with spirit gum. . . ."

"That's it! We're done. And I'm *not* wearing the tail. I won't be able to sit down. Nonnegotiable, or you can find a broomstick and fly to the costume ball by yourself."

Mother sighed as if I had denied her dying wish. "Very well, no tail. But don't blame *me* if no one knows what you're supposed to be."

"Oh, I think they'll know what I am—an idiot in a rainbow leotard and organ-grinder vest with umbrellas stuck on the back."

"You're probably right, dear."

We gathered our tickets from our guest packets and headed out, leaving Mother's purse behind and my fanny pack, too. My little jacket had pockets for money and our room keycard, so everything else got left behind—including Toto a.k.a. Sushi.

The costume party, an adults only affair, was back in the Skytop Ballroom. As Mother and I arrived, the judging was in full swing. We had no intention of taking part in the competition—all costumes had to be handmade, not purchased (or, as in our case, borrowed). Almost everyone here was in costume, whether they were competing or not, and hundreds of characters from the comics, movies, TV, anime, and video games were seated having drinks and snacks.

All eyes were on the finalists parading across a platform before an uncostumed panel of four, sitting at a table just below, making their tabulations. I thought Violet might be one of the judges, but she was not—they were other professionals who were guests at the con.

The ballroom had been transformed since the awards ceremony, a dance floor now taking up the center of the room, candlelit tables scattered on the periphery, a bar against a side wall, DJ in one corner providing music

("Super Freak" playing) (no comment), giving the room a dance-club feel.

I found a postage-stamp table, deposited Mother in a chair, then headed toward the bar to get us ginger ales.

Weaving in and around the partygoers, I bumped into Harlan Thompson, or rather he bumped into me, jostling his drink in hand. He was in no particular getup, unless the tweed jacket with patched elbows qualified as a slightly-gone-to-seed-writer costume.

"Excuse me . . . oh, you're the girl from the bar last night."

Nice to know I'd made an impression.

He raised an unsteady eyebrow as he looked me up and down. "And what are you supposed to be?"

"A monkey."

He frowned. "Needs work," he said, and he and his drink wandered off.

To my dismay, the queue at the bar seemed impossibly long, but I spotted Brad Webster toward the front, and sidled up to him. His costume consisted of a black unitard encased in dozens and dozens of black belts wrapped around and around his arms, legs, and torso. A black satin knee-length cape fell from his shoulders, and at his waist was a pearl-handled knife in a scabbard.

"Brad, hi," I said.

He just looked at me.

I smiled. "Brandy, remember? We talked in the hospitality suite? How about ordering a drink for yourself and two ginger ales for me, and I'll pick up the tab?"

"Sounds like a plan. Cool costume. *Wicked*, right?"

So there, Harlan Thompson!

"Yeah," I said. "It'd be better with facial fur, but I just couldn't go there."

"You'd have nabbed a prize, if you had."

"No, this outfit is a professional job. I'd be disqualified.

Anyway, I'm not much for sewing." My expertise with a needle was limited to giving Sushi her insulin.

He frowned and craned to look behind me, about the most brazen example of a guy checking out my rear view as I ever experienced.

I frowned at him. "Can I help you?"

"Oh. Sorry. It's just . . . aren't you supposed to have a tail?"

"I left my tail in the room."

I would hate to have any of this taken out of context.

I said, "That's a really interesting costume. Who or what *are* you?"

"A sorcerer."

"Any specific sorcerer?"

"A *Dungeons and Dragons* sorcerer."

"Oh! I had friends who played D&D in high school, but I never got into it." I cocked my head. "I thought a sorcerer wore a long robe and pointy hat with stars. Like in *Fantasia*."

With near disdain, he said, "I'm not *that* kind of sorcerer."

"So there are a lot of different kinds, then?" I gestured to my monkey-self. "Like the wizard in *Wicked*?"

Just making conversation, as we waited in line.

But he seemed to take umbrage at my question. "Modern sorcerers are young, and cast natural spells. Wizards are old and need books."

The line was moving, anyway.

I pointed out, "Harry Potter is young, and he's a wizard, isn't he? It's 'Hogwarts School of Witchcraft and Wizardry,' not 'Witchcraft and *Sorcery*.' "

He frowned at me. "You want those sodas, or not?"

These hardcore fans sure could get testy.

I changed the subject. "Your knife looks real."

"It's a *dagger*, not a knife. A dagger's blade is sharp on *both* sides. And, yes, it's real."

"I thought real weapons were banned from the convention."

His expression turned to disgust, but, for once, not at me. "Used to be you could buy swords, daggers, and knives in the dealers' room, but there are stupid laws now preventing that. And for the costume party, we're supposed to limit ourselves to cardboard and rubber and other fake varieties of weaponry."

I nodded toward the pearl-handled dagger in its sheath. "But *that's* not cardboard."

He smiled slyly and raised a shush finger to his lips.

I would be getting into no more disagreements about sorcerers and wizards with this character.

Smiling nervously, I said, "I'm with you, dude. Rubber weapons *do* take away from the reality."

Like witches without green faces. Or monkeys without facial hair.

Finally, Brad had his turn at the bar, and he ordered the two soft drinks, plus a rum and Coke for himself—wonderful to know a guy with a real dagger was knocking back alcoholic beverages—and I paid as negotiated. We said our good-byes with no particular affection for each other.

By the time I had returned to Mother with the sodas, the costume contest had concluded, won by the two-headed good–evil Ash character from the *Evil Dead* movie (Bruce Campbell rules!). Second place went to the sailor-hatted Stay Puft Marshmallow Man from *Ghost Busters*. Tommy may have wanted to keep Hollywood out of his con, but at the costume party, anyway, Tinsel Town kicked the superheroes' collective behind.

Suddenly the lights dimmed, and the music cranked up,

and the dance floor flooded with zombies and caped crusaders and cutesy Japanese anime characters. And I wondered how Mother and I could possibly confront *anyone* about *anything* in this frenetic atmosphere.

Mother leaned close and, with her good diction and stage-trained projection, rose easily above the din. "I had a word with our friend Robert Sipcowski while you were off flirting with that man wearing the belts."

The security chief and his uniformed men were prowling the ballroom's periphery. Maybe they were looking for daggers that weren't rubber.

"A word about what, Mother?"

"I asked him if he'd been at the crime scene when the murder weapon was removed from the victim. He said he had. I asked him to confirm that the name on the gold pen was Harlan Thompson, and he did. He was shocked I knew that, but he *did* confirm it. I was right about something else, too."

I sat forward, excited. "What, Mother?"

"It *was* a Montblanc!"

Smirking, I leaned back and sipped my ginger ale.

The whites of her eyes showed in the green of her face. "Oh, and I surprised him with another question, too."

"What, did you know the color of ink?"

"No. I asked him if I was right in thinking that Tommy didn't have his room keycard on him. And he confirmed that as well."

"What made you think that?"

"Elementary, my dear flying monkey. Violet must have taken it off his body after she killed him. That's how she got into his room to search it, reclaiming Eric's pen."

I was smiling, excitement spiking through me. "Mother, I think you *have* her. I think you have enough for Detective Cassato to arrest Violet."

She was clearly proud of herself. "Well, at least enough to convince him that Violet's the prime suspect."

So we sat in the semidark, smugly sipping our sodas for a while, as I sent my eyes around the room, looking for Violet. Finally, I spotted her at a large, well-populated table at the edge of the dance floor, and gave Mother a poke.

Our prime suspect was dressed as a sexy Little Red Riding Hood, red cape removed and draped over the back of her chair. Holding court with a group of zombie-clad friends, she seemed overly animated, as if trying a little too hard to be having fun, possibly for the benefit of Eric and Helena. The couple, entwined in each other's arms, were dancing slowly nearby to "Love Hurts."

Neither husband nor wife was in costume: Eric wore a bright green sports coat over a black shirt with black slacks; Helena, a short yellow knit dress and blue kitten heels.

I couldn't help feeling a wee bit sorry for the jilted woman, who was trying hard to pretend she wasn't watching them. On the other hand, Violet was almost certainly a murderess, so maybe she had it coming.

Before the music stopped, Eric and his wife moved off the dance floor holding hands, then wended their way through the crowd and out the main doors.

Finally, after a midtempo tune that got few dancers out there, the DJ started another song, an upbeat bombastic one, and Violet's zombie friends got up, one by one, and headed out to the crowded floor. But Violet remained behind, even as other dancers moved past either side of her table, on their way to the floor.

"Now's our chance, dear," Mother said. "Let's go show Little Miss Red Riding Hood what big teeth I have!"

"No, Mother. Maybe we should wait until—"

I was going to say until the DJ took a break, but the

Wicked Witch was up and moving. I caught up, making no effort whatsoever to walk like a monkey, and together we approached Violet.

"Dear," Mother said loudly above the music. "We simply *must* speak with you! There are questions only *you* can answer. . . ."

Violet was staring rather blankly at her glass of red wine.

Mother touched Violet's shoulder, and the woman fell forward, sprawled across the table, her white complexion contrasting with the various shades of red around her, including spilled wine.

In her back was a pearl-handled dagger I had seen before.

A *Trash 'n' Treasures* Tip

To get the most out of the convention, plan each day in advance by using the program booklet to determine what panels and events you wish to attend. Seasoned attendees allow for the unexpected, such as long lines, last-minute changes, and surprise guests—and, in our case, the occasional unscheduled murder.

Chapter Eleven

Con Fine

A sprawled costume partygoer with a knife in her back caused an interesting reaction among those nearby. Smiles blossomed at first, as in, "What a cool costume!" or "Isn't that an outrageous stunt!" Then those smiles turned downward into horror, and couples clutched each other, hands going to mouths, eyes wide, not sure what to believe.

But the loud dance music, and the crowded room itself, meant a relatively small number of attendees had noticed Violet's condition, and no general panic had broken out; at least, not yet.

While Mother stood watch over Violet's body, I hurried off to find Robert Sipcowski, pushing my way through the boisterous crowd, most of the happy revelers unaware of the murder, much less the murderer in their midst (unless he or she had already fled). I considered opening my wings, as that might cause people to make way for me, but in this group, it took more than just being a winged monkey to get their attention.

The head of security was leaning against the wall by the main doors. I waved at him.

"*Trouble!*" I yelled.

I wasn't sure he could hear me over the music, but however relaxed he might look, Robert was a trained pro. His slack body straightened, bored eyes going alert, and he quickly came over and followed me back to Violet's table.

He took one look at the protruding knife in her back, and the blood that had seeped around the wound, and knew at once that this was no comic-con special effect.

Finding no pulse in Violet's neck, he barked tersely into his walkie-talkie: "*Code thirty!*"

Which I knew meant "homicide," because Mother had a police scanner back home, along with a list of codes. I knew those codes by heart, not because I'd memorized them, but thanks to Mother blurting out each number's meaning as it came out of the scanner.

Around us, the crowd of costumed spectators had grown; we were surrounded, though no one encroached upon our space, perhaps out of fear or uneasiness. Possibly, it was out of respect for the late Violet—the second-in-command at Bufford Con, who had just joined its founder in death.

Robert and his team backed the attendees off farther, as the ballroom went into immediate lockdown—doors slamming shut, chandelier lights blazing on, the pounding music abruptly stopped midtune.

For a few seconds dancers on the crowded floor boogied on, before halting midstep, squinting from the bright lights like bar patrons at closing time. Gasps and cries spread through the room like ripples in water, alerting others that something bad had happened, the music replaced by the milling sound of disturbed partygoers. Some of the latter remained standing, but most made their way back to their tables. Here and there attendees were crying, mostly females, a sobbing Wonder Woman weeping nearby.

Robert shouted, "*Find somewhere to sit! If you can't, stand at the rear.*" He pointed. "*No one is leaving!*"

The half-dozen tables nearest Violet's body were cleared by the security chief's crew, keeping civilians away from the immediate crime scene.

When Mother and I started to follow Robert's orders, heading back to our little table, he said, "Hold up there! Not you two."

We put on the brakes, still near the table where Violet slumped like a child napping at a school desk, with only the knife in her back to say she was doing more than slumbering.

Robert frowned at us, apparently not hostile, just enmeshed in the seriousness of what had gone down. "What can you tell me about this before the cops arrive?"

He had addressed both of us, but I wasn't sure we should say anything until the police got here—with his Mob ties, Robert was a suspect. Where exactly had *he* been when Violet was stabbed? He could have been in that crowd that swarmed past her table, done the deed, and repositioned himself along the wall.

So I gave Mother a narrow-eyed gaze and shook my head as if I were straightening my hair, but trying to convey *don't answer* to her.

Mother, however, has never been one to shy away from a question, although her response might be suspect.

She said, "We saw Violet seated all by her lonesome, and came over to keep the dear girl company. We were eager to tell her what a fine job she's been doing with the convention. Such a terrible thing to happen."

"And this is how you found her?"

"Well, she was sitting up and I touched her shoulder and then she sort of . . . flopped forward. So, yes and no."

Robert looked at me. "What about you? Did you see anything? Do you know anything about this?"

"Well . . ."

His frown deepened. "Well *what*?"

I nodded toward Violet. "That dagger belongs to the con's Fan Guest of Honor. Brad Webster."

I was about to add that the dagger being the murder weapon didn't necessarily make Brad the murderer when a beefy security guy hauled over a sullen Brad, arms pinned, the acned young man looking more than a little ridiculous in his cape and all those buckled belts.

"This kid tried to sneak out," the guard told his boss.

"That your knife, son?" Sipcowski asked.

"I'm not saying *anything* without a lawyer," Brad answered defiantly.

Robert nodded toward me. "*She* says it's your knife."

"Dagger," I said.

Then Brad glared at me. "Thanks a *lot*, Brandy."

Robert turned to me again. "You know this guy?"

"I've spoken to him exactly twice. Most recently, he let me cut in line at the bar. I guess he thought that bought him my silence in a murder investigation."

Brad gave me a dirty look. Not as dirty as when I'd confused sorcerers and wizards, but dirty enough.

And they hauled him out to wait for the police.

Who soon arrived, with a forensics team, but with no sign of Detective Cassato or any other plainclothes cop. A uniformed officer interviewed us briefly, taking notes. Around midnight, the partygoers were finally released, after giving the officers their names and addresses; out-of-towners like Mother and me were told not to leave the city without informing the NYPD, and to expect to be asked to make more formal statements tomorrow.

I was relieved Sal Cassato hadn't been among the first responders, as Mother and I might have been kept deep into the night, answering his questions. I felt pretty wrung out, and looked forward to getting back to our suite and getting out of this monkey suit, and I don't mean tuxedo.

But in the otherwise empty elevator, Mother seemed energized by the tragedy.

"Why so morose, dear?" she chirped, a smile on her green face, her pointed hat a little crooked. "The police have their man. Violet killed Tommy, and Brad killed her over it. Case closed."

"I'm not so sure. Brad's a little odd, but he's a fantasy role player, not the type for a real-life killer."

"There's no murderer 'type,' dear. You should know that by now."

The elevator ding signaled our floor, and we stepped off.

"But there is," Mother said solemnly as we walked to our room, "*one* thing about Violet's murder that bothers me."

She wanted me to ask, so I did: "And that is?"

"That we didn't get the credit for solving *Tommy's* murder."

I came to a halt in the hallway. "You can't be *serious*."

"Quite serious, dear. We weren't able to confront Violet about her crime, and the police will consider our explanation of how she killed Tommy irrelevant after her murder, except as it provides a motive for her own killing."

We started walking again.

"I blame your friend Brad," she said.

"He's not my friend."

"Well, he's certainly not *mine*! Not after he and his dagger stole our glory."

"Who cares about glory?"

She frowned and gave her green face a probably witchy cast. "Well, I do. It's a matter of principle—you know I always say, give credit where credit is due."

"Well, I don't want any. Not credit, not glory, not nuttin'. Anyway, I have a feeling Brad is a patsy in this thing."

Her eyes gleamed. She loved it when I talked *noir*.

Stopping in the hall again, she said, "But it *was* Brad's knife, wasn't it?"

"Yes, or at least his dagger. There's a difference."

"That's right, dear, a dagger has two sharp sides."

It was always disturbing to learn that Mother knows such things.

We started walking again as I went on: "Brad made no secret of carrying a real weapon on him—he took a sense of pride in it."

The green face frowned. "You're certain of that?"

I shrugged. "I barely know him, and he told *me*."

She was thinking, wheels turning—I could all but hear the grinding and clanking. "And that was a crowded room . . ."

"Right."

". . . and someone could have easily taken the opportunity to lift that knife without Brad realizing it."

"Someone who knew Brad and Tommy were close, and that Brad and Violet had argued in front of witnesses about Tommy's death."

She was nodding, the black pointed hat bobbing. "Someone who figured Brad Webster was all but *guaranteed* to be charged for Violet's murder."

I opened the door to our suite and let Mother in first.

Sushi ran to greet us and I picked her up. Mother strode over to her commandeered menu board with its suspect list, regarding it as if in an art gallery.

"We have two different murderers now," I said, scratching the little dog's head as I went over to join her.

Mother turned to me. "Yes, a murderer with his or her own motive—perhaps most likely someone who, like us, figured out Violet had killed Tommy, and avenged him."

"Not necessarily. It could be an accomplice in the first crime, cleaning up in panic mode."

She shook her head. "No, Violet had no accomplice. Tommy's murder in that elevator was clearly impromptu . . .

but for now, let's concentrate on Violet's killing. Who had the opportunity?"

At her side, I studied the names she'd written on the board, taking them in order. "Gino Moretti—didn't see *him* there, did you?"

She shook her head. "But it was a costume party, keep in mind. Almost anyone could have attended incognito. Isn't that a wonderful word, *incognito*?"

"Wonderful, maybe. Helpful, no. The suspects who we know were there for sure are, well, obviously, Brad Webster. So he's a yes."

Mother put a check by his name, and every "yes" that followed. Gino had earned a "maybe."

I went on: "Robert Sipcowski, yes. Eric Johansson, yes."

"Yes and *no*," Mother said, raising a finger. Standing at the chalkboard, she was the epitome of every kid's image of the teacher as a wicked witch. "Eric was at the costume ball, *yes*, but left with his wife, Helena, *before* Violet was murdered."

"So he's a *no*. . . . Harlan Thompson, yes."

Mother added the new suspect to the list, making a check mark in the "yes" column, then stared at the chalkboard for an eternity, or, anyway, ten seconds.

Finally, she turned her green mug toward me. "Dear, we simply *must* speak with that boy Bradley Webster."

I frowned. "He's in NYPD custody—how exactly do a couple of tourists from Serenity, Iowa, manage that?"

Her smile was every bit as wicked as Margaret Hamilton's (that's what Google is for, youngsters). "I have a plan. A cunning plan."

I groaned. Whenever she made that particular *Blackadder* reference, I knew I was in trouble. "Can it keep until the morning? I'm bushed."

"This *is* the morning, dear, and there is no time like the

present. Right now, that poor innocent boy is probably in a holding cell—tomorrow he may be in an even more inconvenient location."

"So now you think he's innocent?"

"It's a strong possibility."

"Fine," I sighed wearily. "Can I at least get out of this monkey suit first? Maybe you could *not* go green?"

"No time, dear. We must move quickly."

Mine was not to reason why. Mine was but to do and sigh. "Shall I get our coats?"

"Yes. And Sushi's medication."

"She's had her medication today."

"I don't want you to give it to her. I want her insulin bottle."

"What for?"

"Just get it, dear. And a syringe packet, too, if you please. I'll fill you in on our way."

This evasiveness meant she didn't want to argue with me over whatever "cunning" plan she had just cooked up. I really should have put my foot down. I should have stripped out of the borrowed organ-grinder getup and left my mother to her own devices. Just grabbed my warm little dog and crawled under the covers.

So that's exactly what I did.

Not. Instead we left the room and caught the elevator down to the lobby.

Mother asked the hotel doorman where the closest police station was, and he told her, before hailing us a cab. Taking off her witch's hat, Mother climbed in first, saying to the driver, "Fourteenth precinct and make it snappy." I crawled in after, as Mother added, "Don't let the green face alarm you."

The seen-it-all cabbie said, "As long as your money's green, lady."

"It's really rather multicolored these days, isn't it? But I take your point."

We were already moving, with me sitting forward to accommodate my umbrella wings. Up Eighth Avenue we went, taking a left on West Thirty-fifth Street. The cab dropped us in front of a squat three-story, brown brick and glass building, a seasoned structure that still had window air conditioners. A lettering style screaming sixties read MID-TOWN PRECINCT SOUTH above a smaller CITY OF NEW YORK POLICE DEPARTMENT over the double glass doors.

Police cars were parked diagonally on both sides of the narrow street, front wheels up on the sidewalk to make the most of limited space, and we squeezed between two of the blue-and-white vehicles, then went up three squat wide cement steps and stopped at the doors.

"I'll do all the talking, dear," Mother whispered.

En route, she had told me her plan.

"You bet you will. By the way, this is your dumbest stroke of genius yet."

An eyebrow arched in the green face. "If you have a better idea, I am open to suggestions."

"Not my job. I'm just a flying monkey. You're the head witch."

She nodded, apparently taking that as a compliment, and breezed into the waiting area with me in her embarrassed wake. Things seemed relatively calm, by Manhattan standards, anyway; only a few citizens were seated, waiting to be served and protected: worried parents, battered women, male indigents in from the cold. And now a green-faced witch and a disgruntled-looking winged monkey.

The dispatch area, however, was bustling—behind a bulletproof window, several women and men in navy NYPD attire were busy handling incoming calls, weaving in and out of offices, handing off information sheets to one another. This was the kind of cool but intense professionalism you might see in an air-traffic control room during a violent thunderstorm.

We stood at the window a full minute before a Hispanic female dispatcher could get to us.

"Yes?" She wore glasses, her short brown hair dark, her expression all business. She could not have been less fazed facing a green-pussed Wicked Witch of the West and her flying monkey. (You know, if I was going to be an accomplice, the least I might have is a name.)

Mother, leaning toward the window-embedded microphone, said, "We've just come from the Hotel Pennsylvania, the costume party held by the comic book convention there."

"Is that so?"

"It is indeed so, and I mention that only by way of prelude to a tragedy."

I take that back. I was fine being a nameless accomplice.

Mother was saying, "My son, Bradley Webster, was also in attendance at the costume party, before he was brought here and presumably booked, sometime within the last two hours."

"I can't give out that information, ma'am, unless you have—"

"I *must* see my son. It's a matter of life and death."

"That's not possible, ma'am," the woman—who in her time had presumably heard all kinds of routine matters described as life-and-death ones—said. "You'll have to come back tomorrow."

Mother whipped up some tears. She does have certain acting skills. "When I say life and death, young lady, it is not a figure of speech. If I don't see him, and immediately, he may *die*."

"What do you mean?" For some reason, the dispatcher appeared skeptical.

Mother's eyes and nostrils flared. With flair. "I mean *die* as in Bradley will cease to be, go to meet his maker, kick the bucket, be pushing up daises."

Oh, my God, was she going to go through the entire Monty Python "Dead Parrot" routine? I could have just died. Shuffled off this mortal coil. Rung down the curtain . . .

Now Mother, indignant yet still tearful (green makeup running some), was holding up the small bottle of insulin. She wasn't sticking it up right against the glass, because then the dispatcher might notice that it was veterinarian prescribed.

Mother said, "If Bradley doesn't get his medication *right now*, young lady, you will be responsible. Responsible not just for Bradley's demise, but for the New York Police Department and the city of New York facing a wrongful death lawsuit that will turn this building into a parking lot!"

"Just a moment," the dispatcher said. Eyes widened a trifle, she swivelled to a phone, spoke, her words muffled, then swivelled back. "Wait over by that door."

We stepped aside, moving to where she had pointed, and stood without speaking, Mother not wanting to break character, and me not having much to say, too busy thinking that maybe it wouldn't be so bad getting booked here. They'd probably trade me a nice orange jumpsuit for this terrible monkey costume.

Then the door to the inner workings of the precinct opened and a uniformed African-American officer stepped out, his name tag reading WILLIAMS.

Middle-aged with short gray hair and wire-framed glasses, he wore the wary, weary expression of a public servant who had all too often been assigned to deal with the precinct's crackpots.

We would not disappoint.

"What's this about?" Williams asked matter-of-factly.

Again, Mother explained that "her son Bradley" needed his insulin shot. Reading her audience, she seemed to be going for a less melodramatic approach.

He said, "You can leave the medication with me and I'll give it to the precinct doctor when he comes in."

Mother whipped up some more tears, adding to the tracks on her green face. "But my son must have it *now*!" she said frantically. "Otherwise, the poor boy may go into *shock*. Do you know what that means, officer?"

"I believe I do."

But there was no stopping her. She took a deep breath and went on: "His heartbeat will speed up . . ."

Her hand clutched the dark dress over her heart.

". . . his vision blur . . ."

She swung her head in a dizzying circle.

". . . feet and hands go numb . . ."

She shook each foot and hand, possibly creating a new dance.

". . . after which he will faint . . ."

She briefly mimed fainting.

". . . and go into a diabetic coma . . ."

She closed her eyes and her head hit her shoulder, sticking her tongue out just a trifle.

Then her eyes popped open.

". . . followed by cardiac arrest and *death*!"

So I was wrong about her abandoning the melodrama. But it *was* an impressive performance. She'd accomplished it all on that one breath. Now that she'd run out of air, she grabbed a fresh gulp. "Do you wish to be responsible for that, Officer Williams?"

"Look, madam, the doctor isn't here right now."

"*We* can administer it," Mother offered generously.

Williams frowned. "Can't the boy give himself the injection?"

My mother's unnamed accomplice said, "He faints at the sight of a needle—that's why *we've* always done it for him."

"Both of you?"

Mother said, "I need Brandy along to check the dosage before I administer the shot—my eyesight is bad." She opened her eyes wide; the whites of her eyes against the green makeup was startling. "Glaucoma."

The officer seemed hesitant, but said, "All right. I'll need some I.D. first."

"My dear man!" Mother huffed. Her hat was sitting crooked now, after all that emoting. "Do you see any purses with us? Do you see how we are dressed? We have just come straight from that horrific ordeal at the Hotel Pennsylvania with only our coats, and just happened to have the insulin with us."

"You're guests there?"

"Yes," I said. "Vivian and Brandy . . . Webster."

Please don't call over there. Please don't call over there.

Mother waved a frantic hand. "Sir . . . we're wasting precious time!"

She was wearing him down. Forces of nature can do that to you.

"All right," Williams acquiesced, "you can see your son just long enough to give the medication—but that's all."

"It's all we ask," Mother said. "His attorney will be here tomorrow."

"Fine. You can come back, too."

The officer took us down a hallway and through another locked door, on which a sign said MALE HOLDING CELLS.

We stepped through into a brightly lit square area, off of which were half a dozen small rooms—each about four feet by six, some with doors shut (occupied), others yawning open (awaiting new guests). Our next suite?

"Now isn't this *lovely*!" Mother gushed, as if being

shown charming accommodations at an exclusive resort. "*Your* holding cells have Plexiglas doors instead of bars. Much nicer than ours back home."

Williams asked, "How is it you know that, Mrs. Webster? Has your son been incarcerated before?"

"Uh, no, I am simply very active in local affairs. Helped raise money for the new jail. We could have used the kind of forward thinking I see on display here."

Dryly, the officer said, "Well, I'm tickled pink you approve, lady—now, could we get on with this? I thought you were in a hurry."

"Yes, of course," Mother said apologetically. "Time *is* of the essence—which cell is Bradley's?"

I had already spotted him through a Plexiglas door, seated on a padded bench. He was wearing one of those orange jumpsuits, which struck me as an improvement over his sorcerer costume of many belts. I raised a shush finger to my lips, much as he had to me when we'd discussed his real dagger.

Officer Williams unlocked the cell door, then stood aside for us to enter.

The cell was as sparse as it was tiny. Apart from the bench used for sitting and sleeping, the only other fixture was an aluminum combination sink and toilet, tucked in a corner.

Mother said loudly, "Bradley, darling, it's Mother and your sister, Brandy."

Just in case he didn't know the names of his mother and sister.

"*We're here to help you,*" Mother whispered.

Brad smirked in my direction. "Right. Like turning me over to the police."

Despite his bravado, there was fear in the young man's eyes.

I whispered, "*You shouldn't have tried to run.*"

Outside the door, Williams said, "Stop talking and get on with it."

I whispered, "*Brad, we're looking into Violet's murder. We think you're innocent.*"

Well, we thought he *might* be innocent, but . . .

As if in an operating room, Mother said loudly, "Brandy . . . prepare the insulin, please!" And under her breath, she added, "*Buy me some time, dear.*"

Turning toward the door to hold the officer's attention, I retrieved from my organ-grinder's pocket the sealed syringe and slowly began to unwrap it. Then I took the insulin bottle and, holding it at an angle upside down, stuck the sharp needle into its soft rubber end. Carefully I drew out the liquid.

All the while, Mother whispered rapid-fire questions to Brad. "*When did you miss your dagger?*"

"Not until the lights went up."

"*Anyone bump into you?*"

"Not that I noticed. But it *was* crowded."

"*What was your argument about with Violet in the restaurant?*"

"I thought she should've cancelled the convention out of respect to Tommy's memory . . . but I would never have killed her over it."

"*Did you know that Violet killed Tommy?*"

His eyes popped. "Violet killed Tommy?"

"*Yes. Were you in love with him?*"

"What . . . what does that have to do with anything?"

"*Is there anything else you know that we should?*"

"I heard Violet say she was going to make Eric sorry he dumped her. She thought he was through with that wife of his, but then Mrs. Eric shows up, all lovey-dovey. Listen, what do you mean, Violet killed Tommy?"

Finished with my floor show, I handed the syringe to Mother, who stood with her back to Williams, blocking his view of Brad.

The Fan Guest of Honor's eyes went wide. "Hey . . . !"

"Roll up your sleeve, dear," Mother said, with a wink-wink. "How afraid of needles he is!"

And she faked the injection.

Outside the cell, Mother said to Williams, "Thank you, dear man, you have *saved* my poor boy's life."

"He didn't look sick to me."

"Ah, one can never tell about a diabetic. One moment that person seems fine, and then—*poof*! Pearly gates. Do you have any orange juice?"

I wasn't sure if Mother wanted some for herself, or if this was part of the ruse.

Williams blinked at the apparent non sequitur. "Uh, yeah. In the break room. Why?"

"A little orange juice after an injection is best. Could you see that Bradley gets some?"

"Okay."

Williams escorted us back to the waiting room, and Mother and I proceeded through to the outside. I wondered idly exactly what laws we'd just broken. I had a feeling Mother and I might meet a harder, hardier breed of felons behind bars in New York.

Just as we were going through the double glass doors, Detective Cassato was coming in. Whether his shift was starting or he'd been called about the ballroom murder, I couldn't hazard a guess.

"Why, good morning, Detective," Mother said pleasantly, then to me, "Let us not tarry, dear."

I don't know if Tony's brother would have recognized us had Mother's distinctive voice not emanated from that green face.

And by the time he did make us, we were scurrying along Thirty-fifth toward Ninth.

"*Hey*, you two!" he yelled after us. "*Stop!*"

"Run, dear," Mother ordered, picking up her long skirt, holding on to her pointy hat.

And run I did, wings flapping as I shouted, "Taxi! Taxi!"

I wondered if the monkeys in *Wicked* got any dialogue.

A *Trash 'n' Treasures Tip*

Food at the convention is usually expensive, so it pays to bring along your own snacks and liquids. I buy one bottled water, then keep refilling it from a fountain. And Mother, in the bar, helps herself to popcorn, which is free, after all, although I doubt many patrons bring plastic bags to stuff it in.

Chapter Twelve

Con Clusion

Dearest ones, this is Vivian back for the first half of this chapter, which should delight many of our readers. For those few naysayers among you (you know who you are), I pledge to refrain from using this platform to air my grievances (however numerous and justified they might be). After all, bringing a killer—or killers—to swift justice transcends any need to address (I should say *redress*) unfair affronts to my character and/or my writing style, such as the baseless charge that I go off on discursive tangents when there is a story at hand to tell.

When Brandy and I returned to the hotel from the precinct house, it was nearly three in the morning. I had expected some amount of activity in the lobby—the departure of a few nervous guests after two murders in three days, perhaps, even at this ungodly hour. But who could have anticipated this?

The queue to reception seemed endless and winding, the lone checkout clerk overwhelmed by this unexpected exodus. There was a Fellini-esque air to the proceeding, many people still in their masquerade costumes, bags hurriedly packed, fleeing for home or other hotels.

Added to the macabre carnival atmosphere was the appearance of members of the "Fourth Estate," having gotten wind of another "suspicious death," TV news representatives thrusting their microphones and cameras in the faces of distraught fans held captive in the slow-moving line.

Brandy, seemingly oblivious to all this, was saying, "You know, Detective Cassato will come looking for us. He might be right behind us."

We were standing on the periphery of the commotion. "That's why we must make haste, dear," I informed her.

(I believe writers today are lazy by not using enough variations of "said." There are so many more interesting alternatives, such as "claimed," "commanded," "inquired," "rambled," and "remarked." But I would suggest, for you writing students out there who hang on my every carefully crafted line, that one might draw the line at "hooted.")

"Make haste to do what?" Brandy asked incredulously. "Climb in bed? What other options are there at this hour?"

"Dear, are you feeling all right? Are you well?"

"I'm just peachy keen, thanks for asking."

"Maybe so, but you *look* terrible." Even had she acquiesced to my suggestion of adding Sushi facial fuzz, it wouldn't have helped hide the dark circles beneath her eyes. She was one wilted little monkey.

Make that an indignant wilted little monkey.

"That's because I haven't *slept* for twenty hours!" the girl retorted.

(There's another good one—"retorted"!)

Her Grumpy Gussie attitude did not surprise me. She had become a game participant in my investigations of late, but when time wore on, as in long days such as these, little Brandy got frayed around the edges.

The child always did require more rest than I. (And off

my medication, I hardly ever need sleep. A regular Super-woman!) (Who would have fit right in at this comics con.)

I patted her arm. "Why don't you get a little shut-eye? I'll join you later."

"But where are you *going* at this hour? What are you up to, Mother?"

I gestured toward the security office sign. "There are a few remaining points I need to clear up with our friend Robert."

Brandy sighed. "Okay. But if he's still here, that means he's busy, dealing with the aftermath of Violet's murder."

"Oh, I doubt he'll be too busy for Vivian Borne." That girl needed to be more optimistic when we were out solving violent crimes.

"Well, please don't be too long," she pleaded. (Another good one!) "I don't want to face Tony's brother by myself, should he turn up at our door. And he probably will."

"Never fear. I'll be back in a flash. Like the Flash!"

"Huh?"

"Comic book superhero, dear—the Flash? You really *must* do your research before setting out on an adventure."

"I don't want any more adventures tonight. I mean, this morning. I want forty winks. Settle for twenty."

We parted, Brandy heading toward the elevators as I continued across the lobby, avoiding the newscasters and their microphones and cameras (as much as it pained me to do so).

The door to the security office was unlocked and, after straightening my witch's hat, I stepped into the office. As when Brandy and I first entered here, at the very start of this caper, Robert was not at his desk. He *did* get around. So I took the opportunity to hurry over and begin sifting through his papers on the desktop.

I was just getting started when the security chief entered from the command center, his suit rumpled, his five o'clock shadow nearly lapping itself, another five o'clock mere hours away.

"You *do* realize I could see you," he growled, pointing to a tiny camera-eye high in a corner. ("Growled"—*very* nice one!)

"But of course," I retorted. Another good one (all right, I've made my point) (let's not belabor it). "Just my little joke. Merely wanted to get your attention, my dear fellow."

Actually, I hadn't spotted the darn thing—my eyesight really isn't anything to brag about.

"What do you want?" he asked brusquely.

And I responded, "*Information.*" Just like in the opening sequence of *The Prisoner*, that wonderful 1960s British spy series starring the late, great Patrick McGoohan. (I just couldn't help myself. And, anyway, I seemed to have shifted into my classy U.K. mode of speech, which always impresses.)

"Well, you're not going to get it." Had Robert unintentionally given me McGoohan's standard response? And if so, if the security chief actually knew his pop-cult stuff, did that mean he was flirting with me again?

"Well, that's a shame," I replied. "Then I take it you're not interested in the conversation I had with Brad Webster at the Fourteenth Precinct a mere half an hour ago."

And I turned to go (not really, I was just hoping to get a rise out of him) (no double entendre intended).

He sputtered, "Wait . . . what? You actually got to *see* him?"

(Now I know I promised to back off, but isn't "sputtered" just a lovely way to express it? Would it really have been better writing had I used *He said, spitting*?)

"Indeed I did see the young man," I said, Britishly crisp.

"And what he had to say was *most* interesting. One might say . . . illuminating?"

"How so?"

I raised an eyebrow. "How's your Latin, Robert?"

"My what?"

"Your Latin—as in quid pro quo."

His mouth formed a thin line. "That much Latin I know just fine. Go on, Vivian."

"First, a question. I must determine your role in all this."

"My role? What the hell—"

"What were you doing Thursday afternoon?"

He sighed irritably. "You're going to have to be more specific, lady."

I liked it better when he used "Vivian."

I said, "Brandy saw you coming out of Tommy Bufford's room. Your manner was suspicious, such as wearing latex gloves before skedaddling down the hall. My daughter had a keycard, as that room used to be ours, and went in and discovered the room had been searched."

Robert snorted. "You think *I* did that?"

"I think *nothing*." That didn't come out quite right. "*Did* you search that room?"

He reddened, rather like Yosemite Sam in the old Bugs Bunny cartoons, right before his (Sam's) head turned into a radish. "*Of course* not! I *found* it that way!"

I put one finger to my lips. "Well, it couldn't have been Sal Cassato who 'tossed the place'—he arrived after Brandy."

I didn't go into the fact that the detective had discovered her hiding in the closet. Or, for that matter, that Brandy had found those switched ballot pages in the fridge.

My eyes went to the police photo on the wall. "It must have been dispiriting," I said, not without sympathy, "to have been asked to leave the force. Under a cloud."

His eyes narrowed. "How do you know about that?"

"I have my sources."

"Like Sal Cassato?"

"You were a police detective once, Mr. Sipcowski. Would you ever have divulged your sources? I think not." I gave him my most girlish smile, and it's quite girlish, if I do say so myself. "*Unless* . . . it's in exchange for something I *really* desire."

"That right?"

"Oh, yes. And then I can *sing* like a canary! Put all the stool pigeons to shame."

Robert huffed a sigh. "Mrs. Borne . . . Vivian . . . there was never an investigation. I was never charged with anything."

I tilted my head. "But weren't you rather well . . . *connected*?"

He nodded. "But only in the sense that I had buddies from the old neighborhood who I knew before I joined the department." He added sadly, "And you know how it is, Vivian. You can't prove yourself innocent when the charge is guilt by association."

That was very well put, I thought, and I could relate. On my rare stays at the psychopathic hospital, I made any number of friends whose stigma seemed to rub off on me!

"My dear Mr. Sipcowski," I declared. "I believe I owe you an apology. It seems I have misinterpreted your actions completely."

It takes a big woman to admit a mistake. I have done it before, though none of those instances spring swiftly to mind.

"Robert, I see now that you have been endeavoring to solve these murders yourself. Whether for your own self-esteem, or to repair your tarnished reputation, your motivation is both understandable and admirable."

"Maybe you're right, Vivian." His eyes were unfathomably sad. "But that ship sailed. That kid Webster murdered Violet, and I'm fairly sure she killed Bufford."

"That ship has *not* sailed!" I informed him. "And you are still in the running for its captain!"

"What are you talking about?"

"I assume the police have acquired the pertinent security camera footage."

"They have."

"But am I also right in assuming that you keep a digital backup?"

"We do."

"Excellent! Now, I want to review what was captured by the security camera outside the Skytop Ballroom shortly before, and after, Violet was killed."

He shrugged while shaking his head. "I can do that, but I assure you, Vivian—I've already gone over that footage several times."

"Never discount the value of a second pair of eyes, dear." Of course, the value of *my* eyes was clearly on markdown, but he didn't need to know that.

He shrugged again, but rose to lead me into the command center. Here, other security personnel were at their posts in front of the wall of color monitors whose screens were rotating between various views of assorted security cams throughout the hotel.

Robert sat at one of the computers and I drew up a chair next to him. Soon his fingers were tapping on the keyboard, finding the recording I'd requested, at approximately the time I had seen Eric and his wife, Helena, leave the masquerade party.

We watched the couple exit the ballroom into the shallow lobby area with elevators, Eric in his green jacket, Helena in her yellow dress. Then Eric stopped, drew his wife

close, looked into her face fondly, and kissed her passionately. Finally, they walked on, hand in hand, out of camera
range.

"If you suspect them, you're wasting my time," Robert
grumbled. (Good one!) (Sorry.) "Neither one goes back in
the ballroom before Violet was killed."

"Run it again," I commanded.

He sighed, but complied.

Once more we watched.

Then I said, "That kiss. It's staged."

"What do you mean?"

"It's staged! As in perfectly blocked. See where he hits
his mark for the kiss? Right in front of the camera. The
whole performance looks *stilted*—and I should know, I'm
an actress!"

Not that I'd ever given a stilted performance.

"By *both* of them?" Robert frowned, obviously a little
confused.

"No—just *Eric*. Helena seems surprised by this sudden
display of affection, even caught off balance."

"So you're saying that Eric *wanted* to be noticed."

"Hence the bright green jacket—not exactly the kind of
Nordic attire he's been wearing. And no mask, either, so
you can clearly see his face."

Robert sat back from the computer. "Mrs. Borne, you
can speculate all you like about stilted performances and
unlikely attire, but Eric would have had to go back
through those doors to kill Violet. All the others were
locked from the outside. And he *didn't*."

"Well, he didn't wearing a green jacket."

Robert gaped at me.

I gestured toward the computer screen. "When you
went over this footage, were you on fast-scan mode?
Times two, maybe, or more? Not watching it in real time?"

"Well, yes," he admitted. "Just to be more efficient."

"Speed does not necessarily mean increased efficiency. But I suppose you might still notice a green jacket."

"Yes, and . . . I see what you're getting at."

"Let's go on from here," I said, "and *not* speed it up."

We started where Eric and Helena had gone out of view, and watched intently, as if this were the final episode of our favorite television series.

Approximately ten minutes later, a costumed group of four showed on the monitor, their backs to the camera, moving in a tight cluster toward the ballroom doors.

"Stop!" I exclaimed.

Robert froze the footage.

I pointed to the screen. "There he *is*—without the jacket. All in black. Using that group of partygoers as cover. Can you zoom in?"

Robert's fingers flew across the keyboard as he magnified, then enhanced the frozen image.

"By God, it *is* Eric Johansson!" Robert exclaimed. "The son of a bitch *did* return!"

"Yes, he returned to lift Brad's dagger, stab Violet, then slip out a side door . . . which *can,* I believe, be exited from the inside."

"You're right about that, Vivian," he said, nodding gravely. "He used other guests as cover as he moved by Violet, stabbing as he passed."

From behind us, a security guard asked, "Ah, Mrs. Borne? Isn't this your daughter?"

I swivelled in my chair to see what he had been viewing.

On his screen was Brandy in her monkey costume; she seemed to be throwing something away in a trash can.

I frowned. "Why, she told me she was going back to our room—said she was all tuckered out! Where is that camera?"

"Outside the Skytop Ballroom," the guard told me.

I rose and moved closer.

"What *is* she doing?" I asked myself.

But the guard answered anyway, "Looks like she's diggin' in the garbage."

Robert had joined me, standing behind the guard's chair, and the three of us watched Brandy pulling something out of the can that looked like a white napkin. With a dark red stain on it.

Then she walked toward the video camera, her mouth moving.

"Do you have audio?" I asked.

"No sound," Robert said.

"Is she trying to tell us something?" I asked.

"She's not looking at the camera," the guard said, glancing back at us. "I think she's talking to someone just off-camera . . . *behind* it."

While that "someone" remained out of view, Brandy appeared to be calm. But even with the TV's overhead camera placement, and less than perfect picture—not to mention my less than perfect eyes—I could detect alarm in her expression.

I clutched Robert's arm. "She may be in danger," I said. "We need to get to her . . . toot sweet!"

After leaving Mother in the lobby, I caught an empty elevator, leaned against the back wall, and zoned out. Then it stopped, the doors whooshing open, and I stepped off.

But I found myself not on the fifteenth floor—rather, the eighteenth, having accidentally or perhaps subconsciously pushed the button taking me back to the Skytop Ballroom.

By the time I realized my mistake, the elevator had gone. I was about to push the button when curiosity nibbled at my brain. This was an opportunity to see if the police and forensics team had gone, and if they had, what they'd left behind. . . .

I strolled down to the ballroom, where I found yellow

crime scene tape stretched across its double doors, making a big X.

Mother might have burst the tape and gone in, but I wasn't that ambitious. I was about to head back to the elevators when I spotted something on a nearby narrow accent table.

It wasn't a clue, not really, and if you have any respect for me, no matter how slight, you're about to lose it now.

Abandoned on the little table, on a small paper plate, was a half-eaten piece of party cake.

Need I go further?

After wiping the gooey white frosting off my mouth with the back of one hand (in my defense, I ate forward from the unnibbled side and left a small wall of somebody-else's-cake germs behind), I went to a trash can and tossed in the nasty sliver of cake and its paper plate.

But in doing so, something caught my eye.

No, not more discarded food—I do not eat garbage, I'll have you know. I have *some* pride. Apparently not enough to refuse having a flying monkey costume foisted on me, but *some*.

I reached in and pulled out what I had spotted: a white cloth. A handkerchief with little blue stripes. With the initials *EJ* on it . . . and Rorschach splotches of blood.

I stared at the handkerchief like a chimp trying to read the directions on a can of peanuts. Then it came to me—how that handkerchief had found its way into that trash can, and how that blood had gotten on that handkerchief.

That Eric Johansson, after leaving the ballroom with his wife, must have returned, stolen Brad's dagger, stabbed Violet—the dagger's handle handkerchief wrapped to keep his prints off—then disposed of the damning evidence in a trash can outside the ballroom, a receptacle less likely to be searched.

I frowned, sorry that sweet Eric had turned out to be

not so sweet, but then smiled, taking some pleasure in beating Mother in figuring out who Violet's killer was. Then I carefully folded the handkerchief and tucked it into my organ-grinder jacket pocket.

"I will take that," Eric said.

The writer, wearing a black, long-sleeved shirt and black jeans, stood about twenty feet from me, blocking my way to the elevators.

"Eric, hi," I said calmly. "Take what?"

He shook his head. "We will not play that game."

Violet must have been the one who Americanized his scripts, starting with putting the contractions in.

He gave me a horrible smile and held out a hand. "Give it up," he said ambiguously.

Backing away, I said, "So was it you or Violet who broke into our room?"

Moving forward almost casually, he shrugged. "It was me. Looking for my award and those ballots."

"I didn't guess your part in this. Because Violet *did* kill Tommy, on impulse. But you're the mastermind, aren't you, Eric? You manipulated Violet into fixing that award competition for you. She had no idea, until well after the fact, that you would dump her . . . for your own wife."

I was still backing up slowly. He was moving forward the same way.

He said, "I have never found females hard to handle."

"I bet not. I thought you were pretty cute myself. Using Violet that way . . . you just are not nice, are you?"

"Not nice is a way to put it."

"But seduce and abandon, that's a very old plot, Eric. You won't win any awards for that."

"Perhaps not. But this would have worked out well had that stupid woman not stabbed that clod Tommy."

Me backing up. Him moving forward.

I said, "She couldn't have come forward about your role

in the ballot-fixing without exposing herself. That would have meant risking putting herself in line for a murder charge. Why kill her, Eric?"

Another shrug. "She was not rational. She said she did not care if she went to prison. She lied and cheated and killed for me, she said, and now she would tell the world about me. What else could I do?"

The question was, what could *I* do?

During this exchange, my mind was desperately seeking a solution to my predicament—one that didn't end with me becoming a third comic-con fatality.

I turned and fled down a hallway, my half-open wings flapping, trying doors as I went but finding only locked ones. Eric was walking toward me, taking his time, like the mummy chasing a girl through a swamp, no hurry, no hurry. The corridor and my luck would run out simultaneously. When I glanced back, he was removing his tie, wrapping each end around a hand, then snapping it taut.

But there was a door at the end of the hallway that was unlikely to be locked—marked ROOF with a warning on the door's horizontal bar stating that an alarm would sound if opened.

Fine by me!

All I needed to do was stay alive on the roof long enough for security to respond to the alarm. That's all. Nothing more.

I pushed on the steel bar—no alarm sounded (it was a silent one, right? Right?) and raced up cement steps to another door with a similar bar, though no alarm warning, and then I was out on the roof, nearly knocked over by a ferocious wind that tore at my flesh and my costume with icy fingers.

Up here in the dark, under a million uncaring stars, I could make out neighboring buildings towering around me, silhouetted against the lights of the city. And on this rooftop, I could make out the squat, square shape of an air-conditioning unit, behind which I could hide.

I ran toward it.

But tripped, and landed on my stomach, in an awful belly flop, my chin hitting the hard surface of the roof, momentarily stunning me.

And he was on me, grabbing me by my ankles, dragging me like a sack of wet laundry, pulling me along, away from the noisy-street-traffic sides of the building toward the more desolate courtyard area, where he could toss my body over and feel reasonably assured it would not be found till daylight.

Through all this, I was kicking frantically, my efforts to free myself no match for his tight grip, my screams for help seemingly swallowed up by the wind and the night, two conspirators who were happy to see me go. So I clawed at the roof, breaking my nails, skinning my fingers—not because this might slow my fate, but because at least, dammit, it would prove that my death was no accident.

I could see one possible chance for survival—before strangling me, or knocking me out, Eric would have to let go of my legs, and retrieve the handkerchief. That was key evidence that he needed and I had. He needed to get it, before throwing me off this roof like a sock monkey.

When he had dragged me to the roof's three-foot-high protective wall, I was still on my stomach, his hands still on my ankles. But his grip had eased, since he was no longer hauling dead (or soon to be dead) weight.

"Well," Eric shouted against the wind, "shall we see how well the monkey can fly?"

As he released my legs, I flipped over on my wings, snapping them, and with both feet kicked his kneecaps, and they made a snapping sound, too.

Hollering, he fell backward against the little wall, arms

windmilling as he tried to regain his balance. I was about to give him another kick when a strong gust gave him a final push over the edge, and I didn't have to.

For a moment—as I watched in fascination—it seemed that Eric could fly, even without monkey wings, the rising air from the courtyard below creating a vortex, keeping him momentarily aloft, like some crazy cartoon character who'd run off a cliff and hadn't yet realized there was only a long fall under his feet.

Then the swirling vortex dissipated, and Eric dropped from view, followed by a terrible sound, a *whump* punctuated by brittle breakage.

Suddenly Robert was helping me up, and Mother's comforting arms were around me, holding me tight, my pitiful sobs lost in the wind.

"There, there, little Brandy," Mother soothed. "There, there. No need to cry now."

But it was my party and I'd cry if I wanted to.

And I wanted to.

A *Trash 'n' Treasures* Tip

Most comics conventions have an "artists' alley," where cartoonists sell and sign their work. In addition to offering original comic book pages, the artists often do sketches, frequently for bargain rates. You can ask for a drawing of your favorite character. That's what Mother does—she has a whole portfolio of caricatures of herself.

Chapter Thirteen

Con Tinued

Having no desire to learn of the wonders of a Manhattan emergency room, I declined a hospital visit, instead camping out on the unfolded-out couch in our suite. I traded the monkey costume for a baby blue velour Juicy Couture tracksuit, finally shedding those darn wings. Bandages had been provided by someone at the hotel, and my mummy-wrapped hands looked like a burn victim's. Otherwise I was all right. But this long night was not over. A rumpled, bleary-eyed Detective Sal Cassato showed up around five a.m., and I gave him my account of Eric's attack, which he collected by way of a handheld recorder. A keenly interested and atypically subdued Mother, with a concerned Sushi in her lap, looked on.

When I had finished, Mother admitted to holding back the partial ballots found in Tommy's room that had led us to theorize that Violet had killed Tommy.

"And of course," Mother said, "the rest is history."

"Not quite history yet," Detective Cassato said sharply. "You were withholding evidence, Mrs. Borne. That's a very serious matter."

Mother gave him a languid Southern belle shrug (perfected in a Serenity Community Playhouse production of

The Little Foxes). "Well, I suppose technically you're correct, Detective, but we didn't realize the ballots had any kind of evidentiary value, not until late in the game."

She do declare.

Detective Cassato was reddening. "If you'd handed over those ballot sheets, I'd have come to the same conclusion about Violet myself. Tampering with evidence, removing evidence from a crime scene, obstructing our investigation . . . you could be *charged*, you know."

Mother touched her bosom, poor-little-old-me style, saying, "Yes, and we're terribly sorry for any inconvenience, Detective Cassato. And we do hope that you will find it in your heart *not* to charge us, as we've already been through so very much."

The detective, face set like stone, wasn't buying Mother's flummery. "You *do* realize," he replied, glaring at her, "that had you been forthcoming, your daughter's life might not ultimately have been put in jeopardy."

Actually, what ultimately put my life in jeopardy was stopping to finish a piece of half-eaten cake.

Mother shifted effortlessly into Diane Keaton *lah-de-dah* mode. "Of course, if you want to arrest the mother and daughter who solved the case for you . . . the daughter, as you rightly point out, having been nearly killed by the perpetrator of the second murder . . . well, I'm sure this will all make for fascinating reportage by the local media."

She pronounced "reportage" in the French manner.

I yawned, partly from lack of sleep, but also because I'd been through many a dressing down at the conclusion of an investigation.

"And if I might add," Mother said humbly, "we have learned our lesson here in the metropolis. We will never, ever withhold evidence again."

She intoned this with the utmost sincerity, and I just about believed her.

Just about.

"I have your assurance of that right here, you know," Cassato said, clicking off the small recorder.

Mother gave me a little glance that said: *But not under oath.*

The detective sighed. "There will be no charges."

Which, no matter how tired I might have been, was a relief to hear—our last investigation garnered us thirty days in our county jail, where I gained five pounds from the starchy food. And I'd already packed on a few New York pounds from the excess cheesecake. Stay tuned for *Antiques Diet.*

"You are a gracious and generous man," Mother gushed. "The Borne girls do not easily forget the kindness of strangers."

"Yeaaaaaah," Detective Cassato said, rising. "I'll be needing formal statements over at the precinct house. Brandy, you may be required at Eric's inquest. I'm afraid you're going to have to stick around town for a while."

Mother rose. "We were planning to stay on through the week, anyway. We haven't really had time to do much sightseeing. Do let us know when and where you need us."

He grunted, "Thanks," at this unusually compliant response from her.

While Mother walked with the detective to the door, I stretched out on the couch. I fell fast asleep in seconds, a deep, dreamless state approaching hibernation.

Suddenly Mother was shaking me gently. "Wake up, dear. Wakey wakey."

I pushed up on my elbows, blinking. I was in the big bed now, Sushi nestled nearby—how I'd gotten there I didn't know.

"What day is it?" I asked groggily.

"Still Sunday."

"What time is it?"

"About noon."

"Wasn't our panel scheduled for this morning?"

"They cancelled all morning activities, dear, out of respect for the dead. Not every comic con has three deaths
by violence, you know."

I sat up. "But what about the auction?"

She waved off my concern. "The auction is in an hour,
dear. Do you think you can sufficiently rouse yourself? Or
perhaps you'd like to stay here."

I did not. If we didn't sell that Supe drawing for a fat
wad of cash to finance our new shop, *we'd* be in the soup.
It was the main reason we'd come to this ill-fated affair,
and I wasn't about to miss it.

I eased out of bed, and headed to the shower, initially
bent over but evolving from Neanderthal to Homo sapiens
in under thirty seconds.

The auction, in the Gold Room on level C, was under-
attended, much to our dismay. We'd seen many attendees
bailing, after the costume party killing, and with the
events of the morning cancelled, many other attendees had
taken their early leave, as well.

But those who remained were a die-hard lot (too
soon?), and when our vintage Superman drawing—drawn
by Joe Shuster and signed by him and by cocreator/writer
Jerry Siegel—came up, a heated bidding war broke out.
Three collectors in the room vied with a pair of pickers attending by cell phone, driving the price upward, finally
selling in the high five figures. Joe Lange had predicted we
might fare this well, and we were thrilled.

Earlier, on the long drive to New York, Mother and I
had discussed what to do with the money, should Joe be
right. After Uncle Sam got his share, Mother intended to
treat herself to tooth implants, tired of having her bridge-
work fall into her dinner; I/we needed a new car, now that

the Buick had passed on, was no more, had ceased to be, expired, gone to meet its maker, etc.; and we would stake Sushi to a promising, experimental eye surgery technique so she could see again (if it worked for Soosh, maybe Mother could give it a go).

The rest of the cash would go into our antiques shop, at the moment painfully understocked with the contents of our former antiques-mall stall. Oh, and we held back five hundred bucks that we hoped would cover the damage to the broken monkey wings.

After the auction, Mother and I returned to the suite, where we slept until late morning, Monday. Leaving Sushi in the hotel room, la Diva headed out to troll the antiques shops in the Village while I took a cab up to Norma Kamali's on West Fifty-sixth, where I bought one of her fabulous summer swimsuits. That evening, we had a lovely dinner (or is that supper?) at a Village bistro with Ashley and her beau (cute and nice).

On Tuesday, we returned the *Wicked* costumes, our $500 check pinned to the monkey costume, leaving the bundle with the Gershwin stage door manager. Like any other good tourists, we purchased tickets for that evening's performance, which proved thoroughly enjoyable. True to our word, we did not bother Vikki backstage. We did, however, stand outside the stage doors, behind the metal barricades, where the actress who played Wicked Witch Elphaba autographed Mother's Playbill.

"Stellar performance, my dear," Mother informed her. "But might I suggest one simple addition?"

The actress smiled with her mouth but frowned with her forehead. "Yes, of course."

"You might try using a Western accent, my dear. Are you not, after all, the Wicked Witch of the *West*? A little Southwestern twang would not only be distinctive, but make that point."

After a frozen second or two, the actress said, "Well, I'll take that under consideration. You wouldn't happen to be in local theater back home, would you?"

"Why, yes! How could you tell?"

"Come on, dear," the real witch said to the pretender. "We actors know another actor when we see one."

This thrilled Mother to no end, and the encounter became an anecdote she shared far and wide, though she didn't seem to understand why it always got a laugh.

Wednesday morning, a little gold box was delivered to our suite with a small tag reading, *Vivian*. It was as if a Manhattan admirer had sent her an engagement ring.

But rather than a diamond, the box contained a set of car keys, along with a note reading, *Penn Plaza Parking, #112*.

Puzzled, I looked over Mother's shoulder as she dangled the keys like a single earring she was considering wearing.

I asked, "What's that about?"

She frowned. "I'm not sure, dear."

Leaving Sushi behind, we got into our coats and walked the half block to the parking garage, where, in stall 112, we found a car.

But not just *any* car—a 1960s black Cadillac convertible with tail fins and a blood-red interior.

Mother, squealing with delight, rushed with the keys to the driver's side door.

"You don't have a *license*, remember?" I warned, shivering at the thought of her driving in New York City traffic.

Mother put hands on hips. "There's no law against sitting behind the wheel, is there, Little Miss Buzz Kill?"

"No. Plant your keister if you like, just don't go anywhere."

With an indignant sniff that was quickly replaced by a gleeful smile, she unlocked the car with one of the keys, then slid in behind the wheel. To make sure she kept her word, I came around and got in on the other side.

We just sat there admiring the pristine interior with its chrome wheel, deep front dashboard, and boxy panel with simplistic gauges. Best of all, the vintage car had new car smell!

"Whose car is this?" I finally asked.

"Mine, I think," she said slyly. "Look in the glove compartment, dear."

I did. All I saw at first was an owner's manual in protective plastic. But under it was a white business-size envelope with *Mrs. Vivian Borne* written in a shaky hand.

"Open it," Mother ordered.

I did, removing a letter, along with the title of the vehicle.

"Now read it, dear."

I unfolded the letter. "*Dearest Vivian,*" I said, "*Please accept this gift in gratitude for clearing Gino. And on that other matter, be assured I will keep my word. I never had a better Scrabble partner.*"

I looked at the signature. "Good lord! Isn't he . . . is that . . . ?"

"He is *that*. Indeed."

"The Godfather?"

"Of New Jersey, yes."

"When the heck did you see *him*?"

"After my little visit to the Badda-Boom. I dropped by his nursing home."

I turned in my seat and glared at her. "Mother! You're *not* keeping this car. We're talking about the monster who sent those hit men after Tony—and he and I were almost *killed*."

"Yes . . . and the old sweetie is very sorry about that."

"*Sorry?*"

"Yes, apparently some of his minions, well . . . overstepped." She touched my shoulder. "Dear . . . this is not your decision. The car is mine, not yours."

"Well, I won't ride in it—and I'm not even going to sit here one second longer."

I moved to open the door, but Mother took my arm.

"Brandy, the 'other matter' the Don mentioned in the letter was that he would remove the contract on Tony *if* I proved that his relative, Gino, was innocent."

I looked at her, stunned.

"I kept my part of the bargain," she said. "And he will keep his. This car is just . . . a sort of tip."

"And you *believe* him?"

"Yes, dear, I do. These people have a code. His word is his honor."

"Why didn't you *tell* me—"

"I did not want to raise your hopes. We needed to find a killer first . . . actually, we found two, didn't we? And we needed Gino not to be one of them. No, I couldn't tell you until I knew the outcome. Now, I think in due course you'll find that Tony Cassato will be back in your life."

I believed she believed this . . .

. . . *but could* I *believe it?*

Could I take the word of a notorious organized crime figure?

And . . . *Scrabble?*

Unbidden, my mind started whirling with the possibility of a real future with Tony. I didn't want to think about that, I really didn't; but I couldn't stop myself. . . .

The contract on Tony cancelled.

Could it be true?

Wednesday afternoon, Mother and I returned to the Midtown Precinct, where we spent several hours giving our formal statements to Detective Cassato in his small office. I would not be needed at an inquest because Robert Sipcowski's statement indicated Eric had fallen accidentally to his death.

The detective, in a crisp light blue shirt, navy tie, and pressed gray slacks, looked rested, and was typically businesslike though treating us cordially.

He even shared added information about the murders, specifically his interview with Eric Johansson's widow, Helena.

"Apparently," Detective Casatto said, "she was unaware how deeply Eric had become involved with Violet to further his career."

Mother asked, "Then, Helena had no idea Eric had gone back to the ballroom?"

Cassato nodded. "She said Eric told her he had some business to attend to, and she should wait for him down in the lobby bar. We believe she's innocent in Violet's murder."

"Poor girl," Mother said.

I wasn't sure if she meant Helena or Violet.

"Well," I said, "at least Eric will finally be getting the notoriety he craved."

There was a moment of silence before the detective cleared his throat. "Now, one final matter. We need to discuss the fraudulent way you got in to see Brad Webster—"

"Oh, my!" Mother interrupted, checking her wristwatch. "Look at the time! We have an appointment across town with our book editor—and you *know* how New Yorkers simply *hate* people being late."

We'd have plenty of opportunity to be on time, because our meeting wasn't till tomorrow.

Mother, smiling sweetly, was saying, "Perhaps we can discuss this at a later date, Detective Cassato."

"Ma'am," he said dryly, "there will *be* no later date, else you and me are going to have a problem."

She waved a flirtatious hand. "Oh, I just know there's no problem that the two of us can't solve, if we just put our heads together." She smiled at me. "Doesn't Detective

Cassato have a colorful way of putting things, dear? So very NYPD!"

Not seeming quite so rested now, the detective escorted us from the interview room and down the corridor toward the precinct's waiting room. With Mother in the lead, he caught me by the arm, gently, and whispered, "Tony would like to see you tonight."

And I whispered back, "Where?"

"He'll come to your room. Around seven."

"Fine. Tell him fine."

As soon as Mother and I had returned to our suite, she began redoing her makeup, fussing with her hair, and laying out a new outfit on the bed.

I didn't need to ask her where she was going. After she'd spritzed on perfume, I had a pretty good idea. And I bet you do, too.

You know how thoughtful Mother is when it comes to visiting old friends at nursing homes. . . .

With a final glance in the long mirror, Mother chirped, "Don't wait up, dear!"

"I won't. I know these Scrabble games can go on and on. . . ."

It wasn't until later, while playing with a much neglected Sushi, that it occurred to me to check on the Cadillac keys.

They were gone. She had taken them. She might yet find her way into an NYC slammer. The only question was whether it would be for driving without a license or conspiring with a known criminal.

At a minute past seven, a knock came at the door, and I did something very dangerous in the big city: I didn't bother to look through the peephole before flinging the door open. And then flung myself into Tony's waiting arms.

We backed into the room, and he kicked the door shut, still entwined.

"You've *heard*?" I asked, my words muffled against his barrel chest. "That the contract is off?"

He was trembling, too, something rare in this wonderful beast of a man. I drew back to look into his moisture-pearled eyes.

"It seems to be real, Brandy. It's apparently true, unless . . . unless some horrible trick is being played on me. On us."

"Who told you? Can you trust the source?"

He shrugged and smiled. "You tell me. The Don himself called my brother, gave him a phone number, and said that I should call him."

"And it was *him*? You're sure?"

"No mistaking *that* voice."

"Did he . . . did he tell you *why* the hit was removed?"

Tony's dry little laugh said yes, and he shook his head. "That crazy, ditzy woman . . . that terrible, wonderful mother of yours . . . Brandy, she gave me my life back."

I sighed, but I was smiling. "She'll be incorrigible now."

"*Now*? What has she been, up to this point?"

We had been just inside the doorway during this exchange, and Sushi was jumping at Tony's legs. He picked her up, holding her in one big hand, and we all went over to settle on the couch.

I asked, "So what's next?"

"Well, you're next. Obviously." Tony had one arm around me, his free hand petting Sushi. "But beyond that, I honestly haven't had time to think about it."

"Would you come back to Serenity?"

"Try to stop me."

"Back on the force?"

He nodded. "Yes. I think they'll have me. Maybe not as chief, but they'll find something, and if not, there are other jobs."

"Tony?"

"Hmmmm . . . ?" He was kissing my neck.

"I don't know if I can promise you right now that we'll always be together . . . much as I hope we will be."

He pulled back to study me. "Honey, I understand. When I had to go into WITSEC, we were just getting to know each other."

"Then let's get to know each other some more," I said, and kissed him.

At noon on Thursday, Mother and I had a delightful meal at a French restaurant with our editor, who had heard about the murders, and knew we were involved in the inquiry but not to what extent. Most of what Mother and I did, for good and ill, had been kept out of the media, much to Mother's annoyance.

"Well, I think that's fine," our editor said. "That means you can save the full story for the book."

Which we have.

After lunch, Mother and I returned to our suite to pack and gather our things, and generally prepare for our long drive back to Serenity in our new old Caddy. Sushi, no doubt homesick for her own patch of grass, began running in circles with excitement as soon as we dragged out the suitcases.

Soon we were bidding New York good-bye, with me behind the wheel of the Caddy, Mother riding shotgun, and Sushi snuggled in back on our coats, our luggage and parcels stowed in the car's spacious trunk. The vehicle drove like a boat, but a smooth-sailing one. I had to admit that I loved the feel of the massive ride.

As we tooled along the city streets, making our way toward the Lincoln Tunnel, we garnered looks of envy and admiration from pedestrians and drivers alike.

We had been on the road several hours, having just passed through Parsippany on Interstate 80 (after stopping for fuel—holy mileage, Batman, what a gas guzzler!), when Mother's cell phone chirped its "New York, New York."

"Vivian here. Oh, hello, Phil *darling*!" Then, to me, "It's Phillip Dean, dear."

I had gathered as much, from her fake Hollywood voice.

Phil Dean was a Los Angeles reality show cameraman-turned-producer who had, for the past few months, been pitching a new series for us: *Antiques Sleuths*, a mother–daughter duo who not only solved mysteries in real life, but told viewers the stories behind the curious items that found their way into the Trash 'n' Treasures shop.

Mother was asking him, "Any news?" Then, "Oh, my goodness! Oh, that's *wonderful*! Yes . . . yes . . . I'll call you as soon as we arrive home, daah-ling! Ciao!" She ended the call.

"Bad news?" I asked.

"Dear, we've been green-lighted! Or is that lit? Anyway, the shooting of our pilot is a go go go!"

"When?"

"Early this summer."

"That's great."

Mother didn't seem to notice my lack of enthusiasm as she launched into a monologue of kooky ideas for the series that she was already convinced would follow.

Was it so terrible of me to just want to go home to a little peace and quiet and a lot of Tony?

I glanced over at Mother, jabbering on with elation.

A warmth flowed through me. I really did love this crazy old broad. I owed her *so* much. . . .

So I drove and listened with rapt attention and unflagging interest, matching her clown's smile with my own.

And why not? I could afford to be magnanimous. Because I felt confident that any pilot starring Vivian and Brandy Borne would *never* get picked up by a cable network.

Would it?

A Trash 'n' Treasures Tip

At a recent auction, a 1938 *Action Comics* featuring the first appearance of Superman sold for one million dollars. So, Grandma, Grandpa . . . back when you were parents? If you cleaned out your kid's room and tossed out that funny book, you have no one to blame but yourself that a life of luxury has eluded you and your loved ones.

About the Authors

BARBARA ALLAN

is a joint pseudonym of husband-and-wife mystery writers Barbara and Max Allan Collins.

BARBARA COLLINS is a highly respected short story writer in the mystery field, with appearances in over a dozen top anthologies, including *Murder Most Delicious, Women on the Edge, Deadly Housewives,* and the best-selling *Cat Crimes* series. She was the co-editor of (and a contributor to) the best-selling anthology *Lethal Ladies*, and her stories were selected for inclusion in the first three volumes of *The Year's 25 Finest Crime and Mystery Stories*.

Two acclaimed hardcover collections of her work have been published: *Too Many Tomcats* and (with her husband) *Murder—His and Hers*. The Collins' first novel together, the Baby Boomer thriller *Regeneration*, was a paperback bestseller; their second collaborative novel, *Bombshell*—in which Marilyn Monroe saves the world from World War III—was published in hardcover to excellent reviews.

Barbara has been the production manager and/or line producer on various independent film projects emanating from the production company she and her husband jointly run.

MAX ALLAN COLLINS has been hailed as "the Renaissance man of mystery fiction." He has earned an unprecedented nineteen Private Eye Writers of America "Shamus" nominations for his Nathan Heller historical thrillers, winning for *True Detective* (1983) and *Stolen Away* (1991).

His other credits include film criticism, short fiction, songwriting, trading-card sets, and movie/TV tie-in novels, including the *New York Times* bestsellers *Saving Private Ryan* and the Scribe Award–winning *American Gangster.* His graphic novel *Road to Perdition,* considered a classic of the form, is the basis of the Academy Award–winning film. Max's other comics credits include the "Dick Tracy" syndicated strip; his own "Ms. Tree"; "Batman"; and "CSI: Crime Scene Investigation," based on the hit TV series, for which he has also written six video games and ten best-selling novels.

An acclaimed, award-winning filmmaker in the Midwest, he wrote and directed the Lifetime movie *Mommy* (1996) and three other features. His produced screenplays include the 1995 HBO World Premiere *The Expert,* and *The Last Lullaby* (2008). His 1998 documentary *Mike Hammer's Mickey Spillane* appears on the Criterion Collection release of acclaimed film noir *Kiss Me Deadly.*

Max's most recent novels include *Ask Not* (the conclusion to his Nate Heller "JFK Trilogy") and *Complex 90* (completing an unfinished Mike Hammer novel from the late Mickey Spillane's files).

"BARBARA ALLAN" live(s) in Muscatine, Iowa, their Serenity-esque hometown. Son Nathan works as a translator of Japanese to English, with credits ranging from video games to novels.